The List
A Jack & Jill Mystery

The List
A Jack & Jill Mystery

Jeremiah Peters

STONEGATE BOOKS

Cover design by Adam Pinheiro

Published in the United States of America by Stonegate Books

Publisher's Note: This novel is a work of fiction. Names, characters, places, and incidents are either products of the author's imagination or used fictitiously. All characters are fictional, and any similarity to people living or dead is purely coincidental.

Paperback ISBN 978-1-7328659-3-8
eBook ISBN 978-1-7328659-4-5

Dedicated to my wife, Jodie.
She's the Jill to my Jack.

Chapter One

I **never** knew death could be so lifelike. Over in Iraq, it was anything but.

Here, though …

She looked so peaceful seated against the rear of the library building. Serene. Her skin had an almost translucent glow from the single light bulb that hung over the service entrance. Her long, dark hair curled around the sides of her face and draped over her shoulders. If it were a couple of inches longer, I wouldn't have even noticed the knife in her chest.

I shook my head hoping this was just a dream, a nightmare from which I'd awaken. No luck.

But maybe she wasn't dead. Maybe she was just hurt. Stupid thought. The knife pointed to death. But what if I was wrong? I jumped off the corner of the cement slab that acted as the library's loading dock, where I'd stopped to retie my running shoes. "Hey! Are you okay?"

No response.

I inched forward and cupped my hand above my eyes, shielding them from the stark light. Her sweater had a large, red stain on it, circling the knife's entrance. A puddle of blood stretched across the cold ground. I lifted her wrist to check for a pulse. Nothing.

In the stillness of the dawn, I offered a silent prayer.

Clouds of steam escaped my mouth and ascended into the dull, predawn sky. Most of my fellow students at Springsbury College were still sound asleep.

A dead body behind a Dumpster … The media was going to have a field day with this.

In the past few months, two other girls had been found in a similar state. One was about seventy miles away. The other, thirty. The media announced we had a serial killer running rampant through New Hampshire. With the bodies being left the way they were, they dubbed him The Dumpster Killer.

Just then, a small cry, like a dove cooing, sounded from behind me. I spun around and raised my hands, expecting to see a wild-eyed murderer, wielding a blood-stained blade. Instead, across the narrow road that ran behind the library stood a young girl, her back to the woods. The morning mist played around her feet.

Freaky. It was like something out of one of those horror movies where the children rise from a cornfield or dark woods, seeking vengeance on the adults. I had the queasy feeling that at any moment the girl's elf-like voice would call out to me, "Jackson Hill, I've come for you."

Instead, "Oh," was all she said.

After a moment of dazed confusion, I lowered my hands.

What in the world is a kid doing on campus this early in the morning?

She stared at the body. "Do you have a cell phone?" Her voice was cold, almost detached. Certainly not elf-like. I patted the pockets of my running pants. "No. Why?"

She rolled her eyes as if to say, 'How dumb can you be?' "Someone's got to call the police." She started to leave but turned back. "You stay here. Don't touch anything."

What did she think I was? Stupid? Of course, I knew not to touch anything.

She disappeared around the corner of the building.

That was weird. If I were her, I'd have been frightened out of my wits. Yet here she'd been, in the early morning, behind a building with a strange man and a dead body. Why hadn't she run off, screaming at the top of her lungs?

Then I had a terrible thought. I tensed as a cold wind bit into my face. It was a silly notion, really. Probably fed by the shadowy morning fog and eerie quiet.

Who's to say the serial killer had to be a man? Or even an adult?

The police arrived and cordoned off the area with yellow tape. A few cruisers and an ambulance were parked on the narrow road. About a half dozen latex-gloved officers were busy at work, I assumed looking for clues, occasionally bagging some object. A steady stream of traffic flowed through the back door of the library. The Dumpster sat silently to its right. The stark flashes from the photographer's camera lit the building.

I leaned on the front edge of the dock, as far away from the Dumpster as I could get.

Where's the chalk?

On television, they always do a chalk outline of the body. And how would they accomplish this with the deceased leaning against the building? Would the chalk line flow from the ground to the wall?

I mentally chastised myself. Here I was in the middle of a crime scene, worrying about chalk outlines. The scrape of plastic against metal jolted me to reality as the ambulance attendants pulled a body bag from the back of their vehicle.

Wait. Something's not right.

I jumped to my feet. Where was that young girl? Had she escaped? I caught sight of her, behind one of the cruisers. Satisfied that she hadn't escaped, I relaxed and sat back down.

"You Jackson Hill, the one who found the girl?" A baby-faced officer approached me.

"Yes, sir."

"You're going to have to answer some questions. Don't leave." He spoke in a voice too stern for his youthful look. "You want to sit in one of the cruisers?"

"No, sir. I'm fine."

"Would you like—"

A voice bellowed from the sidelines. "What's the meaning of this?" A tall, silver-haired man fumbled with the tape, trying to gain access to the area. He looked like he'd just crawled from his bed and thrown on wrinkled clothing from the hamper.

A woman followed him. Her long, blonde hair was slightly gray. She had high cheekbones and a slim figure. In her youth, she must have been quite a beauty. She placed a hand on the man's shoulder as he struggled with the tape. From the tender touch, I assumed she was his wife. "Let me—"

He yanked his hand away. "Ms. Fielding, I can do this." *Okay, so it's not his wife.*

"I know." Crestfallen, she backed away. "I'm just trying to help."

Finally, in a great fluster, he tossed the tape over his head and marched toward the center of the action, with the woman close on his heels.

My baby-faced officer raced over.

"Who's in charge here?" The newcomer glared at the scene.

A large, muscular gentleman with close-cropped red hair, approached. He wore a dark sports coat and light brown trousers. "I'm Detective Phillips." He nodded toward the young officer as if to say, 'I'll take care of this.'

Looking grateful, the baby-faced officer hurried away.

"And you are?" Detective Phillips asked.

The man straightened up. "Dr. Roland Spiner. The president of this college."

The woman hovered behind him, remaining watchful, but silent.

"Well, Dr. Spiner, until Detective Thomas arrives, I'm in charge of the investigation."

"Investigation? What investigation?"

The z-i-i-p-p-p of the body bag cut through the air.

Dr. Spiner seemed to catch sight of the activity behind the Dumpster for the first time. His mouth dropped. "What? But—but this can't be happening."

Detective Phillips consulted a small notebook. "Her name was Emily Hamilton. Mean anything to you?"

Ms. Fielding gasped.

Dr. Spiner stared at the body. "Should it?"

"She was a student here," the detective said.

The color drained from the man's face. His legs gave out, and he fell against one of the cruisers. "No ... no ..."

The detective lurched forward to catch him as he slid down the side of the car, but the woman beat him to it.

"Easy," Detective Phillips said. He reached for the door handle. "Do you need to sit?"

Semi-dazed, Dr. Spiner stared at the scene behind the Dumpster. "How could this happen?"

He allowed the detective to take him by one arm. Ms. Fielding held tight to the other. They guided him to the cruiser's door, and the two crawled into the back seat. Before his head disappeared through the opening, he gave one last look at the body. "What's this going to do to our enrollment?"

That was cold.

Speaking of cold, my backside was chilled from sitting on the cement. On top of that, I had to go to the bathroom. I shifted my position and glanced around. All the officers seemed engrossed in their work.

No one will miss me if I sneak away for a second.

As I ducked under the yellow tape, a voice called out. "Hey, you!"

Before I had a chance to answer, someone else joined in. "Hey, kid? You deaf or something?"

Two officers marched toward me. The shorter one, who looked like he had trouble buttoning his shirt around his bulging stomach, spoke. "Where do you think you're going?"

"To the bathroom."

His partner sniffed and wiped his nose. He looked like he'd give the college president a run for his money to win The-Most-Shabbily-Dressed Award. "You can't just walk away. You got to tell someone."

"Sorry, sir."

"You the one who found the body?" the short one huffed.

I nodded. "Yes, sir."

He placed his hand on my shoulder and guided me to the loading dock. "This is a crime scene. You're a part of an investigation. You walk away, it don't look too good."

The tall one pulled a slightly used tissue from his pocket and blew his nose. "We don't know where you're planning on going unless you tell us."

"Sorry, sir, but—"

"Boy! Kids today." He shook his head. "Where do we get them?" His words were directed to his partner, but it was obvious I was meant to hear this condemnation of college students in general and of me in particular.

"Yeah. Not too bright," his partner answered.

"You know …" The tall officer balled up the tissue and stuck it back in his pocket. "Once they graduate high school and go off to college, they think they're all grown up." He eyed me, suspiciously. "Then again, you're too old for a typical college brat."

"Yes, sir."

"A little young for a teacher?"

"Well, I—"

"Late starter, eh?" The short one with the belly poking through his buttons gave a sympathetic look. His insinuation was obvious. Somehow, I must have been too stupid when I graduated high school to go right to college.

Maybe it was because of the early hour. Or the fact that I'd found a dead body. Or a lack of food. Whatever the reason, my temper rose. "Well, sir," my volume increased. "You're right when you noticed I'm older." I stuck out my chest, "I served time in the marines before starting college."

It's funny, at one moment I'm trying to forget my time in the service, and at another, I'm wearing it like a badge of honor. The words poured from my mouth like water through the crack in a dike. Unfortunately, I didn't have a little boy to stick his finger in the hole. I'd like to come up with another reason for my anger, but there was only one I could attribute it to—stupidity. My stupidity. I don't know. Maybe these two simply rubbed me the wrong way. Whatever the reason, I kept going.

"That, sir, is why I am older. And may I also add, as a marine I've been trained to respect those in authority. I'd appreciate it if the authorities respected me."

Suddenly, the area grew very quiet as the surrounding officers' conversations came to an abrupt halt. All eyes focused on me. Even the girl by the cruiser was gawking.

A thick cloud of embarrassment hung over my head.

The silence dragged on until the taller officer snickered. "Wow! A marine."

"We're sorry," the other said.

The two smirked.

"We promise to treat you with all the respect you're due. Don't we, Officer Daniels?"

They laughed.

"Everything okay here?" Detective Phillips walked up.

Others who'd stopped to watch this spectacle took this as a cue to get on with their jobs.

"Yes, sir. Everything is fine," the short one answered. "General Patton here needs to pee."

The detective gave him a stern look. "I've got a job for you. Dr. Spiner and his secretary are in your cruiser. Their homes are on the other side of the campus. I don't think he's in any shape to walk back. Take care of them."

"Will do, sir." He walked away.

Officer Daniels smirked. "But we weren't done with—"

The detective glared. "You're done. I'll take care of Mr. Hill. Get going."

"The two climbed in the cruiser and drove off, smiling and laughing as they did.

"Don't be too hard on them," Detective Phillips said. "They're just coming off a twenty-four-hour shift. A little sleep deprived."

"No problem."

What else could I say?

Another car pulled up. A man got out and slowly scanned the scene. He nodded at Detective Phillips.

"Wait here." The detective trotted over to the newcomer.

I slapped myself on the forehead.

Idiot!

In a low whisper, I mimicked my voice. "I'm a marine so treat me right! Next week, I'll be the king of England."

Idiot!

I sighed. There wasn't much I could do about it now.

Settling back on my perch, I watched as Detective Phillips greeted the man. Then grim-faced, the two talked. Several officers approached the pair, asking questions, receiving instructions, or showing items they'd recovered.

By his attitude and the way everyone treated him, it was obvious this must be the fellow Detective Phillips told the president about, the one who would be in charge. Occasionally, his eyes wandered in my direction. He wasn't looking at me though, but at the Dumpster. At least that's what I wanted to think.

The sun was beginning to peek through the trees. Students lined the yellow tape, curious, all wanting a good view of the proceedings.

How long was this going to take?

Finally, the man broke off from Detective Phillips and approached. "I'm Detective Thomas. You are?"

"Jackson Hill."

"You found the deceased?"

"Yes, sir," I answered, meeting his steely stare.

Detective Thomas stood about six foot two or three. He looked to be of average-to-thin build. "I have a few questions for you."

Did his mouth move? I couldn't tell. It was like speaking to a statue.

"I'll answer as best I can."

"What time did you find the body?"

"I found Emily about six a.m.." I was kicking myself that I couldn't be more precise.

"Emily?" The man showed no signs of emotion, not even the flickering of an eyebrow. "Did you know her?"

I shook my head.

He paused, his stare fixed on me. What was going through his head? "You say you found the body around six?"

"Yes, sir."

"What were you doing out at that hour?"

"Jogging. I was in the military and—"

"So I heard."

Was that a dig? Had someone already told him of my stupid and embarrassing declaration?

I continued, deciding to ignore his comment. "I got in the habit of early morning runs." As I continued with the whole story of how I found Emily, he just stared at me. No movement. He looked like a statue. The Great Stone Face.

I finished.

"Thank you. That's all for now. You'll have to come down to the station for a more complete statement. We'll be in touch about that. Give Detective Phillips your contact information. Meanwhile, please don't leave town without letting the police department know." He stepped away.

I leaped forward. "One other thing."

"Yes?" He turned back.

As inconspicuously as possible, I glanced in the direction of the cruiser, where the young girl stood. She appeared nervous, fidgeting, half hiding behind the car's side.

"I ... er ..." I made my way around the detective so that the cruiser was behind me. "If you look over there," I mumbled, "You'll see a girl by the cruiser. She looks like she's trying to hide. Do you see her?"

His eyes barely moved. "Yes."

"She was there, too," I announced in a somewhat dramatic whisper. "When I found the body."

For a nanosecond, I thought I saw a glimmer of something on his face. Maybe an emotion. But it quickly disappeared. "And?" he said.

"She appeared out of nowhere, acting like she was guilty of something. It seems odd to me ... a high school kid wandering around that early in the morning."

I couldn't tell if the detective was taking me seriously or not. It almost looked like he smirked. Then he paused, and the petrified look returned to his face. With a coldness in his voice, he said, "Thank you, Mr. Hill," and walked away.

"Get those cameras behind the line," Detective Phillips barked.

The Manchester television station had arrived. They scurried around like hungry field mice, trying to snatch up tidbits of information. Who could blame them? How often did a serial killer come their way?

I was on the receiving end of dubious stares both from reporters and fellow college students. Let's face it, if I were them, I'd be staring, too. Being the only civilian on the wrong side of the yellow tape made me fair game. I felt like a freak in a sideshow. 'That's the guy! He's guilty,' was probably what they were thinking.

"It wasn't me," I wanted to yell. "What about the girl?"

To suspect her was crazy, I knew that, no matter what my earlier fantasies had been.

The onlookers, shock and disbelief on their faces, parted, making room for the ambulance. A couple of girls were crying. One found comfort in the shoulder of the young man next to her.

Could this possibly be happening? Here was someone who was so alive just a few hours ago. And now …

I caught sight of Detective Thomas by the cruiser. He was interrogating the girl, leaning over her and speaking in a low tone. She shook her head. Her eyes welled with tears.

Then something happened that took me by surprise. Detective Thomas signaled to an officer. They loaded the girl in the cruiser. The officer got in and drove away.

Chapter Two

The police escorted me into the library and allowed me to exit through the front door. This way I avoided the media and the crowd. I headed back to my residence hall for a hot shower.

Pulling a towel and some clothes from the drawer, I paused to stare into the mirror hanging over the dresser. A fatigued face stared back. Right then, the weight of the morning's events hit home. I sank onto the edge of the bed.

"Oh, Emily." I moaned, fell back onto the mattress, and stared at the ceiling. "What happened?"

Should I have told the police about last night?

Then again, I'd given them all the pertinent facts and answered their questions honestly.

Didn't I?

The bed felt so soft and comfortable against my aching muscles and side. I lay there replaying last night's scene over and over in my head.

It hadn't been a busy night for book browsing in the library. Just a smattering of students. I had a paper on Shakespeare due in a couple of days. After locating the needed books, I wound my way through the bookshelves and tables to the main desk.

"May I help you?" the girl on duty asked. The ID hanging around her neck read Emily Hamilton.

I slid the books across the counter. "Checking these out."

She only half glanced at them, keeping an eye on a trio of troublemakers—a girl and two boys—across the room, seated at a large, wooden table. They were making a general nuisance of themselves—laughing too loud, slamming books on the table, things like that. With every outrageous noise they made, one of them would cast a sneer Emily's way. A person might suspect they were trying to be obnoxious on purpose.

"You all right?" I asked.

"Fine." She held out her hand.

"What?"

"Library card." Her face was rigid.

"Whoops." I fumbled through my wallet. All the while she watched the table. I nodded in that direction. "Do you want me to talk to them?"

Her mouth dropped in horror. "No … I mean … thank you, but … I have everything under control."

No, she didn't. Her eyes were red, probably from crying. Her lips were pulled tight like she was trying to control her temper.

I leaned on the counter. "It's okay to ask for help."

"Did you find your library card?" The coldness had returned.

I stood up straight. "No."

Emily jumped at a loud scraping noise. The three troublemakers had shoved back their chairs.

"Let's get going," the girl said.

Gathering their belongings, they strolled by the desk. I figured Emily would yell at them. At least glare. Instead, acting all mouse-like, her face stayed focused on the counter.

I recognized one of the guys from my psych class. Don Henderson. With half a grin, he nodded in Emily's direction. The other one, a big guy—big like he crushed cars for a living—hung his head, a kind of sulky look on his face. The girl was on his other side, wrapping her arm through his. I couldn't get a good look at her though. The large one was in the way.

Once the three exited the building, I turned to Emily. "I can't find my library card. I must have left it in my room."

"Sorry. No card. No books."

"But I can show you my other IDs."

She took the books. "It's the rule."

"Come on. I'm a student here."

She shook her head and repeated, "It's the rule. Go back to your room and get your card."

Just then I spotted two other guys from the class entering the library. They too had Shakespeare papers due. What if they nabbed the books before I could run to my room and get my card?

I checked my watch—10:15. The library closed at eleven. "Look. Can you hold the books here?"

She opened her mouth ready to protest.

I raised a finger to stop her. "I know. I know. It's against the rules but come on. I was willing to defend you against those morons. That's got to buy me a few points." I smiled.

She sighed. "Fine. I'll hold them here 'til closing. That's in forty-five minutes. Be back by then, or they'll be returned to the shelf."

"Thanks." I headed toward the exit, shouting over my shoulder, "I'll be back to see you before closing."

An odd tingling crept up my neck. Someone was watching us. Across from the main desk, in an alcove next to where the three troublemakers had been, someone sat in an overstuffed chair, face hidden behind a magazine.

Why would that feel important?

I raced out of the library heading to my room. But when I stepped through the front door, somehow, I was back by the Dumpster. There sat Emily ... dead.

I walked inside again. Then, taking a deep breath, I stepped through the door. Once again, instead of facing the college's quad, I was at the back of the building. I looked around. Everything was as it was when I first discovered Emily. The dull light of morning. The knife in her chest.

I studied the scene closely. Maybe there was something I'd missed.

I didn't think I'd moved, at least I don't remember stepping forward, but all of a sudden, I was crouched by the body. Emily's face was drained of color. Though it was a long shot, I lifted her wrist. Nothing.

As I turned to leave, her dead eyes snapped open. Her hand grabbed mine.

"Jack." Cold mist poured from her mouth. "Where were you? I needed you."

"No!"

I jumped off my bed and ran halfway across the room before screeching to a stop. My heart was pounding. Sweat rolled down my face.

It was only a dream.

My growling stomach momentarily took my mind off the nightmare and the pain in my side. The clock read 11:30 a.m.

No wonder I'm hungry.

I showered and dressed at breakneck speed, then headed out.

A yellow flyer was taped on the glass entrance to the residence hall: All Classes Canceled for the Day

That was it. No word of explanation. Not that any was needed. Bad news had a way of spreading at the speed of light. With this being a Saturday, canceled classes would have a minor effect. None on me.

Outside, I was greeted by a crisp, cold breeze.

The campus lived up to the brochure's description. "Springsbury College, a small liberal arts school, is nestled in the foothills of the White Mountains."

If nestled meant postcard pretty, it certainly was. The large grassy quad in front of me was dotted with trees whose leaves had begun to show their fall colors. Vine-covered stone and brick structures surrounded the campus, giving it the feel of a quaint New England town. Majestic pines poked their heads over the tops of the buildings.

It usually took only five to ten minutes to get to the dining hall. Not today. As I started there, I was set upon by passing students, all wanting a firsthand account of my discovery of Emily's body.

"What was it like?"

"Was she alive when you found her?"

"Did she say anything?"

"Was there anyone else there?"

I answered as concisely as I could, not wanting to say anything that would incite more questions.

As I passed the administration building, two women emerged and fell in step behind me.

"It's crazy! My ear is starting to hurt," the younger of the two complained. "I can't believe he called us in to work on a Saturday."

"I've been here twenty years," the older one answered. "I don't remember ever getting so many calls."

"I'm just thankful we can break for lunch."

"I think the president's losing his mind over this."

"Can you blame him? How many parents have threatened to pull their kids?"

"And the questions they're asking—'Should the school close until the killer is found?' 'Why was the girl out alone at night?' 'How many security guards are on staff?' Honestly! I'm only a secretary. I don't have all the answers they want ..." Their voices trailed off as they veered left on a different walkway.

I paused outside Hatch's, one of the largest residence halls on campus. Several cars were parked in front of it.

Odd. That's not allowed, except on Moving in Day.

Just then an older man emerged, pulling a suitcase.

A girl was trailing after him. "But Dad, I don't want to live at home."

"I don't care what you want. You'll be safer."

In the short time I stood there, similar scenes played out three or four times. Parents taking their children home.

I was vaguely aware that someone had approached.

"What's going on?" Don Henderson stood there, unwrapping a chocolate bar.

I'd only known him a short time and can say, positively, we were not friends, just acquaintances. I don't think we could ever be more than that. Something about him bothered me. Every strand of his perfect sandy blond hair fell in place like it had just been blown dry. His complexion, still holding the remains of his summer tan, appeared to have never seen a fault or a pimple. To me, this guy's looks were too good to be true.

I nodded toward the building. "Parents taking their daughters home."

He bit off a chunk of the bar. "Why?"

Could it be possible he hadn't heard the news? Seemed unlikely, but there it was. "I guess they're concerned about the murder."

"What?"

"This morning a girl was found dead, behind the library."

His dark eyebrows knit together. That's something I noticed about Don when we first met. Dark—almost black eyebrows—matching the eyes, but not the blond hair.

"Who?" he asked.

"Emily Hamilton."

Don stopped chewing.

"Did you know her?"

"Yes—Yes. I mean, not well … But I knew her."

"She worked in the library." Knowing the trouble he and his friends had given her, I added with sarcasm in my tone, "You remember? You were there last night."

"What … What happened to her?"

"Stabbed. Left by the Dumpster."

He remained transfixed, staring at the parents piling their daughter's belongings into the cars. "Stabbed … Behind the library … but—"

"You okay?"

Before he could answer, a voice called out, "Jackson Hill!" A police officer, about my age and sporting a wide grin, approached. "I thought I recognized you from this morning. Good luck on my part. Now I don't have to go searching for you."

"Searching for me?"

"Uh-oh, Hill." The corners of Don's mouth drew up. "Looks like they caught you." Obviously, he'd recovered from the shock of the news. "Officer, I can vouch for young Hill, here. He didn't mean to do it."

Puzzled, the officer tipped his head to the side and studied the two of us.

Don laughed. "Well, I've done all I can. I leave you to justice." He walked away.

Jerk.

"We tried to call," the officer said. "Your phone went right to voice mail."

"Oh. It must be shut off." I hate cell phones.

"Could you come with me, please. Detective Thomas has a couple of questions he'd like to ask you."

"Did I do something wrong?"

He shook his head. "He just wants to cross his i's and dot his t's. That's all."

Three or four people slowed as they passed by, trying to eavesdrop. Whenever there's a police officer on the scene, people expect the worst. A drug bust, a theft … a murder. I felt like a car wreck on the side of the road, with all the passing vehicles slowing for a good look.

"But—but I'm starving." I edged toward the dining hall. "I haven't eaten since last night. Kind of got caught at the murder scene."

He gave me a sympathetic look. "Tell you what. I haven't eaten either. How about we do a drive-thru on the way."

I was tired and hungry. The last thing I wanted to do was spend hours at a police station. "I don't know …"

"My treat."

I grunted. "All right."

"That's great! Let's go."

We headed to the parking lot and climbed into his patrol car. I happened to glance back at the quad filled with curious onlookers, students and faculty alike.

Why did Detective Thomas want to see me? The solution seemed obvious. Since I was the one who'd told them about the creepy girl, they needed a more detailed account.

The officer started the engine. "I'm Officer Grant—Jason Grant."

"Nice to meet you."
"So, I hear you were in the marines."
I sighed.

Chapter Three

True to his word, Officer Grant hit a fastfood drive-thru. After getting our order, we pulled into a parking spot and ate. I devoured a chicken sandwich, large fries, and a strawberry frappe in under five minutes.

"Pretty gruesome business, huh?" Officer Grant took a sip of his drink.

"The murder?"

He nodded.

"It's sad. I saw some parents taking their kids home."

"Who can blame them?" he said.

"Administration wants to believe things are safe. They're not."

"Really?" His eyes narrowed.

I grunted. "Have you checked out the security on that campus? Even with it being tightened, it's not enough. Between being bordered by woods and their thousand feet of road frontage, I could list hundreds of entry points. Unless they built a wall around this place," I continued after taking the last sip of my frappe, "and hired fifty security guards to patrol, it's vulnerable."

He had the oddest look on his face as he studied me. "You sound like you've put a lot of thought into this."

I shrugged. "I guess it's my training."

With our food finished, it was a short ride to the station. Before we left the car, he said in a sheepish tone, "About those two guys this morning ..."

"Which two?" As if I didn't know.

He looked around. "The ones who were giving you a hard time. Don't worry about them."

I lowered my head. "Ever say something you wish you hadn't?"

"All the time." He laughed. "It really wasn't that bad. You should see how they hassle me, always trying to get my goat. I think they're jealous of our age." He opened his door. "Come on. Let's go."

I appreciated his trying to make me feel better, but I couldn't take back what I'd said. It's too bad people aren't built like computers, with delete keys. Life would be a lot easier, less embarrassing. "Let me ask you a question." I closed the door and looked across the top of the car at him. Maybe it's because we were about the same age, or because he had shown me some compassion, or maybe it was simply because he bought me some food. Whatever the reason, I felt like I could trust this man. "What's this detective like?"

"Detective Thomas?"

I nodded.

"Good guy. Tells it like it is. Of all my superiors, I trust him the most."

"Doesn't show much emotion. Does he?"

He smirked, leaned in closer, and whispered. "Sometimes we call him the Old Man of the Mountain."

I stifled a laugh, recognizing the reference to the famous New Hampshire rock formation that, before it tumbled down, had resembled a man's face.

We walked into the police station and past a row of folding chairs that ran along the right side of the room. A sergeant sat at a tall counter, behind a sheet of glass. As we approached, he looked up from some paperwork.

"Hey, sarge. I have Mr. Hill here to see Detective Thomas."

"He can have a seat in there." He pointed at a door to my left. "I'll let the detective know he's here."

"This way, please," Officer Grant said.

I followed him into another room. A large table sat in the center with several chairs around it.

"Have a seat. He'll be with you shortly." Officer Grant left, shutting the door.

Time stretched on forever. How long had I been waiting? Obviously, his "shortly" wasn't exactly my definition of the word. I stood and crossed to the door, pushed it open a few inches and peered out. Maybe they'd forgotten me.

Between shuffling papers, fielding questions from other officers, and answering the phone, the sergeant was keeping busy. Directly across from me—on the other side of the counter—another door was constantly opening and closing as a variety of people entered and exited.

Must be an important room.

Then I laughed. For all I knew, it was where the officers ate their lunch.

The door to the "important" room opened, and lo and behold, that girl from this morning walked out. She was followed by what I assumed was a plainclothes officer. Then again, maybe it was her father.

She'd changed her clothes. Funny how I'd noticed. I tried to remember what she was wearing earlier but couldn't. All I knew was she looked different, maybe not as short or elf-like as she appeared in the morning fog. Not as menacing. I'd peg her at about five foot. Her long blonde hair hung down to her waist. Her eyes were red. Probably from crying. The man escorted her around the counter and to the line of folding chairs.

She caught sight of me and scowled.

What's she upset about?

The door to the other room opened again, and Detective Thomas emerged. He marched across the main office. I let the door shut and returned to my seat just as he entered.

"Mr. Hill." He acknowledged my presence with a nod and sat opposite me, placing a few papers on the table in front of him. Then he removed a wire-bound notebook from his shirt pocket and flipped it open. We sat quietly as he concentrated on whatever was written in it. More time dragged by. Finally, he turned his attention to me. "I have a couple more questions."

"I don't know what else I can say."

He continued speaking, ignoring my small protest, almost stepping on my words, his voice low and even. "You stated you didn't know Emily Hamilton." There was a pause. Pale blue eyes focused on me. I couldn't get the image of the Old Man out of my head.

No emotion. Just stone.

"Yes."

"Then," he said, remaining calm and yet somehow having an accusing tone to his voice, "why did she make a date to meet you last night?"

"But—but—" Though I hadn't done anything wrong, I felt guilty. A reaction to being in the police station, I suppose. "What are you talking about? There was no date—"

"You still contend you didn't know Emily Hamilton?"

"Yes ... no."

"Which is it? Yes or no?"

"No." I shook my head, hoping it would add extra emphasis to my innocence. "I knew of her. I'd seen her working in the library, but I didn't know her." My mouth went dry. "I saw her last night—"

"Last night?" Detective Thomas sat back and folded his hands in his lap. I guess that was the signal for me to continue. Maybe confess to the murder or something.

I took a deep breath. "Yes. I went to the library to get some books on Shakespeare."

"Shakespeare?"

I nodded. "I have a big paper due on Monday. Haven't started yet." I hesitated, waiting for a comment about my procrastination.

Nothing.

"The library was pretty empty. Go figure. Friday night and everything. People probably had better things to do with their time." I chuckled. "Except for those of us who put off our work until the last minute."

Another pause. The detective remained statue-like.

Tough crowd.

"I found some books and headed to the checkout. Emily was there, working on a couple letters. I caught sight of the heading. Dear something or other."

"Did you see a name?"

I concentrated. "There were a couple of them. Other pages were torn or crumpled." I shook my head.

He wrote something in his notebook.

"From behind me, I heard this commotion. Three people were laughing and acting like idiots."

"How so?"

"Slamming things down, throwing papers back and forth at each other. Emily wasn't too happy with them. She was all red-faced and shaking."

"Did you recognize any of them?"

"Don Henderson." I hoped the sneer hadn't come through in my voice. I tried to think of any other detail I could share. "He likes to eat chocolate."

"Chocolate?"

I smirked. "Always munching on a candy bar. As a matter of fact, he had one in his hand, and there were a couple of wrappers on the table." I concentrated for a minute. "The other one, a male, I've seen around campus. He has a nickname of some kind. Bash or Hammer ... I think he goes to my church." I shrugged. "All I can tell you is, the man is a mountain. Must be six feet seven."

"And the third?"

"It was a girl. I know that because I heard her giggle when she pushed the books off the table. Only got glimpses of her. Sorry."

Detective Thomas kept scribbling in his notebook. "Continue."

"Like I said, Emily was at the main desk. I'd say she was about five feet six. Long dark hair. She was wearing the same sweater I found her in." I lowered my head and my voice. "Of course, last night it wasn't covered with blood."

"Mr. Hill, we know what she looks like."

"Sorry."

"Please continue."

I told him everything I knew, how Emily wouldn't let me take the books without a library card, and how I had gone to get mine, promising to return and pick up the books from the checkout desk. "But it wasn't a date."

"So, did you see Emily again?" the detective asked.

"No, sir. I didn't return until 11:15. The library was locked up. All the lights were off."

"How far is it from the library to your room?"

"About five to ten minutes."

"And you left there at 10:15?"

I returned his stare. "Give or take."

"And you didn't get back until quarter past eleven?"

I was hoping he wouldn't pick up on that. "Yes."

He placed the notebook on the table. "Is there something you're not telling me?"

I tried my hardest to maintain eye contact. That's the key to not letting them know you aren't quite telling the truth. In this case, if I had, all it would have served to do was get me in deeper trouble. Unnecessary trouble. "I took a while to find the card … then I had to go to the bathroom …"

Detective Thomas stared at me, unwavering eyes. Did he suspect?

I cleared my throat. "Like I said, by the time I got back the library was closed, totally dark. I climbed the front steps. The doors were locked."

"That's it?"

"That's it."

"You're not omitting anything?"

"Not that I know of."

"And no one can corroborate your story?"

"Well …" I thought for a moment. "There was the security guard?"

He picked up the notebook. "Security guard?"

I paused before answering. "Yes, sir."

"Why didn't you tell me about him before?"

"I didn't think it was important."

"From now on, please share all information, whether you think it's important or not."

"Sorry." I hung my head, feeling like a schoolboy being scolded by the principal.

"Tell me about the guard."

"Not much to tell. When I returned to the library, the guard saw me trying the door and asked what I was doing."

Again, he jotted something down. "We haven't spoken to campus security yet. We'll see if they verify what you've said. Anything else you'd like to add?"

"No, sir."

"So, you never made a date with Emily?"

"No, sir."

"You simply planned on going back to get some books from her?"

"Yes, sir."

"And that's your whole story? Nothing left out?"

"No, sir." I nodded, but as I did, I remembered something. "Wait. There was someone else. A girl ..."

The detective poised his pencil, ready to write. "Who?"

"I ran into her outside the library, on the stairs."

"When?"

"When I came back at 11:15."

His eyes narrowed. "Was she going up or down?"

"Down."

"Coming down?" He placed the pen on the table and gave me a stone-faced glare.

"Yes, sir."

"As if she were coming out of the library?"

"... Yes, sir."

"Mr. Hill." He rubbed his temple. "This is another one of those important pieces of information that you should have told us. Is there anything else you're concealing?"

"I'm not concealing—"

"You're not telling." He almost raised his voice.

I looked him square in the eyes. "Sir, I am not withholding any information. As for knowing Emily, I didn't. At least if I did, it was simply as the girl who worked at the library. As for the guard, since I did nothing wrong, I didn't think I needed someone to verify my whereabouts. As for the girl—" I shrugged "—I have to admit, that did slip my mind."

"Tell me about her."

"Like I said, the library was dark. I was walking through one of the stone archways at the top of the stairs. It was all shadows. I remember thinking they needed some security lights. That's when a figure collided with me. Her belongings slipped from her arms and scattered on the steps."

"What did she look like?"

I shook my head. "I couldn't see her too well. It was dark. I knelt and scooped up a couple of her books. When I went to hand them to her, she recoiled, then grabbed them and ran away."

After a minute of scribbling in his notebook, Detective Thomas looked across the table at me. "Is there any other information or evidence you've neglected to tell us?"

The hair on the back of my neck bristled. "No, sir. That's all I know."

"Are you sure?"

"Yes, sir."

He glanced back to the notebook. "Now, from what I understand, you've been in this area for a short time."

"Three or four months."

"And before that?"

"I was in the marines."

"So I've been told."

Again, I bristled. "What's that supposed to mean?"

"It means," he said slowly and deliberately, "so I've been told." He stared. I wasn't sure if he was waiting for a response or was simply studying me. "Thank you for coming in, Mr. Hill. If you'll take a seat in the booking area, we'll get someone to drive you to the college." His attention fell back to his notebook.

I stood but remained by the table, waiting for him to acknowledge my presence.

Finally, he looked up. "Is there something else?"

"Just wondering what gave you get the idea that I'd made a date with Emily?"

"It came up in our investigation." He went back to his papers.

That was it. He was done with me, so I turned and left.

With all the information Detective Thomas thought I'd withheld, it wouldn't surprise me if I were their chief suspect. But honestly, the girl on the stairs was the only thing I'd forgotten to tell him.

The girl on the stairs.

I smiled.

Why? I hadn't seen enough of her to know whether she was pretty. We hadn't had an engaging conversation. Why had the thought of her seemed so pleasant? Then it hit me.

Her perfume.

The wonderful, intoxicating perfume made me wonder if the face matched the scent. I paused outside the door.

Should I go back in and tell Detective Thomas?

With a shrug, I decided against it. What was he going to do? Line up all the girl suspects and have me sniff them? I doubted it very much.

Officer Grant leaned on the desk chatting with the sergeant. Seeing me approach, he asked, "Are you ready to go?" He pointed to the line of chairs where the blonde girl sat. "I'm about to take Jill back. There's plenty of room for you."

So that's her name. Jill.

Jill scowled in my direction.

I cringed. "No, that's okay. I'll walk."

"Suit yourself." He turned to the young girl. "I'll be right with you."

I was thankful when the door closed behind me, putting a layer of protection between me and the scary elf. I was halfway across the parking lot when the pain in my side ground me to a halt. I buckled over. "Not now!" For a couple of minutes, I remained hunched over, breathing slow and steady. In and out. In and out. Finally, I straightened up.

Just then, a cruiser slid to a stop next to me. Officer Grant rolled down his window. "You okay?"

I rubbed my side. "Overdid the run this morning. Paying for it now."

He hopped out and opened the back door. "Come on."

I peered in. No Jill. It wasn't until I climbed in that I saw her sitting up front.

We exited the parking lot and were part way down the street when she turned to me. "Thanks for trying to blame a murder on me," she said in a soft and sad voice.

I felt a twinge of guilt. "You were there. I—I had to tell the officers. I'm sorry."

"Before you try to take on the role of detective, don't you think you should get your facts straight? Since I called the police, told them about the situation, and was remaining on the scene, they already knew I was there."

I hadn't thought of that. I turned my head, avoiding her stare. Officer Grant snickered.

"Oh," Jill said. "and by the way, Watson—"

"Watson?"

"You're not bright enough to be Sherlock."

Officer Grant coughed. It seemed to me he was trying to hide another snicker. "Sorry. Must be coming down with something."

Jill continued. "You were there too."

"Your point?" I said.

"All the proof you gave to the police about my guilt is also proof of yours."

"But, I—" I choked on my words. She was right. I couldn't deny it. Hoping to bring some sunlight into the dismal cruiser, I changed the subject. "What's a kid like you doing on a college campus anyway?"

Her brow creased. "Kid?"

Officer Grant shifted, uncomfortably. "Er … You two hungry?"

"We ate on the way here," I reminded him.

Jill turned farther around to face me. "What do you mean, kid?"

Officer Grant cut in. "Maybe Jill's hun—"

"So, are you a prof's kid?" I asked. "Or are you visiting an older sister or something?"

Jill's mouth dropped open. "Older sister?"

"Yes."

She shook her head as if hardly able to believe what she was hearing.

"Oh, look!" Officer Grant pointed. "There's the campus. We're almost back. How about if—"

Jill blushed. "I'm at the school because I go there."

"No way!" I chuckled. The dark expression on her face said she was not amused. "Honest? You go to college? Are you one of those child geniuses or something?"

She turned and faced the front. When she spoke, her voice was quiet, almost broken-hearted. "I'm twenty-three years old."

"Really?" I was honestly amazed by this revelation.

Officer Grant steered the cruiser through the main entrance of the campus.

"Jason." She spoke to Officer Grant. "Could you drop me off here. I ... There's somewhere I need to go."

"Sure." Officer Grant pulled over.

Jill hopped out. She closed the door and walked away.

I scratched the back of my head. "Man, what's wrong with her?"

"You're a terrible judge of age, aren't you? And of a girl's feelings."

"Huh?"

"Jill's always been kind of sensitive about how young she looks."

"Really?" I watched the retreating figure. "I don't know. She's kind of cute."

"But you didn't say that, did you?"

I went to open the door. "Should I—"

"Let it go." He grabbed my arm. "Trust me. I've known Jill since high school. She needs time to cool off."

I felt a pang of guilt. I hadn't meant to hurt her feelings. Sometimes, I guess, I don't pay attention to what I'm saying. But then, just as quick as the guilt came, a memory flashed in my mind—an image. That person reading the magazine by the checkout desk, last night in the library … It was Jill. I could see her as clear as day. She was there.

An idea hit me. "Officer Grant," I said. "How did the police get this crazy notion that I had a date with Emily?"

He went to answer but stopped. He looked to where Jill had just slipped around the corner of a building.

"I thought so." With a grin, I tipped my head in her direction. "Something tells me little Miss Jill likes to eavesdrop on conversations."

Officer Grant didn't respond.

Sunday morning arrived. I'd promised a chaplain friend from the hospital that once I was discharged, I'd get involved in a church. Seeing as the pastor of the Springsbury Community Church was a friend of his, and that he took me in when I first came to town, it seemed only right for me to go there.

The church was a mile and a half from the college. Taking a nice walk was good for me. That's the little white lie I swallowed. The simple truth—I didn't have a car yet.

Pastor Roberts was a good preacher. Of course, being new to the faith I didn't have many to compare him to. He didn't have the flare or razzle-dazzle of some of the television evangelists. Frankly, this was a plus.

The Good Samaritan was his sermon this Sunday. I sat on the right side of the sanctuary among a congregation of about one hundred and fifty. For some reason, I was having trouble concentrating. Why?

At the part in the story when the Samaritan drops the fellow off at an inn, I figured it out. Across the sanctuary, over to my left and about four rows up, sat a gaggle of girls watching me. Whoever they were, they derived great enjoyment in looking my way and giggling. I'd like to say they were middle schoolers, but with my recent disaster in the game of age-guessing, I wasn't willing to put money on that.

Finally, someone in the pew behind them nudged their backs and signaled for them all to behave. They obediently straightened up and gave their full attention to the pastor.

Thank you, whoever you are.

The nudger glanced my way. My heart sank. It was Jill. Wasn't there anywhere I could go to get away from this girl?

With a sudden, sheepish look, she melted into her pew.

The service ended, and the congregation meandered toward the doors, gabbing and chatting as they did. Jill tried to corral the group of girls.

I sighed. Maybe I'd been a little hard on her and should try to make amends. After all, if we're attending the same church, we should probably be civil to each other. As I stepped into the aisle, a passerby almost ran me over.

"Sorry," he mumbled.

"No pro—" My word cut short by his sad yet familiar face. It was one of the three who'd been giving Emily a hard time at the library. The big guy. Tank or Bash or something like that.

"Wasn't paying attention to where I was going." He ran his thick-fingered paw through his blond hair and cast a forlorn look at the floor.

"Like I was saying," I answered, "no problem."

"Hey, Boomer," someone called from behind me.

Boomer. Hmmm. Suits him.

The big guy had no trouble peering over the top of my head. He waved a hand at whoever called, nodded at me, and was off in the direction of the voice.

I continued toward Jill. She was so busy collecting the girls that when I walked up behind her, she didn't notice me.

"Hi there." I tried to sound as friendly as I could.

She turned around. At that moment I knew what a slug must feel like when a girl looks at it. Kind of a self-conscious feeling. Jill's face registered horror with a speck of anger added in for good measure.

The gaggle reverted to giggling, cupping their hands around each other's ears and whispering who knows what.

"Girls," Jill said, sternly.

They quieted, but still mild giggles and silly stares seemed to be the standard of the day. Why in the world do girls have to do that? Whisper secrets to each other. It's so annoying.

I cleared my throat. "I wanted to say I'm sorry for any misunderstanding we've had."

Jill softened. She brushed a strand of her long, blonde hair over her left ear and stepped toward me. "That's okay."

Yes! I was getting through.

"It's just ... you look so young."

The girls' noise level rose.

Jill threw dagger looks at them.

Not wanting to lose this goodwill between us, I thought I'd try some humor. After all, I could be a pretty humorous guy. So I've been told. "Plus, you are kind of short. I mean, you probably could have been an understudy for one of the munchkins."

Her mouth dropped.

The giggling stopped. In unison, the gaggle took a step back.

"I—I didn't mean to—"

"No—No." Her face flushed. "It's ..." The words seemed to stick in her throat. "Thank you for the ... apology." She spun on her heels and escaped into the crowd of girls. A couple of them put their arms around her shoulders as they marched toward the other side of the church.

Oh boy.

Jill was desperately trying to listen to Pastor Roberts' sermon on the Good Samaritan, but the three girls sitting in front of her were causing trouble. Something had them all giggly. Being middle schoolers from her Sunday school class, she felt sort of responsible for them. She leaned forward and nudged them. "Quiet."

They turned and faced front. However, one of the girls gave a lingering glance to the right and smirked.

Jill looked. There sat Jack. Her face flushed.

Oh, wonderful. Is he going to think I've been staring at him?

Lisa, another middle school student, sitting on Jill's right, checked out Jack. "He's cute."

Anna, on Jill's left, must have thought her two cents was needed. "Very cute."

Jill's jaw tightened. "What's that matter to me?"

Lisa turned in her seat to face Jill. She whispered, "Don't *you* think he's cute?"

"Tell us!" Anna's hushed voice was filled with urgency.

Lisa giggled. "I mean, we've seen you gawking at him."

"Gawking … at *him*?" Jill grunted. "I—I don't know what you're talking about."

The two shared a look, huge grins on their faces. Leaning close to Jill they sang in a whispered voice. "Jill and Jack sitting in a tree. K-i-s-s-i-n-g—"

Jill placed a hand on each of the girl's knees. "If you girls don't settle down, I'm going to tell Mrs. Roberts."

It had the desired effect. The girls faced the front and remained quiet the rest of the service.

How can middle school girls be so perceptive?

Service ended. After greeting a few friends, Jill started gathering her students to discuss their upcoming apple picking trip.

A familiar voice called to her. "Hi there."

Her mouth fell. It was him. What did he want? Did she have a stupid look on her face?

Her stomach tightened as the girls giggled and whispered to each other.

"Girls," Jill said, sternly.

Jack stepped forward. "I just wanted to say I'm sorry for any misunderstanding we've had."

What a nice thing to say.

She brushed a strand of her long, blonde hair over her left ear and edged toward him. "That's okay."

The girl's noise level rose.

Jack had the silliest grin on his face. "Plus, you are kind of short. I mean, you could probably have been an understudy for one of the munchkins."

Jill's mouth dropped.

Her students stopped giggling. In unison, the gaggle took a step back.

Jack waved his hands. "I—I didn't mean to—"

"No—No." Jill was at a loss. How could he think of her that way? Was he kidding? Was he trying to hurt her feelings? "It's … Thank you for the … apology." Embarrassed, she escaped into the crowd of girls. A couple of them put their arms around her shoulders as they marched toward the other side of the church.

"Don't worry, Jill," Anna said. "He's not worth it."

That was the problem. Jill felt he was.

Chapter Four

As usual, I was one of the last people to leave the sanctuary. Pastor Roberts stood by the front door, warmly greeting the remaining few stragglers as they departed. He saw me approaching. "Well, what questions do you have for me today?"

I scratched the back of my neck. "Am I that predictable?"

Tapping a finger on his lip, he considered. "I don't think predictable is the right word. Maybe inquisitive. Why don't you join Mrs. Roberts and me for lunch? It'll give us a chance to talk."

"I don't want to impose."

"Sure, you do." Mrs. Roberts came up behind us, her face beaming. "You can't live on college food. Every once in a while, you need a good home cooked meal."

"What are we having today?" I asked.

She considered. "I think we're sending out for Chinese."

With a twinkle in his eye, the pastor snorted, "A good home-cooked meal."

Pastor and Mrs. Roberts were a wonderful couple. I'd say in their mid-fifties to early sixties. The best word to describe Pastor Roberts would be—Gentleman. It fits him so well. He didn't run off at the mouth or lose his temper too quickly. He was smallish in stature, with a bit of a high-pitched voice and thinning snow-white hair combed straight back over his head.

Mrs. Roberts was, to be polite and diplomatic, a husky woman who stood a couple inches taller than her husband. She had a true Christian spirit which showed by her willingness to open her home to me when I had needed a place to stay. And now, on an almost weekly basis, she invited me for Sunday dinner.

"We'll see you next door." She headed outside with me and the Pastor following.

As Mrs. Roberts crossed the parking lot to the parsonage, Pastor Roberts paused at the bottom of the church steps. "We'll be home shortly," he called after her.

Though the sky was bright with sunshine, the air remained cool—typical of an early fall day. Cars rushed along Route 97, which ran in front of the church, through the center of town and out toward the college.

Pastor Roberts sat on the step. He looked up at me. His brow knit with concern. "Sit, please."

I sank next to him. "Problem?"

"You tell me?"

"I—I don't understand."

"You heard me announce about Emily this morning. From what I understand, you found her."

"That's right. But I'm fine. Honest."

"Jack, when you came to us, you'd already been through quite a bit—"

"I'm fine," I snapped. I looked away, suddenly feeling flushed and guilty for my reaction. "Sorry."

Pastor Roberts placed a hand on my shoulder. "That's all right, son."

I shook my head. "I've been interrogated by the police and hounded by morbid college kids. I guess I am a little frustrated." I glanced over at him. "I gotta admit, I didn't even know she came to church here."

He nodded as his gaze lingered across the street. "For over two years now. She used to be so happy. I can remember her and her friends laughing and joking." He frowned. "But as of late I've noticed a distinct change in her. A sense of sadness. I don't know why. Maybe the stress of college. And now this." He lowered his head. "Who'd have ever thought our small community would be invaded by a serial killer?" He shrugged, sadly, and rose to his feet. "I wanted to make sure you were okay. With all you've ..." His words cut off. "You know I'm here whenever you want to talk."

"Thank you." I stood, and the two of us crossed to the parsonage. "May I ask you about another girl?"

He gave a crooked smile. "Another girl?"

"No, no, It's nothing like that."

Pastor Roberts laughed. "Relax, Jack. I'm only joking with you. Besides, there's nothing wrong with a young Christian man looking for a young Christian woman. What better place to find a prospective bride than in the church?"

I shuffled uncomfortably. "I'm not interested in her in that way. Believe me."

"Fine. So, what's this other girl's name?"

"Jill."

"Really?" It was a single word. That's all. And the pastor tried to make it sound normal, but when he said it, his voice cracked.

"What's the matter?"

"Nothing." We walked a few more steps in silence. When he spoke again, there was an air of nonchalance in his voice. "So, what did you think of Jill?"

"Well ..." I scratched the back of my head. "I think I hurt her feelings." I proceeded to explain about our encounters.

When I finished, he chuckled.

"I don't see what's so funny."

"I'm sorry." We walked across the gravel sidewalk and onto the whitewashed porch of the parsonage. He opened the door, and the two of us stepped inside. "I simply think it's amusing, your continuing to run into a girl you're not interested in."

"What?" Mrs. Roberts called from the kitchen area. "Is Jackson Hill noticing girls?" I started to protest but was cut short. "Wonderful Christian girls make wonderful Christian wives. And, if I may say, I've seen some of our girls sneaking glances at you."

"Sweetheart." The Pastor's eyebrow rose. "Let's not go there." As we headed into the kitchen, he turned and confided in me. "Mrs. Roberts has a bit of a matchmaker in her." Playfully, he jabbed my ribs. "Be careful. She'll be fixing you up with some young thing before you know it."

"So, who did you meet?" Mrs. Roberts rushed up to us, champing at the bit.

"Don't hound the boy." Pastor took me by the arm and steered me away from his wife. "He'll tell you if he wants to."

"I was only asking. There's no harm in asking."

"Martha."

The warnings were getting more serious. Pastor Roberts actually called his wife by her first name. I laughed. "Honest, Mrs. Roberts. I'm not interested."

"Of course. Of course."

I sat at the kitchen table, picked up a cookie from a plate, and took a bite. "The girl's name is Jill."

"Really?" She slid a chair next to me and sat. "So?"

"I think that will be quite enough," Pastor Roberts interrupted. "Honestly, dear, if you keep badgering Jack, he'll never want to come to our house again."

Mrs. Roberts looked crestfallen. "I was only making polite conversation."

"I know what you were doing." Pastor Roberts gave his wife a look that said, "drop it."

She ignored this, turned to me, and in a singsongy voice said, "So … Jill?"

Pastor Roberts spoke in a slow cadence with an extra meaning to his words that I couldn't quite figure out. "He had a run-in with her. In truth, he insulted her. Called her a munchkin or some such thing."

"Man!" I shook my head. "Is she sensitive about her height!"

Mrs. Roberts frowned. "We can't have that. Can we? I mean, you should probably apologize."

"I tried." I lowered my voice. "But I think she's a bit crazy."

Pastor Roberts broke into a fit of laughter.

Mrs. Roberts scowled at him. "No, no. I'm sure it was just some sort of misunderstanding." Deep lines formed in her forehead as she chewed on a fingernail. "Yes. Just a misunderstanding." Suddenly her face brightened. "How about if I give you her phone number. You can call to say you're sorry."

Pastor Roberts cleared his throat. "I don't think that will be necessary. By the way, Martha. Have you ordered the Chinese food yet? Jack and I are hungry."

"Fine!" She huffed, marched to the counter and pulled a large selection of restaurant takeout menus from the drawer. In a great flourish of annoyance, she rifled through them until she found the appropriate one. "No reason to get upset. All I'm doing is talking."

The pastor peered over the top of his glasses at his wife. "Oh, really?"

I kind of suspected Mrs. Roberts' real intentions were more than just talk. Though I didn't give it much thought. As far as I knew, I was the farthest thing from Jill's mind. "I tell you what, Mrs. Roberts," I chuckled. "When I'm in the market for a girlfriend, you'll be the first to know."

"Jack, my boy." Her face beamed. "People your age are always in the market."

Chapter Five

Later that evening, rain pelted my window. Drops, like thousands of tiny, frigid arrows fell in the quad, ready to sting the skin of anyone who ventured out. Even the dumbest person would have the sense to stay inside tonight.

I hate rainstorms.

As I studied the terrible weather from the warmth of my dorm room, two figures caught my eye. They were in the shadows on the side of a maintenance shed, which sat on the edge of the quad.

I squinted, my vision impaired by the deluge.

Definitely two people. Looked like a guy and a girl. They were skirting between the darkness and the bit of light thrown from the streetlight.

Without warning, he grabbed at her, but she fought back.

Is this how it started for Emily, leaving the library, unaware that someone was waiting to attack?

My jaw tightened.

No way was I going to let that incident repeat itself. I ran from my room and pushed past a couple of students in the hall. They hollered their protests as I rushed to the stairwell.

I have to get there in time.

Halfway down the first set of stairs, I vaulted over the railing and landed on the stairs below, continuing in this way until I reached the first floor.

Groups of people clustered in the lobby. I'm sure they thought I was insane as I slammed through the front doors and out into the bitter weather.

A cold blast of wet slapped my face.

A scream.

The grounds keeper's shed was located across the walkway, about thirty feet into the quad.

Another scream. An angry one.

Good. She was still alive and fighting.

I was close enough to see that the one being attacked *was* a girl. The other figure wore a bulky coat and a hat pulled over its head.

"Hey!" I raced toward them.

The struggling stopped. They both looked my way. The assailant backed off and disappeared around the side of the shed.

He had about a seven-second head start on me. If I hurried, I could catch him. My feet slapped into the puddles, splashing the water against my legs.

The startled girl's mouth fell open. Then, with a glance in the direction of her assailant, she slumped to the side, fell against the building and whimpered. She slid toward the ground.

I was torn. Do I chase or offer aid? There really was no choice. It would be foolish to chase and catch the guy only to leave her hurt or bleeding.

"Are you all right?" I asked as I reached her side. "It's okay. He's gone." There was a definite note of disappointment in my voice. Maybe I should have chased him.

The girl wiped the rain from her face. "I'm—I'm fine."

The eave extended three or four feet, offering some protection from the rain. A couple wooden crates were piled there. I helped her over, and we used them as seats.

"Are you sure?" I asked.

"Thanks to you." Her black hair was plastered to her head, drenched from the rain. Mascara streamed down her face. She was quite a sight. She pulled her windbreaker tightly around her neck.

"Who was that?"

She paused before answering. "I don't know. He jumped out from behind the shed."

"Are you sure you don't know who it was?"

She nodded.

"You need to report this."

"No." Her answer came out quicker than I expected.

"Why not?"

She shook her head. "No. No harm was done."

"But—"

"Besides what good would it do? I'm sure attacks like this happen all the time. He was probably after my pocketbook." Her hand slid along the strap around her neck until it touched the bag at her side. "He didn't get it though."

"Still, security should know, especially with what happened behind the library."

It took a second, but her eyes lit up. "You don't think ... Oh, no!"

"Easy." I tried to steady her. "It's going to be okay."

She hugged herself and rocked slowly. "This is so terrible."

"Can I walk you back to your residence hall?"

"No, I'm—" Her words dropped suddenly. "Maybe in a minute. First, could you do me a favor? I lost my books in the scuffle, somewhere by the back of the shed. Could you get them for me?"

"Of course." I hopped up. Just at that instant, the rain picked up. It was as if it knew I was venturing out, mocking me. Maybe I volunteered for this mission too quickly. But then again, I was already soaked. I glanced at her, hoping she'd realize any books caught in this deluge would be ruined and reconsider.

A smile peeked out from under her hair. "I'd really appreciate it."

Taking a deep breath, I stepped into the rain and sloshed through the muddy ground. I did a preliminary scan. "I don't see them."

"They're farther to the back," she called, her voice nearly drowned out by the sound of the rain hitting the roof.

"Of course they are," I grumbled under my breath. I searched for what felt like a half hour, but it was probably closer to three minutes. "You were very brave, fighting like that," I yelled.

No answer.

She probably couldn't hear me over the storm.

I looked around a bush on the side of the building, gently kicked through a large puddle toward the back. All my efforts came up empty. No books. I was wasting my time.

"What's your name, by the way?" I said as I made my way along the side of the shed.

Again, no answer.

"I'm Jack." I rounded the corner and stepped under the eave. "Sorry, there are no books out there …" I stopped. The bench was empty. I sighed. "And there is no girl up here."

Now, that's odd.

The girl said it was no big deal. I disagreed. Whether she wanted to report it or not made no difference to me. Security needed to know.

Their office was in the basement of the administration building.

The frosted window pane in the door had a single word painted on it. Security. The *e* and half the *r* were missing.

I knocked.

Nothing.

I knocked again.

No response.

I turned the knob and opened the door.

A slightly balding man sat behind a wooden desk with large chunks gouged from its edges. A bag of chips was ripped open, its contents scattered along the surface. The man was scribbling on a report of some kind.

"Excuse me." I inched forward, dripping puddles on the floor. "I knocked. No one answered."

"Uh-huh." He didn't look up, just kept writing. "Usually by the fourth or fifth knock people figure they can walk right in."

"Oh."

"What do you need?"

I stepped forward, my sneakers making a loud and uncomfortable squishing noise. "I want to report an attack."

"An attack?"

"Yes, sir."

"Anyone hurt?"

"No, sir."

"Who attacked you?"

"Not me. A young lady."

He looked beyond me to the door. "Where is she?"

"She … She didn't want to report it."

He pushed his report aside. "I see. And what's her name?"

I paused. "I don't know."

Rolling his eyes, he picked up a chip and put it in his mouth. "Look …" He chewed for a few seconds, staring at me.

"Jack."

"Look, Jack. If she doesn't want to report it, it probably wasn't anything serious." He shrugged. "A lover's spat. A disagreement between friends."

"But with what happened to Emily—"

His face lit, and he pointed at me. "Wait a minute. I know you. Aren't you the one who found the dead body?"

"Her name was Emily."

He raised an eyebrow. His expression changed as if seeing me in a new, less-than-favorable light. "You always go looking for trouble?"

"No."

"Funny how it finds you."

"I resent your implication."

He picked up another chip and motioned with it as he spoke. "Tell you what. Get the girl to come in and file a report. We'll check into it. Frankly, if she wasn't hurt, and she doesn't want to file a report, chances are she's protecting someone, or she doesn't think it was that big a deal."

"But—"

"I know what it's like for you ex-military types." He took a deep breath while giving me the once-over. "Want to jump right in and solve all the problems, bring justice wherever you can." He straightened up. "Hey, I was in the army. Like I said, I know what it's like. Why don't you just leave the crime solving to the pros. Enjoy college life."

"Thank you." I marched out before I said something I'd be sorry for.

"You military types," I muttered. "He doesn't know me at all."

The rain had eased a bit.

He knows what it's like? Hah! Army. They're just the cleanup crew for the marines.

I stormed back to my room, fuming. How could he ignore what I was telling him? Emily was dead. Another girl had been attacked. And he wasn't going to do anything about it!

At the top of the steps to my building, I paused, my hand on the door.

Just because he isn't going to do anything, didn't mean I can't.

I glanced in the direction of the admin building.

"Well, Mr. I-was-in-the-army, you're about to have my help whether you like it or not."

Chapter Six

Once back in my room, I calmed down. Security was probably doing their best. However, with hundreds of access points to this campus—more than they could possibly manage—I doubted their best was good enough. So, I determined to do my part by keeping my eyes open for any trouble. Nightly patrols of the perimeter would be a good place to start. No one would complain about that. It wasn't like I was going to suit up in military gear or carry a weapon. I'd simply go for a walk.

A vigilant walk.

For the rest of that week, the murder was the main talk on campus. The constant harassment by curious students wanting my eyewitness report had an unexpected consequence. It ended up being an icebreaker. Let's face it, being the new kid on the block (plus being a few years older), I'd remained kind of standoffish from everyone else. Finding Emily gave me the opportunity to talk to a lot of people.

With all my new acquaintances, there was one I tried to avoid. Jill. Was it my fault she was so height sensitive? I imagined how neat and clean it would have been if she was the killer. Kind of stupid, I know, but if she were tossed in jail, my problem of trying to avoid her would have vanished.

I guess, just like me, she'd been jogging that morning. I considered this and vaguely remembered hearing footfalls during my run. It must have been her. But there was still one question that bothered me. Why in the world had the police taken her away? I hadn't received that treatment. Why her?

Monday evening, armed only with a small flashlight, I began my patrols. All was quiet. As a matter of fact, Monday and Tuesday went by without incident.

Wednesday, though, I had a minor problem. I didn't make it back to the residence hall until after curfew. That meant dealing with Mrs. Oswald.

Mrs. Oswald. I winced and groaned.

She was one of the math professor's wives who also doubled as a monitor. Since the first two Dumpster killings, each residence hall had one—someone who signed people in and out and made sure curfew was followed. All the other exits to the building had been alarmed. The only way into the building was the main entrance. There was no way to get around her.

Something about her rubbed me the wrong way. Maybe it was because she reminded me of my Aunt Helena, a rotund woman who perpetually pinched my cheeks and crushed me with her bear hugs. I have vivid memories from my childhood of hiding in the hall closet when she'd come to visit.

On top of that, once Mrs. Oswald discovered I'd been in the marines, she treated me differently from the other students. It was difficult to understand, but she babied me. I'm sure she didn't mean any harm. Her father was a marine, and I guess some whacko family code of honor obliged her to look after me.

Tonight, I didn't feel like being babied or pinched.

Thankfully, as I watched her through the window, wondering how to get in without answering all kinds of foolish questions, she left her station. I assumed for a bathroom break. Great luck. I'd have to keep an eye on this. It could be to my advantage if this were her regular routine and I was ever out after curfew again.

On Thursday night something odd happened.

I was about halfway through my rounds, crossing behind the library. All signs of the crime scene had been removed. Things were getting back to normal. I guess we'd all like that to happen. Unfortunately, my nightmares had returned. I was trying to cope, trying to trust in the Lord.

I continued on, behind Simmon's, one of the residence halls, when something stung the bottom of my left foot. I hobbled over to a bench by the building, sat down, and pulled off my shoe. A vigorous shake dislodged a pebble.

Just then a branch snapped. I stiffened and shined my flashlight toward the dark woods across the road. Nothing appeared out of the ordinary. Odd. The sound hadn't seemed to come from that direction anyway.

As my flashlight's beam slowly scanned the area, something whacked me on the head. A shoe fell to the ground in front of me. I rubbed my new pain while looking for whoever had thrown it.

"Er, excuse me," a female voice timidly called.

With the echo off the building, it was difficult to pinpoint where it came from.

"I said, excuse me," she repeated in a firmer voice. "You're in my way."

I looked up and down the road. All was quiet. Was I imagining things? The voice sounded oddly familiar. But was that possible? Maybe I was dreaming. I picked up the small sneaker.

No. Dreams don't throw real sneakers.

"Who's there? Where are you?" I asked each question with growing perplexity.

"Here," the voice called from above.

I directed my light up. There was Jill, about two floors up, precariously clinging to the ivy vines that covered the building. One shoeless foot dangled in the breeze. She clung to the side of the building like a human fly. Her shoed foot rested on a large vine, holding all her weight. Her shoeless one gingerly searched for a safe place to perch.

"What are you doing?" I asked.

She answered in a what-do-you-think-I'm-doing? kind of tone. "Trying to get down."

I held up her shoe and smirked. "Did you lose something?"

She glared at me.

"I assume this is yours." I struggled to stifle a chuckle. The whole situation seemed like an old *I Love Lucy* episode. "Can I do anything to help?"

"Get out of my way." She continued her slow descent.

"What are you doing up there?"

She sighed. "Trying to get down."

"You already said that."

"And you already asked me what I was doing up here." Her words dripped with sarcasm.

"True. But I mean, why are you even up there?"

Before she could answer, her bare foot jerked as if she'd stepped on something sharp. She yelped, lost her footing, and fell.

You'd figure a little bit of a thing would have fallen slowly, kind of like a leaf wafting in the breeze. No such luck.

My instincts kicked in, and I leaped into action. Like a graceful deer, I sprang forward. Jill landed in my arms like a well-thrown pass. My momentum took me forward into a somersault. Then I sprang to my feet with Jill safe and secure in my arms, a look of admiration on her face.

Uh-huh. That's what happened in my mind's eye. The reality was different. As I raced to catch her, my shin hit the edge of the bench. I stumbled to the ground, and Jill—like a sack of rocks—crash-landed on top of me.

We lay there for a few seconds. I was checking to make sure I hadn't broken any bones. Jill lifted her head from my chest. Slightly dazed eyes locked onto mine. The corners of her mouth turned up.

"Are you okay?" I asked.

The sound of my voice chased her dazed look away. It was replaced by one of panic. She pushed off me and hopped to her feet. "Of course." She brushed dirt and grass from her clothing. "Why do you ask?"

"Are you serious?" I got up. "You just fell ten feet."

"Oh, that. I'm fine. Are you all right?"

I felt my side. It hurt, but not too bad, considering. "I'm okay, but you never answered my question. Why the imitation of a wall crawler?"

"Trying to prove a point."

"Which is?"

She picked leaves and twigs from her hair. "Nothing. Don't worry about it." She held out her hand.

"What?"

"My shoe."

I looked at it, sitting on the bench.

"Please."

I fumbled behind me for her shoe while keeping my eyes focused on her. "It's not safe for you being out here at night, climbing up walls." I handed it to her.

She reddened. "Other one, please."

"Huh?"

She held out my shoe, the one I'd shaken the pebble from.

"Sorry. Wrong one." I exchanged them.

Jill plopped on the bench, quickly tied her shoe, and was off.

That is one crazy girl.

I looked up at the vine-covered wall, puzzled.

What was she doing up there?

Except for Jill's wall-climbing, my nightly walks had revealed nothing. Maybe security was right, and the attack I'd witnessed was a lover's quarrel. I really couldn't be sure of what I'd seen through the dark and the rain. As for the Dumpster Killer, even though nothing new was being reported by the police, I was sure they had everything under control.

Saturday morning, after I completed three miles of my five-mile course, I hobbled back to my room. My right leg was leading a revolt against me. My hip had joined its side.

Before I could get in the door, the phone rang.

7:30. Who'd be calling me this early?

"Hello, Jack?" A gravelly voice said. "Pastor Roberts here." He went into a coughing fit.

"You sound awful." I sat on the edge of the bed and removed my running shoes.

"I feel awful. Sorry for calling so early. It's about Emily's funeral."

I yanked off my sweaty shirt. "That's this afternoon, right?"

"Correct. I'm not going to make it. The church elders are all away at the discipleship seminar. I was wondering if you could go to represent us?"

"Me?"

Another coughing fit. It sounded like he hacked up a lung. "Yes."

"But I'm new in the church. How could I be your representative?"

"Relax. I'm not asking you to eulogize or anything like that. I'd simply like someone to be there to talk to her parents. Tell them how sorry we are, and that if there is anything we can do, to let us know." The phone line went silent. "It would really be a big help."

I surrendered to the pitiful sound of his voice. "Okay. But I don't have a car. How will I get there?" Emily's home church, where the funeral was being held, was about an hour away.

Again, the line went silent.

"Let's see what I can arrange." He clicked off.

While awaiting his return call, I jumped in the shower. After drying and dressing—about twenty minutes later—the phone rang again.

"That was quick," I said as I answered.

"Jack?" It was a woman's voice. "This is Mrs. Roberts."

"I was expecting a call from your husband."

She laughed. "I gave him orders to get to bed. That's the best place for him. However, I've gotten you a ride to the funeral."

"Oh …" I was half hoping they wouldn't be able to find me one. After all, I really didn't know Emily.

"Bernard will take you. He said for you to be in the parking lot of the administration offices at noon."

"Bernard?"

"Bernard Anderson." She said the name as if it should mean something to me. "You know Bernard."

I scratched my head. "I can't say that I do."

"That's funny. He says he knows you."

"Really?" I tried to think of a Bernard. No face came to mind.

"He's probably in one of your classes. He was good friends with Emily, from what I understand."

"He doesn't mind driving me?" I asked.

"Bernard was thinking about skipping the funeral. Riding together will give him the strength and support he needs."

"Okay. Noon at the admin parking lot. Tell the pastor I hope he's feeling better."

"I will. Bye!"

At 11:30, I was finishing tying my Windsor knot. Dressed in a blue sports coat and dark dress pants, I headed for the door.

People who are perpetually late drive me crazy. I think it's a selfish thing. They have no respect for others. I, on the other hand, always try to arrive ahead of schedule. Today was no exception. By 11:45 I was scanning the admin's parking lot. Though there were several parked cars, I saw none with a driver in it.

Where is Bernard? For that matter, who is Bernard?

Oh, well. I'd find out soon enough. Some orange and yellow leaves rode through the air on a cold wind. I stuck my hands in my sport coat pockets, trying to keep them warm. It didn't help much.

Since I was representing the church, I considered the appropriate thing for me to say to Emily's parents. I recoiled remembering my first funeral. I was fourteen years old when my uncle died of cancer. At the funeral, when I approached the family, all I could think to say was, "How ya doin'?"

I was the butt of jokes for years to come.

I tried to come up with the proper words. "Hi, Mr. and Mrs. Hamilton. I'm Jack Hill. I'm from your daughter's church."

No.

"I'm from the church she's attending while at college … or while she was at college. She doesn't go there anymore, obviously."

I slapped myself on the forehead. "Of course, she doesn't go there anymore! She's dead."

Why was I making this so hard? I searched and searched for the right thing to say. "I'd like to say I'm sorry … I'd like to express my condolences." Yes! That sounds official. "Express my condolences."

"Jack?" A voice called from behind me.

This must be Bernard.

I turned and discovered I did know him. "You're Bernard?"

Boomer blushed. "Not many people call me that."

"Mrs. Roberts does."

The toe of his shoe scraped in the gravel. "Mrs. Roberts has known me since I was small. Her and Pastor Roberts used to serve at a church closer to my dad's."

"Your dad's?"

"My dad's the pastor officiating at" —the big guy grimaced— "Emily's funeral."

His show of emotion surprised me. Mrs. Roberts said Bernard and Emily were close friends, but his actions in the library said something different. "Frankly, I didn't think you'd be going."

"I wasn't planning on it, but my dad … he said I should." His eyes were puffy and red.

I thought it best to change the subject. "So, where's 'Boomer' come from?"

"It's the nickname I picked up in high school." He half smiled and shrugged. "Football, you know."

I nodded. It was easy to see why they'd call him that. The man towered over me. If he hit someone—Boom!

They'd be down for the count! I glanced at my watch. It was noon on the dot. "We'd better be going. Where's your car?"

"My car?"

I nodded. "Mrs. Roberts said you'd give me a ride."

"I was going to, but then I realized I wasn't coming back to the college tonight, so I called her back. She said to meet you here, and she'd take care of everything."

I looked at my watch, annoyed. "It's getting late. Whoever is driving us, better get here soon."

While waiting for our ride, we stood in confused silence, not having much to talk about. It was true, I was acquainted with Boomer. He was in my biology class. Beyond that, we'd had zero personal conversations.

Boomer stared at the ground.

His attitude puzzled me. In the library, I'd have sworn he could barely stand the sight of Emily. Yet here he was, apparently broken up over her death.

After a couple of minutes, a car—I guess that's what you'd call it—jolted to a stop next to us, the gears ground as it was thrown into neutral.

Boomer backed up a step from the yellow hunk of metal. "This must be our … ride."

My watch read ten past twelve. Whoever this was, didn't win any prizes for thoughtfulness in my book. The driver's door opened, and Jill emerged. My jaw dropped, and I developed a sinking feeling in the pit of my stomach.

She looked at Boomer. "Sorry I'm late."

"Hey, Jill," he said. "You our ride?"

"Yup."

"Wonderful," I grumbled.

Chapter Seven

"Ready to go?" Jill directed her question solely at Boomer. Whether she didn't see me in the big man's shadow or chose to ignore me, I wasn't sure.

With his face scrunched up, Boomer pointed to the car. "What is that?"

"This is a 1972 Ford Pinto." Jill proudly patted its top. "My dad's first car."

"That thing seriously runs?" I asked.

For the first time, Jill acknowledged my presence with a frown. "Very funny." Then, turning from me as if I were an insignificant gnat, her attention returned to Boomer. "Mrs. Roberts called. Said you needed a ride to the funeral." She pointed to the car. "Hop in."

Boomer pulled on the handle, and the car door creaked open. We both went to get in.

"Oh …" Jill stared at me, a deadpan expression on her face. "Are you coming, too?"

"I … I thought Mrs. Roberts had set it up."

She climbed behind the wheel, rolling her eyes, and mumbling under her breath. "She set it up all right."

"What?" I leaned over and peered through the open door.

"Nothing," she sighed. "No problem. One of you has to get into the back, though."

I volunteered, not imagining that Boomer's large frame was a good match for the vehicle's small rear seat.

"We'd better get going, or we'll be late," she said.

"Boomer and I were here on time," I muttered as I fell into the back seat.

Boomer climbed in and slammed the door shut. The car listed in his direction.

Jill's slightly vexed eyes watched me through the rearview mirror. She grabbed hold of the stick shift and ground the car into first gear. It lunged forward, pushing us back against our seats.

The trip was quiet, that is, in terms of the conversation. The physical ride was another matter. The engine emitted a variety of grunts and grinds. Jill busily fiddled with the stick shift, while talking to the car as if it were alive. "Come on," she coaxed. "I know you can do it."

Every stop sign and every traffic light was torture to the engine as she jerked the car from one gear to another. Sometimes she eased up on the clutch too quickly or accidentally hit the brake instead and tossed me forward.

"Sorry," was her standard response.

But I'm not sure how sorry she really was. Once, as I struggled to an upright position and was wiping a smudge of dirt off my face, which I'd received from smashing into the rear of the front seat, I thought I saw her grinning.

Oh yes. She's enjoying this.

Boomer was wedged in front like a bear in a bird cage. He sat perfectly still, deep in a brooding contemplation.

As I said, it was a quiet ride.

The funeral was at two o'clock with calling hours from one to two. Much to my amazement, we arrived alive. Boomer extracted his large frame from the tiny car and tipped the front seat so I could escape. I wanted to hug a tree or something but decided against it. Probably a little over the top.

"That was an experience," I whispered to him.

He wasn't listening, though. He stared at the church like it was a slaughterhouse and he was part of the herd, then plodded toward the front door.

Jill came around the side of the car, and we walked together toward the back entrance. "I'm surprised you came. I didn't think you knew Emily," she said.

"Pastor Roberts asked me to share the church's concerns with the family."

"Are you ready?"

I thought of the line I'd practiced during the ride over. I could have told her I was all set. Instead, I said, "I guess something will come to me."

Jill choked back her response as we approached a rather sullen-looking man in a dark suit holding open the church door. We'd hardly entered the building when she stopped. "Something will come to you?"

"Do you have a problem with that?"

"Yes. I do. Pastor Roberts puts a lot of stock in you. The least you could do is try and live up to it. Give what you're going to say some consideration. Weren't you a marine or something? Aren't you supposed to always be prepared?"

I winced. "That's the Boy Scouts. Not the marines."

I could have put an end to the whole silly discussion by simply letting her know I was ready with what I was going to say. Instead, I remained quiet, a lump of pride swelling in my throat. Who was this busybody to question me? Besides, my silence was revenge for the black and blues I'd received at the mercy of her driving.

The less I said, the angrier she grew. I don't know why, but it gave me great pleasure to get under her skin like this. "Don't worry." I smiled. "Everything is going to be okay."

Her face reddened.

I turned and walked away.

We reached the staircase which led up to the hallway outside the sanctuary. I stepped aside and gave a gallant wave of my hand. "After you."

She pushed by me. "I'm glad to see you're so confident. I'd better stick close in case you need some help."

"Hey! I resent that. Listen, shorty, I don't need to be babysat."

She came to an abrupt stop and sighed, deeply.

"What's eating at you, anyway?" I said.

"Eating at me?"

"Yes."

She spun from her perch, one stair up, and stuck her finger in my face. "For one thing, what do you have against short people?"

"Nothing," I smirked at her. She looked kind of cute, standing there. Being up a step, she was almost my height.

"I'd stack my short stature against your lack of brain power any day."

"What?" Now she'd hit a nerve. "What do you mean my lack of brain power?"

Jill leaned in for the kill. "Everyone knows marines are kind of slow."

"Hey!"

"I hear their boot camp is almost twice as long as the army, navy, or air force boot camp. Do you know why?"

I shook my head.

She tapped my chest. "It's because marines are dumb, and it takes them twice as long to learn stuff."

We stood toe to toe; red face to red face.

I was flustered. But, before I could respond, a voice called from the top of the stairs. "Err ... guys."

In unison, we turned our heads to look.

Boomer was peeking over the railing at us, along with a small group of people, all with shocked expressions on their faces. "You might want to hold it down. This is a funeral."

The anger in my face melted into embarrassment. Jill turned a bright red.

"Sorry," we both muttered.

We proceeded up the stairs in silence.

The casket, surrounded by floral arrangements that filled the air with their heavy scent, was placed at the front of the church. A couple stood to its left. *Must be the parents.* They looked to be about forty-five to fiftyish. From there, a long line of mourners wove its way to the back of the sanctuary waiting to pay their respects. Dutifully, we took our place at the end of the line—Boomer in front, followed by Jill, and then me. I glared at the top of her head.

Why does this girl have to be so aggravating?

We moved forward at a good pace, and before too long were at the front. Boomer approached Emily's parents. It looked as if he was trudging his last mile. Mr. and Mrs. Hamilton had just released the hands of another couple. Red-eyed, they turned to Boomer.

Mrs. Hamilton's eyes brimmed with tears. "Hello, Boomer."

"Mrs. Hamilton." He choked as he spoke.

She threw her arms around him and wept. "I am so glad you came."

Mr. Hamilton didn't wait for his wife to release her hold. He grabbed Boomer's hand. "Bernard. So good to see you."

Boomer clung to Mrs. Hamilton. "I'm so sorry."

"We know, sweetheart. We know." They pulled apart. Mr. Hamilton stepped closer, and the three shared a time of private grief.

"How could something like this happen?" Mrs. Hamilton asked.

Boomer shoved his hands deep in his pockets. "I ... I don't know."

"It just doesn't make sense." Her lip quivered.

"The police say it was that serial killer," Mr. Hamilton said. "I don't know what to think."

Jill tensed and mumbled something under her breath.

"Dear." Mrs. Hamilton addressed Boomer. "You were close to her. Had she been okay? Was someone threatening her?" She searched deep into the boy's eyes.

Jill and I were standing close enough to hear what should have been a private conversation. A sudden surge of guilt shot through me. I looked at Jill, about to suggest that we take a couple steps back. As I did, I noticed a tear rolling down her cheek. She was visibly shaking.

I placed my hands gently on her shoulders and stepped back, guiding her along with me. She offered no resistance. Instead, she reached up and touched my hand, seeming to accept it as a source of comfort and strength. She looked at me, her eyes brimming with tears.

Mr. Hamilton wrapped his arm around his wife's shoulder and pulled her into him. She buried her head in his chest, took a deep breath, and tried to regain a shred of composure. "I'm sorry."

"No. I'm sorry. Really, I am." Boomer turned away from the couple and headed toward the casket. Each step grew slower and more agonized, as if he were dragging large weights. Getting only halfway there, he abruptly stopped. Then with a sorrowful gaze in its general direction, he lowered his head and walked away.

Having wiped her tears, Jill crossed to Emily's parents with me a couple paces behind her. She held Mrs. Hamilton's hand. "I want to express my condolences for your loss."

Wait a minute. That's what I was going to say.

It was petty of me, but I wanted to sound original, not like I was copying the mourner in front of me. A bead of sweat rolled down my forehead. I crept forward.

Jill continued. "Emily was such a good friend."

"It's so good to see you again, Jill," Mrs. Hamilton said.

My mind raced, trying to come up with some other way to express—

"Mr. and Mrs. Hamilton," Jill waved a hand in my direction. "This is Jack Hill. He's from the Springsbury church."

What are you doing? I'm not ready yet.

It was too late. Mr. Hamilton extended his hand. Reluctantly, I took hold, and we exchanged a firm handshake.

Now what? I had to say something. It felt like we'd been shaking hands for five minutes when finally, I blurted out, "I am so sorry for your loss. On behalf of the church, I'd like to express my condolences."

The man looked at me with sad, yet sincere eyes. "Thank you, Jack. We appreciate that."

Hallelujah! I didn't say How ya doin'?

I was stepping away when Mrs. Hamilton asked, "Were you good friends with our daughter?"

I paused. A knot formed in my throat. How could I tell them I barely knew her, and our only interaction was a disagreement over a library card?

"Well, we went to the same church ... and also school."

"Oh." Mrs. Hamilton smiled. "Did you have any classes together?"

"No ..." I fumbled for the right words. "Usually I'd uh ... see her in church ... or in the library."

They both stared, waiting for me to add more, but nothing came out.

Silence.

Then, like a godsend, Jill stepped in. "Pastor Roberts is very sick today. He asked Jack and me to let you know how much your daughter is going to be missed."

"Thank you, Jill," Mrs. Hamilton said. Then she added, "Didn't you and Emily teach Sunday school together in Springsbury?"

"Last year we taught the middle schoolers," Jill smirked. "It was an interesting experience, to say the least."

Mrs. Hamilton hugged Jill. "I know Emily really appreciated your friendship."

Once more, Mr. Hamilton shook my hand. "Thanks again for coming."

Jill and I moved on. Pausing by the casket, we bowed our heads and paid our respects to the young woman who lay there looking like she was asleep.

Just like that morning by the Dumpster.

Boomer sat alone in a pew on the right side of the church, about halfway down the aisle. His eyes were focused on some invisible spot on the front wall.

"Can we join you?" Jill asked.

Somehow, I don't think he was in the mood for company, but with a slight groan, he slid over and made room for the two of us.

We sat and waited.

By the time the service began, the church was filled to overflowing. It lasted a little over an hour and was beautiful yet sad.

An uncomfortable quiet settled over the three of us as we followed the line of cars to the cemetery. Boomer's face was drained of color. He stared out the side window as we turned into the entrance, between large stone pillars. Rows of oak trees lined the road, with fields of granite markers beyond.

I broke the silence. "Earlier, did I hear you say you won't be coming back with us?"

"No." Boomer's eyes remained focused on the passing graves. "I'm going to spend a couple days with my folks."

Jill spoke. "It was a nice funeral." Then she added in a hushed voice, "Don't you think?"

"No." He hung his head. "It was lousy."

We pulled up to the grave site. Before the car had stopped moving, Boomer flung open his door. The car rocked as he extricated himself and trudged toward the grave. Jill and I followed the group of mourners.

The graveside service was short. When it finished, the funeral director thanked everyone for coming and extended the family's invitation to join them for a meal at Angelo's, a local restaurant. Then he took a step back.

The crowd stood still. Emily's parents were huddled together near the front, staring at their daughter's casket. People glanced to their neighbors. I think everyone was wondering what was the proper thing to do. Do you leave or wait for the family to make the first move? What's graveside etiquette? Much to my relief, a young couple broke from the group and walked to Mr. and Mrs. Hamilton. This was the signal that everyone was waiting for. Almost all at once people began to disperse.

Jill approached. "Would you mind if we skip the mercy meal? I'd really like to get back on the road."

From my experience, mercy meals can drag on. By the time you get to the restaurant, and everyone finds a seat, then the food orders are taken, a couple of hours could pass. I was glad Jill wanted to skip. I glanced at my watch. It was 3:30. "I'd like to get going, too."

"Let's say goodbye to the Hamiltons first."

It took us about fifteen minutes to get through the crowd which had formed around Emily's parents, all hugging, shaking hands, and offering their final condolences. By the time we got to the car, it was almost four o'clock.

"You can sit in the back," Jill quipped as she climbed in. "If it would make you feel safer."

I turned a puzzled look her way.

"I mean with my terrible driving and all."

I tried to sound as apologetic as possible. "I'm sorry that I insulted your driving."

"And my height?"

"And your height."

"And my car?" She smirked.

I paused. "Well, you've got to admit, this car is ... different."

Now she gave a full smile. "Hey, leave Matilda alone."

"Matilda?"

"Yes." With great affection, she patted the dashboard. "I call her Matilda."

"You name all your cars?"

"All of them so far ... but, then again, this is my first one. And it's really my dad's."

"How long have you been driving it?"

"Counting today?" She turned the key, and the motor revved to life.

I nodded.

"One day." With a thump and a yank, Jill threw the car into first, and we jolted forward.

"And how long have you been driving a standard?" My head slammed into the seat.

With a twinkle in her eye, she grinned. "Counting today?"

I stared at her. "This is your first time driving a standard?"

She nodded. "Mrs. Roberts said Boomer needed a ride. I couldn't let him down. How'm I doing?" Jill grabbed at the gear shift and struggled to put the car in second gear. The crankshaft ground and groaned, but eventually kicked in.

I grasped the window frame.

"Afraid?" she teased.

When we'd reached the entrance to the cemetery, Jill downshifted. The car stalled and coasted onto the main road. As we continued creeping forward, she frantically tried to restart Matilda. The frustration on her face grew in proportion to the line of cars behind us.

"Pull over," I said.

"What?"

"Just pull over and let the other cars go by."

She yanked the wheel to the right, and we glided down a slight incline to the curb.

I hopped out, went around to the driver's door, and opened it.

She pulled it partway shut. "What are you doing?"

"Let me drive."

"You don't think I can do this." The anger rose in her voice.

"I don't want to die coming home from a funeral. It would make a heck of a story for the newspapers, but we wouldn't be too happy."

Jill crossed her arms in front of her. "No. I'm doing fine."

"Jill," I spoke softly. "I'm sure you can handle it, but there's nothing wrong with accepting a little help."

The defiance in her eyes disappeared.

"Besides," I added. "I'd like to see how Matilda drives."

"All right." She climbed out, then added sheepishly, "She really is a good car."

"I'm sure she is."

Jill got in the passenger side. Then I unsuccessfully attempted to get behind the wheel. The driver's seat was pulled so far forward I couldn't fit. I was about to make a comment about her shortness but bit my tongue. Instead, I quietly made the proper adjustment to the seat and hopped in.

"I know this was my first day of driving a standard, but how'd I do?" She had a hope-filled look on her face.

"Not too bad at all." I lied while shifting into first.

"I mean, I've watched my dad drive. I thought, 'How hard can it be?'" She settled back into the seat. "So, how long have you been driving a standard?"

"Including today?"

Chapter Eight

Once Jill got over the fact that I'd hijacked the driving duties, we settled in for a pleasant ride.

About thirty minutes down the road, she said, "You're not doing too bad, Leatherneck."

I winced. "How about I won't call you shorty, and you won't call me Leatherneck, Jarhead, or any other cute names that refer to marines."

"Sorry." Her eyes twinkled. "I was just kidding around."

"I understand."

"Anyway, you're not doing too bad … Jack."

"That's better." With the tension draining from the car, she sat back and stared out the window. Occasionally, a gust of wind would send a hurricane whirl of falling leaves across our path.

"Is Jack your full name, or is it short for something like John or Jonathan?"

"Jackson."

"Jackson." She considered it. "Nice name."

"You can call me Jack." My stomach rumbled. "Sorry. I'm starving."

"Me too. I haven't eaten since breakfast. Maybe we should have stayed for the meal."

I thought for a second. "Hey, I know a little diner about five minutes from here."

"Ralphy's?" She brightened.

"You know the place? How about stopping for a bite? My treat."

"Sure," Jill said, but then she shrank back. Her face flushed. "I mean, I guess if you want to, but you don't have to pay. I have money."

"It's no problem." I grinned. "It'll make up for all those short jokes."

"But—"

"I insist."

She hesitated. "Okay. If you insist."

"It's a date then."

Her face reddened.

Within five minutes, we were at the restaurant. Ralphy's was one of those old, silver diners. It had been modified, though, with the addition of a large dining room off to one side, cluttered with a patchwork of tables of various sizes and shapes. It wasn't too crowded, so we were seated right away.

"Whoever outfitted this place must have shopped at a used furniture store," I said.

An older, balding man emerged from the kitchen and took our drink order.

As he walked away, Jill whispered, "That's Ralphy. He does all kinds of jobs from waitering to cooking."

"You come here often?"

She nodded. "It's one of my dad's favorite places."

"I've heard you mention your dad a couple of times. What about your mom?"

The smile slipped from her lips. "She died a few years ago."

"I'm sorry. I don't know why I ask such stupid and personal questions."

"No, no. That's okay. I mean, I miss her a lot. I truly do. She's in a better place. Knowing that helps." She pushed back her seat. "If you'll excuse me, I'll be right back."

"Where're you going?"

She gave an amused look. "You really do ask some stupid and yet personal questions. Nature calls."

"Oh. I guess you can't get more personal than that. I mean," I fumbled for the right words. "Where you're going, you go alone." I shook my head. "Not that I had thought to go with you … I mean … It's not like you need help or anything." I slapped my hand against my forehead. "Please stop me before my foot goes so far into my mouth that I'm chewing on my ankle."

She laughed, graciously. "I'll be right back." I watched her walk across the room. With her slender build and petite stature, it was easy to see why I'd mistaken her for a high school girl. I use the word petite because I dare not say short again. I grinned. *Well, you know what they say. Good things come in small packages.*

A couple of minutes later, she returned and slipped into her seat. "You look deep in thought."

"Thinking about the funeral."

"Oh, by the way, what you said to Mr. and Mrs. Hamilton was nice."

"Well," I chuckled. "I'm not sure if I needed the extra help."

Her brow puckered. "Extra help?"

"I was handling it pretty well—"

She shook her head. "That's what I said. I don't understand."

"You kind of stepped in."

Her mouth dropped. "You looked like you were floundering."

"Floundering!" My volume level went up a notch. "You just agreed, I handled it pretty well."

She snorted and raised her volume to match mine. "Pretty well? Okay, I'll give you that. But all of a sudden, you didn't seem to know what to say."

I replayed the scene in my mind. She was right, but no way was I going to admit it. "Maybe you misinterpreted what you saw."

"Maybe," she replied in anger. "And maybe you need to hear the advice that a wise person once told me."

"What?" I yelled.

She leaned forward. "I'm sure that you could have handled it, but there's nothing wrong with accepting a little help."

I glared. "And what wise person gave you that tidbit?"

"You did! Earlier when you wanted to take over driving." She sat back and folded her arms, looking very much like someone who'd just captured my king in a game of chess.

"Oh." I paused. When I spoke, my voice was much quieter. "That's annoying, you know?"

"What is?"

"Throwing someone's advice back in their face."

"Are you two ready to order, or should the bell ring for the next round?" Ralphy stood by the table, an amused grin peeking out from under his long, thin nose.

I glanced around. We'd become the center of attention for several customers.

"I think we're going to need a couple more minutes," Jill said, civility restored to her voice.

"Okay. I'll come back. Meanwhile, try to be good to your girlfriend." He winked at Jill and walked away. "She seems nice."

"She's not my girlfriend," I wanted to holler after him. "She's only my ride to the funeral." But I caught myself before I spoke. Instead, with a huff, I opened my menu and placed it in front of me, blocking my view of this infuriating person.

The strained silence covered us like a heavy dew. I listened to the silverware at other tables clanging against the plates. I think I could even hear the ticking of the clock on the wall. The pleasant conversation had changed in an instant, and the former tension had returned. It was so frustrating and awkward.

Having a sudden desire to get away, I shoved my seat back and stomped off toward the men's room, not giving even the slightest glance back to see if she was watching. Once inside the bathroom, I stood in front of the sink, gazing at my reflection in the mirror. I shook my head and chuckled.

What a dummy. She was right. I was floundering.

So why did I let Jill get to me? Maybe it was all I'd been through the past couple of days—not only Emily's death and funeral, but on top that, being the one who had found the body.

A sudden sharp pain stabbed my right side. I drew in a quick breath through clenched teeth, bent over, and grabbed the edge of the sink shaking my head. After about thirty seconds, it subsided. The doctor said over time these attacks would decrease in intensity, and hopefully, they would eventually go away for good.

It's funny. I straightened up and examined myself in the mirror. With my shirt on, a person couldn't see any difference from one side of my body to the other. I collected myself and left the restroom, all the while thinking, *Maybe I owe Jill an apology.*

But that thought disappeared as I approached our table. There, leaning over Jill, was Detective Thomas. Poor Jill. Her lip was quivering. Her eyes were blinking rapidly, trying to hold in the tears as the detective wagged his finger in her face, grilling her.

My back stiffened, and I stormed forward. "Detective Thomas."

He, along with all the restaurant's patrons, jolted at my shout. When he turned and saw me, his brow knit with confusion.

The detective was on the right side of Jill's seat. I took a defensive posture on the left, with Jill sandwiched between us. I straightened my shoulders, trying to look as imposing as possible. "I realize you're in the middle of a murder investigation, and Jill and I were at the scene of the crime, but that doesn't give you the right to follow us or interrogate her whenever and wherever you like!"

Detective Thomas turned his glance from me to Jill.

"Jack—"

"Quiet, Jill," I said. "I can handle this."

"But—"

I put my hand up, halting her plea. "It's one thing to drag me to police headquarters. It's quite another thing to buttonhole us here at a restaurant, of all places."

He remained perfectly calm. "And are you with her?"

"Yes, I am."

"I see." His voice grew quiet. "Did you drive here together?"

"I don't see that that's any of your business." I placed a hand on Jill's shoulder "And I am not going to let you bother Jill!"

She looked at me, her expression a mix of admiration and pity.

I waved a finger in the detective's face. "Maybe she should let her father know how the local police have been treating her." Happy that I'd won the victory, I puffed out my chest and stood triumphantly.

"Jack." Jill touched my hand and nodded to my adversary. "Detective Thomas *is* my father."

"Huh?"

Like a balloon with a hole in it, my chest deflated.

Chapter Nine

"Your father?" This was one of those embarrassing times that will play over and over in my brain to remind me of how stupid I can be. I hoped I'd fallen asleep in the bathroom and was having a bad dream.

Wake up! Wake up!

No such luck.

Jill nibbled on a strand of her hair. "Jack." She gestured toward Detective Thomas. "This is my dad. Dad ... You know Jack, right?"

Detective Thomas remained stone-faced. "We've met. May I join you? I promise not to use bamboo shoots or thumbscrews." Without waiting for an answer, he pulled out a chair and sat down.

I shuffled and cleared my throat several times. When I finally regained my composure, I looked at Jill. "Did I put my foot in my mouth again?"

She smirked and patted my hand. "All the way up to the knee this time."

"Detective Thomas." My face burned with embarrassment. "I'm sorry, sir. I didn't mean any disrespect. When I saw you standing over Jill, I assumed you were bothering her. I—"

He gave an almost approving look. "That's okay. It's nice to see chivalry isn't dead."

"Daddy, as I was telling you before Jack came to my rescue, Mrs. Roberts called and said Boomer—You know Boomer?"

He nodded.

"He needed a ride to the funeral." She studied the tabletop. "Er … I didn't know about Jack at the time."

"So, you took it upon yourself to take my car. A standard shift by the way." Detective Thomas leaned forward, his eyes fastened securely on Jill's. "You don't know how to drive a stick."

"Well, I—"

"How in the world did you think this was acceptable behavior?"

Jill fidgeted in her seat. Finally, she blurted out, "Jack drove."

The detective turned to me. "Is that true?"

"What?" Why in the world had she thrown me under the bus?

"Of course, it's true," Jill said quickly, not giving me a chance to open my mouth.

He raised a hand in front of his daughter. "I want to hear it from him." His eyes bore into me. "Is it true?"

"I … um … That is—"

"Daddy. You're scaring him."

"I'm not scared," I protested. The slight quiver in my voice said otherwise. I'd survived boot camp. I'd seen action in the Middle East. Somehow this conversation with this girl's father struck fear in my heart. Gathering my courage, I announced, "I drove the car here."

"I see," Detective Thomas said. "And you know how to drive a stick?"

I deftly avoided the question. "What? Are you kidding?"

"Honestly, Daddy," Jill held her hands out, palms up. "What was I to do? I wanted to go to the funeral and didn't have a ride. I couldn't get in touch with you …" Her words trailed off.

The detective hesitated. "I was concerned, that's all. Imagine my shock when I pulled into this parking lot and saw Matilda sitting there. I almost called it in as a stolen vehicle."

I smirked. "Who would steal that—"

Jill kicked me under the table. "So, anything new on the case?"

Detective Thomas picked up the menu. "No."

She frowned. "Nothing at all?"

He ignored her and turned to me. "Have you two ordered yet?"

"No, we haven't."

"Why are you avoiding my questions?" Jill raised her voice, slightly.

"I'm not avoiding them, sweetheart. There's just nothing to say."

Ralphy approached the table with our beverages. "You joining the match, detective?"

"What?" Detective Thomas's brow creased.

The waiter laughed. "This table's been a bit volatile tonight." He turned to Jill's dad. "I brought your usual. A lemonade. Are you people ready to order?"

Jill ordered a salad. Her father and I ordered burgers and fries. Ralphy walked away, scribbling it all down on a small pad of paper.

"How was the funeral?" Detective Thomas asked.

Jill considered for a moment. "It was nice. But poor Mr. and Mrs. Hamilton."

"It's sad," her father answered. "A senseless murder. Sometimes these serial killers have no rhyme or reason."

Jill's face darkened. "Serial killer?"

Detective Thomas groaned. "Let's not start this again."

"Why not? Emily's murderer was not the Dumpster Killer."

Not the Dumpster Killer?

"I know you feel that way, but—"

"But nothing," she shot back at her father. "Emily's death has nothing in common with the other two."

I shrugged. "I don't know. It seems pretty cut and dry to me." The words were barely spoken before I wished I could take them back.

"Cut and dry?" Jill's eyes flashed. "How in the world is it cut and dry?"

Detective Thomas answered in a matter-of-fact tone. "She was stabbed with a knife, just like the first two victims."

Jill folded her arms. "Yes, but the knife didn't have a pearl handle like the others."

The detective frowned. His voice lowered to almost a whisper. "That information hadn't been released to the public. How did you know?"

Jill shrank down in her seat. "When I was home a couple of days ago, I kind of … opened your report … and read. Just a little."

"Jill Thomas!"

"Well, you left it on the kitchen table."

A quick look in my direction stifled whatever admonishment Detective Thomas wanted to share. "We'll talk about this later. In private."

Jill sighed. "Can I at least ask what other evidence the police have to link Emily's murder to the Dumpster Killer?"

"She was found in a sitting position by a Dumpster," the detective answered.

"Anyone could place a body in that position," Jill snorted. "Honestly, in my opinion, you have no evidence at all."

"That's your opinion," the detective said.

"That's it? And you dismiss anything I have to say just like," —she snapped her fingers— "that?"

Detective Thomas reached out to touch his daughter's hand. "It's going to be all right."

She pulled away from him. "Don't patronize me!"

"I'm not," he said, calmly. "I know Emily was your friend. This must be hard for you."

Red-faced, Jill looked at the ceiling, her eyes brimming with tears.

"If you have evidence that leads our investigation in any other direction—"

Her voice cracked. "Evidence? What makes you think I have any evidence?"

Detective Thomas paused. "I didn't say you did. I was speaking in general terms. If anyone has any evidence that leads us in a different direction, we'll follow it."

Jill wiped her face. "It's just so … frustrating. The other girls who were killed were … were …"

"Call girls." Her father filled in the appropriate word.

"Emily was *not* a call girl."

"I know." There was great sympathy in his voice.

"And what about you?" she retorted.

The table fell silent. After a moment I realized Jill was glaring my way. "Me?"

"Yes, you. Emily was going to meet with you that night. Don't deny it. I heard the two of you."

"Well, *Inspector* Thomas," I said sarcastically, "as I've already told the police, there was no date. She was holding a library book for me."

"Jill." Detective Thomas touched his daughter's shoulder. "The food will be here soon. Why don't you go splash some cool water on your face and calm down."

"I'm fine," she growled.

"I know you are, but I'd like to have a word with Mr. Hill … in private."

She grunted, rose from the table, and stalked off.

Detective Thomas waited until his daughter was out of earshot before he spoke. "She gets quite emotional."

"You can say that again. Whatever you do, don't call her short."

"Yes, I know."

"Do you realize I've known her for less than a week, and I bet we've had a dozen fights already?"

"Hmmm."

"Good ploy, telling her you wanted to talk to me in order to get her to calm down."

"What makes you think it was a ploy?" Again, his cold, emotionless stare was pointed in my direction.

"Oh."

"So." He picked up a salt shaker and examined its contents. "What did you think of Matilda?"

I chose my words carefully. "Interesting car."

"Yes, she is."

"I'm surprised Jill let me drive her."

"Hmmm."

Again with the hmmm. What did it mean?

"You know, Jack, Jill is my only daughter. I don't know if she's told you, her mother is deceased."

"Yes, sir. She did."

"I've done my best to protect her ... raise her. Not easy. I keep a pretty close watch on her."

"I can imagine." I jokingly added, "I can also imagine if you'd known she wanted to give me a ride to the funeral, you'd have squashed that idea. I mean with a killer on the loose."

"No," he said in a calm voice. "I trust you."

I smiled. "You do?"

He took a sip of his lemonade. "I did a background check."

My smile disappeared.

"Don't take offense. You're involved in a murder case."

"I ... I understand." Curiosity got the best of me. "So, what'd you find out?"

He paused and looked me straight in the eye. "I don't think you're the killer."

"That's a relief."

"But I could be wrong."

I laughed, thinking he was joking. He didn't join in. Instead, he slowly stirred his drink, his eyes never leaving the glass. "So, you're a marine."

"Yes, sir."

"Served in the Middle East."

"Correct."

"Decorated."

I shifted in my seat. "No big deal."

He glanced at me. "A hero."

"No, sir." I bit my lip.

"No?"

"Just doing my job."

"That's not what I heard."

"Then you heard wrong." I picked up my root beer and shoved the straw into my mouth so hard and fast it jammed my front tooth. I watched the liquid level go down as I drank.

The food and Jill arrived at the table almost at the same time.

"Everything looks good." Jill sank into her seat and sighed deeply. "I'm sorry I got so upset. It's—"

"You don't have to explain, dear." Her dad patted her shoulder. "No one your age should have to lose a friend in such a terrible way. I promise you, we're doing all we can in this matter."

She sighed. "I know. These last few days have been ... difficult."

Detective Thomas reached toward me. "If you don't mind, we hold hands when we say grace."

After accepting both his and Jill's hands, Detective Thomas bowed his head. "Dear Lord, I thank you for sending Jack to help drive Jill to the funeral today. Be with the Hamilton family. Help them rise above this sorrow and find peace with you. We thank you for the sure knowledge that Emily is one of your children and is safe in your arms. Now, Lord, we thank you for this food before us. In Jesus name, Amen."

"Amen," Jill echoed.

Our conversation turned to college life. No more talk of murder. I found out that Jill was an art major and was surprised to discover she lived in my building.

Toward the end of the meal, I asked, "What floor are you on?"

"I'm on the second. I'd hate to walk up all those stairs to the fourth floor, like you."

"How did you know I was on the fourth floor?"

"You ... you must have mentioned it."

"That's funny." I thought back over our conversation. "I don't remember saying anything about it."

She shifted in her seat. "Really? I'm sure you did."

Jill's dad interrupted. "Well, I have to get going." He nodded toward me. "It was nice seeing you again, Mr. Hill."

He kissed Jill on the top of the head. "Keep the car at the college. Maybe having a set of wheels would be a good thing. After all, I don't use Matilda that often. She just sits there in the garage."

After Detective Thomas left the table, I asked, "So, you come from around here?"

Jill nodded. "On the other side of Springbury."

"But you don't commute. You live on campus."

She pointed to her father who was at the counter, talking to Ralphy. "He thought it would be a good experience for me. Besides, he works a lot of night shifts and feels I'd be safer on campus … Safer!" She shook her head. "That's a big laugh."

"Don't worry. Your dad will catch the killer. Whoever did it is bound to make a mistake sooner or later. Serial killers usually do."

She snorted. "You're an expert now."

"Well, no, but"—I stuck a fry in my mouth and spoke between chews—"you always hear stories of killers being caught."

"There are also stories about ones who get away."

"I was only trying to—"

"I know what you were trying to do. Take my father's side."

"I wasn't taking anyone's side."

She threw her arms in the air. "Is it an unwritten law that military men have to defend the police, even when they're wrong?"

"Standing up for law enforcement's ability to do their job *is not* taking your father's side," I argued. "What's wrong with you?"

"Wrong with me?" She sat back, startled. "Nothing. Why?"

"We were having a nice conversation … hardly argued the whole meal, which is quite an achievement for us. All of a sudden, you go whacko on me."

"Whacko on you?" Her eyes widened.

Before Jill could throw a piece of lettuce at me, Ralphy intervened. "Would you like to order some dessert?"

Jill's head jerked in his direction. "Dessert?" She made it sound like he was suggesting some type of poison.

"Yes." He nodded with a smirk. "Typically, it's something you eat after a meal. I thought dessert might help. I mean, now that the referee has left, I'd hate to see the battle start up again." He handed Jill a menu. She glanced in my direction to see if it was okay. The waiter picked up on this. "Don't worry about your boyfriend paying for—"

"He's not my boyfriend."

"Of course, he's not." He chuckled. "The detective paid the check and left extra money for dessert. He said you two could use some sweetening up."

"He did, did he." Jill seethed.

I found Detective Thomas's joke kind of funny. "I'd love some dessert."

"*You* would!" She turned away from me, fuming.

I pulled my seat closer to hers and leaned in. "Come on, honey. Let's share a strawberry frappe. One glass and two straws."

"I'd rather share with a diseased pig." She placed her hand against my face and pushed it back. Then turning to the waiter, she smiled sweetly. "But I will have the apple pie, ala mode."

"And you, sir?"

Never taking my eyes off Jill, I said in a dreamy voice, "I guess I'll have the same. Could you heat that pie?"

"Sure." He headed to the kitchen.

With my elbows on the table and my chin resting in my hands, I continued gazing at Jill.

Several slow seconds ticked by.

She tried to ignore me, casting only the occasional uncomfortable glance my way. Finally, she burst. "Cut it out!"

"Cut what out?" I was the picture of innocence.

"You know what. You're mocking me."

"I'm having a little fun, that's all."

She turned away and crossed her arms. "I don't think it's funny."

"I'm sorry," I laughed. "And while I'm apologizing, I owe you one from earlier. You were right. I was floundering at the wake."

"Oh, no," she said, her attitude suddenly changing. "I think you did a good job."

I shrugged. "I guess so. Though I wonder why Pastor Roberts asked me to speak for him. I saw other people there who've been going to the church a lot longer than me."

With her finger, she absentmindedly drew tiny circles on her napkin. "Maybe Pastor Roberts trusts you. Maybe he sees something in you."

"Two apple pies ala mode." Ralphy set the desserts in front of us. "I'm glad to see the fighting has stopped, and that you two lovebirds are cozying up."

Jill blushed. "We are not lovebirds."

"No?" He flashed an impish grin. "Could have fooled me."

Jill watched him walk away. "You know, some people are just plain weird."

I dug into my apple pie. It was delicious.

"Look, as long as we're apologizing," Jill said. "I'm sorry for pulling you into the middle of the argument with my dad about Emily's death. And I'm sorry for overreacting about you taking my father's side."

I shoveled in another bite of the pie. "I understand. Emily was a good friend of yours. This must be a difficult time."

She nodded. "Honestly, I'm not usually this ..." She struggled to find the right word.

"Whacko?" I suggested.

I half expected her to blow up, but she didn't. Instead, she looked down at the table. "My dad is so sure it's a serial killer."

"Jill." I tried to sound sympathetic, not wanting to upset her again. "You have to understand where he's coming from.

At this time, as much as you don't like the idea, everything he knows points in that direction."

"Everything he knows ..." The sentence faded off as her gaze skipped back and forth from the table to a wall at the far end of the restaurant.

Chapter Ten

Jill strolled along the walkway to her building, daydreaming. She felt strangely warm on this cool October evening—exhilarated. She and Jack had just returned from an impromptu date.

And the waiter kept mistaking us for boyfriend and girlfriend.

She grinned. But then her stomach started to ache as she was hit with a wave of guilt. Emily's funeral was this afternoon. This wasn't supposed to be a fun day. She shook her head trying to come to her senses. But it was no use. The harder she tried not to, the more she thought about Jack, the way he'd raced to rescue her from the evil detective's interrogation.

She couldn't help but smile when she thought of that dab of ketchup stuck on the side of his mouth for about half the meal. It was so cute.

Her daydreaming was interrupted by a steady stream of students traveling in the opposite direction. At first, she thought nothing of it, but as the numbers picked up, she remembered what night it was.

Abbott and Costello.

The school's student government sponsored a movie night once a month with free popcorn and soft drinks. It was their way of combatting Saturday evening drinking and wild parties. Last spring, they'd shown a couple of Abbott and Costello movies. Much to the surprise of many, these old black and whites were big hits, developing an almost cult-like following. Overnight, events like Abbott and Costello look-alike contests and *Who's on First* skits popped up.

Tonight's film was *Abbott and Costello Meet the Invisible Man.*

Jill checked her watch. 7:20. The movie started in ten minutes. If she hurried, she could change into some comfortable jeans and get there without missing too much. She raced into her building and up the stairs toward her room. The place was deserted.

As she reached the landing to her floor, she tripped and caught herself against the open door. It crashed into the wall. The noise echoed through the stairwell. Once it died down, the air was filled with an oppressive silence.

Jill gripped the door handle, transfixed to the spot. Her heartbeat quickened. How many times had she come through this door, slamming it against the wall? How many times had she walked this hall without a second thought? But usually, there were other people around. Now she was all alone. Being afraid was foolish, she knew that.

But it had never felt so deathly quiet.

She eyed the doorway, suddenly certain that when she passed through, someone or something would be waiting to attack.

"Don't be an idiot," she said aloud. "You're letting your imagination run away with you."

Just then, somewhere down the hallway, a door latched.

Jill swallowed hard.

Probably a stray student. Nothing says everyone went to the movie.

She gathered her strength and took a deep breath.

Move girl!

With clenched fists, she strode forward two brave steps through the doorway. No one sprang at her. No one grabbed her. Still, that feeling of doom persisted. With each room she passed, her pace quickened.

Room 33 … 32 … 31 …

The utility closet next to her room had no number.

Finally, she reached 30. Her room. A lump formed in her throat. Her eyes widened. The door was slightly ajar.

I'm sure I closed it.

She fought to control the rising fear, to push her heart back down into her chest. Pulling at every strand of common sense she could muster, she reasoned that in her rush to get to the funeral, there was a possibility she hadn't pulled the door all the way closed.

Her outstretched palm pushed it open, and she made a quick reach for the light switch. The fluorescent bulb sprang to life, illumining the yellow painted block walls. She rushed in, swung the door closed, and pressed her back against it. Between her heart pounding and her heavy breathing, she thought for sure a person could be a mile away and hear her. Her eyes swept the small rectangular room. Clothing, books, and papers were strewn across her bed, desk, and dresser.

She frowned. "How did—"

Suddenly, muffled footsteps ran down the hall, growing quieter as they moved away. With newfound courage, Jill charged into the corridor. It was empty. Whoever had been there was gone.

Was this simply a case of another student running a little late, like her? That feeling of foreboding grew one hundred times stronger as her eyes locked on the room next to hers. The utility closet. The door was wide open.

Wasn't that closed when I walked by?

After Jill and I returned to campus, I decided to go for a walk to clear my head. Besides, sitting for most of the day had gotten me a bit antsy. I needed some exercise. I shuffled my feet through the piles of brightly colored leaves gathered along the sides of the road that led to town.

Though I love the fall, I admit it gives me a touch of melancholy. Trees become bare, their branches like crooked fingers stretch into the moonlit night. The chilly air was a reminder that soon the snow would fall. No flowers, no green grass. For a season, the world would die.

Death ... Emily.

I wasn't able to get the image of that young girl lying in her coffin out of my mind. What if I'd stayed at the library? What if I'd been there to protect her? A strong wind blew against my face. I shivered.

About twenty minutes later, I was back on campus walking through one of the college's parking lots toward my room.

A shrill voice cut through the night air. "What do you mean? I have a right to put up these signs!"

Two security guards stood at the edge of the lot bordering the woods. A woman was there, holding a hammer in one hand and a sign in the other. *No Trespassing.*

"No, ma'am. You can't post that sign. Now if you don't move on, we're going to have to call the police."

The woman stood defiantly, almost daring them to take action against her. She was short and kind of stocky. Curly, gray hair scurried out from the edges of her ball cap. After a few seconds of the guards not backing down, she tossed the sign on the ground. "Fine! You haven't heard the last of me!" She stormed off, but not in the direction I expected. She didn't walk toward the road or a car. Not even toward the campus. But into the woods. And the security guards didn't stop her.

Deciding it wasn't any of my business, I continued toward my building. Once inside, I was amazed at how empty it was.

Must be a lot of Abbott and Costello fans.

I jogged up the stairs to the fourth floor. Imagine my horror, as I approached my room. There sat Jill, slumped against my door, eyes closed, perfectly still, peaceful. The last time I found a young girl seated that way was …

I rushed forward. "Jill!"

Her whole body jolted like one thousand volts of electricity had shot through it. "What?"

At the sound of her voice, my heart started beating again. "I didn't mean to scare you. You were just …"

For a moment, she looked confused. But then what I was thinking must have sunk in. She got to her feet. "Sorry."

"What are you doing here?"

She sighed. "Can we talk?

Every floor in the hall had a small kitchenette and lounge. Upon entering my floor's, Jill sat at a small table, trembling slightly. It was only 8:30. Most people were still at the movie or doing other things. Except for the occasional person walking by, we were all alone.

I held up a canister of imported Swiss cocoa I'd brought from my room. "Mrs. Roberts knows I like hot cocoa. She gave me this. It's real good stuff. Want some?"

Jill nodded. "I'm sorry to bother you. I don't know where else to turn." She grew quiet and just sat there, arms wrapped around herself, head bent low.

I removed two mugs from the cupboard. After preparing them, I placed the steaming beverages on the table and joined her. "What's the matter?"

She cleared her throat. "Here's the thing. You and my dad say it was a serial killer—"

I rolled my eyes. "Not that again."

"Listen." Her voice cracked. "He said if there were more evidence ..." She cradled the mug between her hands and took a sip. "This is very good."

"Thank you. You were saying."

"Yes." Her voice lowered to a guilty whisper. "Maybe there is ... more evidence, that is."

I sat up straight.

She checked the door. "I want to show you something, but before I do ..." She glanced at the door once again.

"Oh, stop being so melodramatic."

She glared at me, but it only lasted a second then melted into an imploring look. "I need your word that you won't go running to the police or to my father."

"Jill, I don't know if—"

"Jack!" Her soft blue eyes filled with tears. "I have to trust someone. Please be that person."

I'm a sucker for soft blue eyes. "Okay. I promise."

With a relieved look, she pulled her chair closer to mine. "As you know, Emily and I were roommates last semester. But this year, we split up. I got the job of RA, Resident Advisor, for my floor. One of the perks is a private room. I left some of my clothes with her, though. Just a couple of things. We didn't wear the same size, because I'm smaller." She pointed a finger in my face. "If you dare make a comment—"

"Not a word."

"A couple of my sweaters were a little baggy on me, and she liked them, so I left them for her to wear. But just to borrow. I planned on getting them back. I figured at some point I could try to shrink them."

On and on she went about her and Emily's clothes sharing and other related stories. After a couple of minutes, I shut her off, hearing only the wah wah wah that adults made on the old Charlie Brown cartoons. Bit by bit, I grew more impatient, swimming in useless facts. "Excuse me. What does any of this have to do with Emily's murder?"

"I'm getting to that." She sounded annoyed. "There was one sweater she liked a lot. As a matter of fact, she helped me pick it out. She said big and baggy looked good on me." Her eyes glistened. "Makes you kind of wonder whether she was planning on borrowing it all along."

My patience was exhausted. "Jill?"

She raised her hands in surrender. "Okay, okay." Then taking a deep breath, she exhaled. "I think I may have a vital piece of evidence in the murder investigation." She rummaged through her pocketbook, pulled out a piece of paper and unfolded it to its 8 ½ x" x 11" size. She slid it across the table for me to see. "It's Emily's handwriting."

My interest piqued, I picked up the page. It looked to be a list of some kind. At the top, scrawled in large letters were the words Blood Money. A thick black line, the kind made by a large, blunt-tipped marker, underscored this. Written on the left side of the page were names or initials and dollar amounts. I noticed some of them were followed by the letters *pd*. At the bottom of the list was another thick black line drawn across the sheet. The list read as follows: BA.—$10, Nicki F.—$10 pd. Then there was a set of initials I couldn't make out, followed by $50. I skipped over it for now. The last set read Don H.—$80. I held the page closer to scrutinize the set I'd skipped.

"Is that a DRS or an ORS?" I asked.

Jill squinted. "I'm not sure. It's kind of hard to tell. It might be a PRS."

I gave it one more look. "Maybe. But what's this all supposed to mean?"

"Don't you see?" She pointed to the heading. "Blood Money."

"I see just fine," was my somewhat impatient response. "Well, whatever it is,"—I picked up my mug and took a sip of the cocoa— "it must have been pretty important. Otherwise, she wouldn't have bothered to write it down."

Jill snickered. "Emily was a list freak. She had them for everything. Schedule for the day, homework to do, shopping items."

"She sounds organized to me. Nothing wrong with being organized."

"Maybe. But I think she was just a little compulsive about it."

I didn't argue the point. My views on organization would probably only start another argument. "She was collecting money for something. But I don't see what this has to do with Emily's murder."

"Look at the names and initials. Anyone look familiar?"

"Don H, BA, Nicki F, PRS?" I shook my head. "They could be anybody."

She picked up the page and gave a rather condescending groan. "Well," she pointed to one set of initials. "BA is probably Boomer Anderson."

"Bernard," I corrected.

"Don H. in all likelihood is Don Henderson, and Nicki F. is probably Nicole Foster." This last name came out with a sneer. "They're the three people who were giving Emily such a hard time in the library the other night. The night of the murder."

"What about the other one?" I pointed to the initials we hadn't been able to decipher.

"I'm stumped on that one. But the point is, here are people who've shown an obvious dislike for Emily. I'd almost say it bordered on hatred. Then she turns up dead, and they're all on a list labeled Blood Money."

"A dislike for Emily?" I said. "Or were they just being idiots at the library?"

"I don't think so. I have a feeling it's more than that."

"A feeling?" I smirked.

"Yes. Besides, did you see the looks they were giving her that night? There was some definite anger running through that room. It was unnerving. Especially from Nicole and Don."

With the same attitude I'd give to fairy dust and flying reindeer, I dismissed Jill's intuition. "But what does all this have to do with clothes shopping?"

"Pardon?"

I took another sip of the cocoa. "Your baggy sweater story."

She twisted her fingers together and giggled. "Oh, nothing … really."

"There has to be some reason you subjected me to that anecdote."

She fidgeted, looking like a child caught out of bed during nap time. "She—she was wearing one of my sweaters the night she was killed."

"I don't understand." I shrugged my shoulders. "What's that got to do with this list?"

The color drained from her face. "It's going to sound a sick. Even morbid. I don't know how else to say it." She took a deep breath. "The morning you discovered Emily … I'd found her first."

"What?"

"Please. Hear me out."

I sat back in my seat.

She focused on her hands which were folded on the table, thumbs nervously rubbing together. "As you know, I was jogging, too. Er, I … recently took it up. I'm not half as good or as fast as you."

Though I appreciated the compliment, her reason for telling me this was unclear.

She continued. "As I was coming around the back of the library my left calf tightened. I decided to take a break on the loading dock. I must have been sitting there for about a minute." Jill's head cocked to one side. Her eyes squinted as she remembered the scene. "Then a kind of eerie sensation tickled the back of my neck. Like someone was watching me. That's when, from the corner of my eye, I saw something behind the Dumpster." She gasped as if reliving the scene in her mind. "At first, I thought she was asleep. But that seemed kind of stupid. Then I thought maybe she was sick." She trembled and began to cry. "That's when I noticed the knife."

I placed my hand over hers. "It's okay."

She took a deep breath and continued. "Now here's where the story gets a little freaky." She chuckled. "Please don't think I'm a nut or something."

"Too late for that." I smiled.

"I look back at it now and realize I must have been in shock. Maybe it was my way of dealing with the whole thing. I noticed she was wearing my sweater. That was okay. I guess I wouldn't want it back now." She laughed, a weak laugh, at her attempt at humor. "But then I saw the bottom hem was in a small pool of blood." Her eyes took on a faraway look. "I thought 'That's not good.' For some reason, I couldn't stop focusing on that stupid hem. It was driving me crazy! So, I decided to move it." Her hand stretched forward, reaching for an invisible sweater. "As I pulled the hem back, I noticed this piece of paper in the sweater's pocket. I wondered what it was, so I carefully pulled it out." She pointed to the paper on the table. "It was the list."

Chapter Eleven

"You just took it?" I shook my head in disbelief. "Why? A souvenir?"

"Don't mock me!"

"I'm not. I'm just trying to fathom why Jill Thomas, the daughter of a police detective, removed evidence from a crime scene."

Jill sat there, sputtering. When she finally answered, her voice was strained. "I know it sounds crazy. And once I removed it, I realized how wrong it was. But somehow the idea of reaching into Emily's pocket to put the paper back seemed morbid." She shuddered.

I crossed my arms. "But the idea of taking it out, to begin with, was okay?"

"I was worried about the hem … and the blood." She covered her face with a shaky hand and cried out, "At the moment, it seemed like the right thing to do. You think I'm crazy, don't you?"

Just then, voices sounded in the hallway, saving me from answering. Our conversation halted while three students walked by.

I leaned closer and spoke in a hushed tone. "After you took the paper, what did you do?"

"If you must know, I looked at my hand and realized … I realized I'd gotten some blood on it." Jill's face paled. "Looking at Emily, the scene finally sunk in. My head swirled. My stomach churned. I was just able to make it across the road and into the woods before I threw up."

I felt a twinge of sympathy. "I remember my first combat experience." I rose, crossed to the cupboard, grabbed a pack of cookies, and brought them to the table. "You don't need all the details. After the battle, I came across some dead soldiers. Friends of mine. I … I had the same reaction."

Maybe misery does love company. Jill's face brightened slightly, probably at the thought of me vomiting. "Really?"

I handed her a cookie. "Really."

She dunked it in her cocoa. "I felt so stupid. I was coming out of the woods when I saw you standing there."

"And warned me not to touch anything." I raised an eyebrow. "Kind of ironic. I'm amazed you didn't run."

"Why would I run?"

My eyes widened. "Someone you don't know is kneeling beside a dead body. I could have been the killer."

"Oh, no," she said. "I knew you weren't the killer."

"You did? How, pray tell, did you come to that conclusion?"

"Well … I … that is …" She fumbled a few seconds before blurting out, "I just knew. It was a feeling I had."

"Just like your feeling about this list?"

"Yes." She gave her head a single strong nod. "And just like I was right then, I'm right now."

"Maybe. But I think you need to go to your father—"

"You don't understand."

"Sure, I do. You tampered with evidence."

"What?" She tried very hard to put on an angelic face. "What do you mean?"

"Come on. You took that paper from Emily's pocket. Who knows what else you disturbed? Now you're embarrassed to let your father know. Maybe you think it will make him look bad. The great Detective Thomas's daughter tampered with a crime scene."

She didn't answer me, at least not with words. But her face spoke volumes. Unfortunately, I must have been reading a different book, because I didn't understand her expression. She peered into my eyes, searching them. For what? I wasn't sure.

"Why did you wait until now to tell me about this? Why didn't you tell me earlier at the diner?"

"I wasn't going to tell you at all. But something's happened." Jill proceeded to explain about her unlocked door and hearing someone in the hall. "It may be nothing. Probably just my imagination."

"Probably."

Her face fell. I think she was hoping for more sympathy on my part.

"Has anything like this happened before?" I asked.

She scrunched her shoulders. "Not exactly."

"What's that supposed to mean?"

"The last RA was a bit of a general. To get back at her, residents would pull pranks. I hear a couple of times they broke into her room."

"There's your explanation." I smirked. "You're a bit of a general."

She shot me a stern look.

"Just kidding."

She continued. "What if the killer knows I have this list and broke into my room, searching for it?"

"That doesn't make any sense. How would he know? Have you shown it to anybody else?"

"No."

"See. You and I are the only ones who know about it, and you and I are the only ones who were behind the library that morning."

Jill's brow creased, deep in thought. "I suppose."

"Do you want to know what I think?" I asked. "With all that's gone on recently, you've got your imagination working in overdrive, seeing spooks where there aren't any. That silly piece of paper means nothing."

She stirred her cocoa. "But doesn't it seem odd that three of the names on it match the three troublemakers in the library."

"Coincidence. They'd match hundreds of people on campus."

She pointed to one name on the paper. "Well, I doubt that Boomer is the killer."

"Why not?"

"Did you see him today?"

I thought of that big hulk of a guy who sat beside me at the funeral, hands clamped to his knees. Of his sulking attitude in the car. "Yes. He's taking Emily's death awfully hard. What was going on there?"

"They used to be boyfriend and girlfriend."

"No way!"

She nodded. "Going together since high school. Practically engaged."

"Then what happened?"

"I don't know." She shook her head. "It was last semester—in the spring. For some reason, they broke it off."

"Who did the breaking?"

She thought back. "I think it was a mutual thing. That's when Emily's whole attitude changed. She gave up teaching Sunday school. Went into a funk."

I said, "At one point during the funeral Boomer looked like he was going to jump out of his skin."

"It was obvious why."

"I guess I'm not as smart as you."

"I guess not."

I ignored her dig. "Please enlighten me."

"His dad opened the service to anyone who wanted to share memories about Emily. I think Boomer felt like he should get up. His dad thought so, too."

"You know, I thought I saw the pastor glare our way a couple of times."

She nodded. "Imagine if Emily was your girlfriend for, I don't know, maybe four or five years. You break up for whatever reason, but still have feelings for her. Now you're too ashamed or afraid to speak. It must have been torture for him."

I considered this. She was probably correct about the reason for Boomer's attitude today. But she was wrong about this paper and the murder. I was sure of it. The list had nothing to do with the murder. But all this talk had aroused my curiosity. "What about the other people on the list?"

"Well," she looked back at the paper. "As I said, this PRS person is a mystery, but this one could be Don, Boomer's roommate. I don't know much about him. I think he's a psych major."

"I know him." It came out as a grumble.

Jill looked at me, puzzled, for a second. Then, with a shrug, her attention returned to the paper. "Nicole Foster is the Nicole F."

"I don't know her."

It was her turn to grumble. "Believe me, you don't want to know her."

"Why not?"

"Watch out for that one," Jill warned. "She's trouble. She's a cheerleader for the football team. Pretty," Jill sneered. "I guess."

I shrugged. "Is there a problem with that?"

"She's one of those who *knows* she's pretty. Likes to use her looks to lead men around like they have rings in their noses."

I chuckled. "I'm pretty sure I can handle myself."

Jill gave a derisive laugh. "That's what all the guys say."

"Oh, come on. I'm not some high school boy." I scooped up the two empty mugs and brought them to the sink. "I was in the marines, after all. I'm not going to be bowled over by someone's good looks."

Jill rolled her eyes. That was so irritating. It's all she ever did—roll her eyes at me.

"There you go again," she said. "Honestly, are you looking for ways to sound pompous? Is that going to be your defense whenever you do something wrong?" She mimicked my voice. 'It's all right, sir. I was a marine. I'm older than these other yahoos.'"

I remained quiet.

Jill abruptly stopped and with remorse in her voice, whispered, "Sorry."

"Do—Do I really come across like that?"

She blushed, looked away and answered in a quiet voice. "Sometimes."

Talk about bursting your bubble. I sank into my chair.

Neither of us knew what to say. Thankfully, laughter erupted from the hallway. Four girls being chased by a young man with a water pistol raced by.

I stood. "I gotta go."

"Wait. Could you do me a favor? Come and check my room."

"Your room?"

She nodded.

I stared at her, wondering what she was talking about. Then I remembered. With all the talk about the list, I'd forgotten about the supposed break-in. "Are you sure I'm not too pompous?"

Red-faced, she turned away. "I guess I deserve that. Never mind." She stepped toward the door.

With a bit of harumph, I said, "Hold on."

We headed to her room, where I checked under the bed, in the closet, and everywhere else she'd let me. "No boogeymen."

"Thanks."

I scanned what I thought were the results of an invasion into her privacy. Clothes tossed about, drawers half open, papers scattered around the floor by the desk. "Boy, they really trashed this place."

"Huh?"

I pointed to some of the debris.

Jill turned a light shade of red. "Oh, that."

"What do you mean, 'Oh, that'?"

With a bashful shrug, she said, "Some of that might have been me."

My mouth dropped open. "You? Are you sure someone broke into your room, or do you just need a maid?"

"But,"—she pointed to the door—"I heard someone running in the hall."

"Somebody could have been late for the movie."

She pressed on. "And my door was unlocked."

"Maybe in your rush to leave for the funeral, you forgot to close it all the way."

"But what about the utility closet next door? It was open."

I sighed. "Is it possible your imagination is running away with you?"

She didn't answer.

A grin spread across my face. "The good news is, I can assure you no one is in here now."

She scanned the room, nervous.

"Listen, I have to go if that's okay."

She followed me into the hallway. "Jack, I truly am sorry for calling you pompous."

I shrugged. "If you could put up with all my short jokes, I guess I can take a little criticism."

She smiled. "Remember," she said. "You promised me you wouldn't tell my dad anything about the list."

"Don't worry. I'll keep my promise. But, honestly, I don't think this list means anything."

"How do you know though?"

I gave a lopsided grin. "I have a feeling."

"Very funny."

With that said, I left. Halfway up the stairs, I looked back in the direction of the second floor. *Me? Pompous?*

Chapter Twelve

About six Sunday morning I went out for a run. My residence hall, Barrett's, had floors divided into two sections—the East and West. East was girls. West was guys. Most of the other buildings didn't bother with such things. Mine must have been a throwback to a different time. The only thing really separating the two sides was the large stairwell in the center. Usually, the doors leading from this great divide were wide open, and you were free to wander where you wished. Sometimes girls would roam about in their bathrobes or pajamas. I found this a bit unnerving and it took a while for me to get used to.

As I approached the staircase, a noise came from the girl's side. Metal scratching on metal.

Odd. Nobody's usually up at this hour on a Sunday.

I took a couple steps forward and peered down the hall. The lighting was subdued, still in night mode. Everything was silent. Then I spotted someone huddled by one of the doors, about halfway down, the one with the yellow warning tape hung across it. Emily's room.

Up until a couple days ago, I hadn't even known we were in the same residence hall, let alone on the same floor. Though not officially a crime scene, the police had restricted access to her room while the investigation was ongoing. Also, I think they were giving the family time to come in and gather her possessions.

The figure, dressed in a dark hoodie, was fiddling with the doorknob.

I called out, "Problem there?"

He froze. Was this the same person I saw attacking that girl in the quad?

"Everything all right?" I asked, trying to sound official.

No response.

"I said," —I spoke louder— "is everything all right?"

The intruder seemed to recover from the shock of hearing my voice. Recomposing himself, he took a step toward me. As he did, a large smile sparkled from under the hood. "You startled me," a friendly voice spoke—a female voice. For the life of me, I had thought it was a male under that sweatshirt. Boy, was I wrong.

With one smooth motion, she reached up and pulled the hood back, shaking her long, black hair from its hiding place. It fell around her shoulders. "I didn't expect to see anyone up so early," she said.

I recognized her voice but from where? I took a couple steps closer.

Her eyes flashed with a note of recognition. Then her mouth fell open. "You! What are you doing here?"

That's when it registered. Though she looked totally different when she wasn't dripping wet, with hair plastered to her head, it was the girl I'd rescued from the attacker.

"Is everything all right?" I asked.

She quickly regained her composure and again flashed the pearly whites in my direction. "Of course. You startled me, that's all. Why do you ask?"

I pointed toward the yellow tape. "No one's supposed to be in there."

"Oh, that." She giggled and looked at me from under her long lashes.

Dark, round eyes stared deep into my own. Gorgeous eyes. They went along with the rest of her. With her olive-colored skin, I'd guess she was of Middle Eastern or Mediterranean descent. I won't say she was the most beautiful woman I'd ever seen, but she had to have ranked in the top ten. At least at this college.

"Please don't tell anyone." Her lips formed into a pout. "You wouldn't want to get me in trouble, would you?"

"Well … no, I guess not." For some reason, my face was growing warmer. "But why were you trying to get into Emily's room?"

With one finger, she traced a line along her long, slender neck. "Looking for my necklace. I let Emily borrow it and would hate to lose it. Besides, I need it for tonight." Again, she giggled. "I have a date."

"Funny time to come looking for a necklace."

"I know, but I figured I could slip in and out and not bother with anyone. Who'd have thought you'd be here this early."

I shrugged. "Going for a run. Sorry, you can't get in. The door's locked. I'm Jack, by the way." I extended a hand.

"Nicki. Nicki Foster."

Nicki Foster. I stiffened. This was the girl Jill warned me about.

She must have noticed my reaction because she took hold of my hand. Compassion-filled eyes looked into mine. "Are you okay? You're not sick or anything?" Her long lashes fluttered.

Why would Jill warn me about this girl? She didn't seem dangerous. She seemed nice. I caught a whiff of her perfume—a wonderful, intoxicating scent—and realized I'd met her even before our encounter in the rain.

"You're new to the school, aren't you?" she said. "I've only seen you around campus this semester."

For some reason, the thought of Nicki seeing me around campus pleased me. "Do you mean you've seen me other than when you ran away from our rainstorm rendezvous?"

She blushed. "Sorry about that. So, did you transfer from another school?"

Funny how she changed the subject without giving a reason for deserting me that day. "No," I said.

Her nose wrinkled, slightly. "Kind of old for a freshman, aren't you?"

"I was just discharged from the marines."

Nicki's eyes lit up. "Really!" She tipped her head to the side. "You don't look like a marine."

I chuckled. "What do they look like?"

She struck a muscle builder's pose. "Six feet two. Bulging arms."

"Hey! I've got muscles." I laughed while flexing my biceps.

"I'm sure you do. But not those big ones." Scrutinizing eyes ran up and down my form. "And you don't look to be more than six feet tall."

"Five feet ten and one half, but who's counting."

She laughed. "Where were you stationed?"

I stammered out, "The Middle East."

Nicki's smile faded. "I'm sorry. If you don't want to talk about it, we don't have to. Let's change the subject. What do you think of this whole murder thing?"

"Terrible."

"The police had me in for questioning. Can you believe that? Somehow they got the idea I was the last one to see Emily alive."

I squirmed. "Were you?"

She shrugged. "I don't know."

"But weren't you at the library that night?"

She nodded. "Yes, I was there ... studying."

"I know. I saw you with two other people." I tried to sound as casual as possible. "And after the library closed?"

Nicki's eyes narrowed. "Hey, wait a minute. You're the person I ran into on the stairs."

"Among other places."

For a moment, her face reddened. She recovered and gave a playful slap to my chest. "You naughty boy. Are you the one who told the police I was there?"

I nodded. "What was I supposed to do? They told me if I turned state's evidence, they'd go easier on me."

We laughed.

"Seriously," I said. "I didn't mean to get you in trouble."

"That's okay." She leaned in close and whispered. "I hear you're the one who found Emily."

"Yup."

"Did you find anything else?"

"Like what?"

"I don't know. Something that might be a clue."

I shook my head.

"Do you think the police have any leads?" She looked at me, waiting for an answer.

I shrugged. "I don't know."

"They didn't say anything to you?"

"Why would they?"

She giggled. "You, being a marine, I thought maybe they'd take you into their confidence, let you help or something. Let's face it, you're obviously more mature than these other college boys." Her eyes took on a dreamy quality. "You've seen the world, haven't you?"

Exactly!

Jill says I'm pompous. But experience and age have nothing to do with pompousness or pomposity or whatever the word is. Two different things. Nicki had such keen insight. I admired her for that. "You seem very interested in the murder."

She waved her hand, dismissing the notion. "Don't get me wrong. I was just wondering, Emily being my good friend and all."

"What?" A voice sounded from down the hall, by the stairwell. Jill stood there, hands on hips.

"Oh, hello, Jill." There was a distinct coldness to Nicki's tone. "It's always such a pleasure to see you."

"What are you doing here?" I asked.

"A good friend of Emily's?" Jill scoffed as she marched toward us.

"Well ... yes." Nicki fidgeted.

Jill snorted. "You couldn't stand her."

"That's not exactly true. Maybe we didn't always see eye to eye, but—"

"You mocked her. Made fun of her faith," Jill hammered her point.

Nicki's eyes widened. "I think you're exaggerating."

"Oh, come on! Tell the truth."

"Girls," I interrupted. "I think you should keep it down." I glanced at the closed doors. "People are trying to sleep."

If cold looks were rated, the one Jill gave me would have been a sub-zero—a popsicle maker. She opened her mouth to protest, but quickly closed it.

Nicki stroked my arm. "Good point, Jack." She looked at her watch. "I have to be going, anyway." She sauntered down the corridor.

How could I have ever mistaken that figure for a guy?

Before she entered the stairwell, she threw me an over-the-shoulder glance. Her eyes flashed with her smile.

Had she caught me staring? Did it really matter? I had the distinct impression Nicki enjoyed being stared at.

"See you." Her hair flew around as she turned toward the staircase.

"Hold on," I said. "I'll walk with you."

"That would be wonderful."

I'd taken a couple of steps when Jill said, "Wait for me."

Nicki mumbled something under her breath. I didn't ask her to repeat it, for fear of re-igniting the argument. The three of us headed off. From the looks Nicki was giving Jill, I don't think she appreciated her tagging along.

As we ventured down the stairs, Jill smiled at me. "I had a wonderful time last night."

I squinted. "What? In the kitchen, drinking hot chocolate?"

"No, silly." She gave an awkward pat to my arm. "At Ralphy's."

"Oh."

She paused. "Yes. Er … it was a wonderful time."

I looked at her, bewildered. "Okay."

"The two of you went out last night?" Nicki asked.

I shrugged. "Stopped for something to eat after the funeral."

Nicki cast a wary eye at a smug and satisfied-looking Jill.

What's that all about?

We'd reached the second-floor landing. Jill took a step toward her hallway, hesitated and turned to Nicki. "Was there some group you and Emily belonged to?"

Nicki's brow creased. "Some group?"

"Yes. Maybe she was the treasurer, and you owed dues." Jill's eyes narrowed. "Or did you owe her money for some other reason?"

I lowered my head and sighed.

The color drained from Nicki's face. "I have no idea what you're getting at."

"None at all?" Jill asked.

"None."

I interrupted. "Jill found this list with your initials on it—"

"Jack!" Jill looked at me as if I'd just pushed her grandmother off a cliff.

"List?" Nicki's hands fidgeted. "I don't know anything about a list." Then, as an afterthought, she added, "Oh, by the way, where is it?"

Jill's hand instinctively reached for her pocketbook. "Does it matter?"

Nicki's fingers tapped nervously on the landing's metal railing. "No. Just wondering. If my name is on it, I'd like a look."

"Are you concerned that maybe the police have it?" Jill asked.

Nicki scowled. "Why would I care?"

"You're the one who asked where it was—"

"I was just making conversation."

Jill's voice rose. "Obviously, you care."

Nicki followed suit. "I was just wondering!"

"Time out!" I raised my hands between them. "I thought we were going to lower our voices."

"Me too," Nicki chimed in.

"But I did lower my voice," Jill insisted.

"For less than ten minutes," Nicki said.

"Correct. So now it's later. People should be awake."

Before I could protest, Jill looked at Nicki, steely-eyed. "Why is your name on the list?"

"I don't know!" She squeezed my hand, hard. Her eyes pleaded with me. "Really! I don't know. What's so important about this silly list, anyway?"

"It's okay, Nicki." I returned Jill's cold stare. "Jill is under the impression it has something to do with Emily's death."

"I don't understand," Nicki said. "I thought the murder was the work of the Dumpster Killer."

I nodded. "It was."

"You're wrong," Jill said, flatly.

I sighed. "Jill thinks this list will lead to Emily's killer."

"How?"

"Ask her." I descended three stairs, leaving the two girls on the landing.

Jill glared at me before turning to Nicki. "It's possible this list might contain the name of the killer."

Slowly, Nicki's puzzled look changed to one of shock. Then to anger. "And my name is on this list?" For a moment, I thought she was going to hit Jill. But instead, she stabbed a finger at her face. "You think I killed Emily?"

"Easy, Nicki." I stepped back up to the landing. Maybe leaving these two alone was not a good idea. "Jill didn't say that."

"But that's what she's implying, isn't it?"

I didn't answer.

Nicki's face flushed. "For your information, I have no idea why my name is on any old list. For all I know, it's a list of people who have overdue library books."

"I'm sorry." I touched her shoulder. "Please don't be upset."

"Well, I'm not sorry," Jill announced.

We were playing good cop-bad cop, and one thing was for sure—Jill was the bad cop. She was like a pit bull. "If you were such a good friend to Emily, tell me this. Why weren't you at the funeral?"

Nicki stuttered and stammered. "I had a doctor's appointment that I couldn't miss."

"Why were you at the library after closing hours the night of the murder?" Jill stuck her finger in Nicki's face. "Don't try denying it. Jack saw you leaving."

"I won't deny it." Nicki pushed the finger aside. "I went back to apologize to Emily for my earlier rude behavior. The door was locked, so I left."

"Then," I added quietly, "when I ran into you on the library stairs, why did you look so guilty?"

There was no hesitation in her answer. "Not guilty. Frightened."

"Why?" Jill snapped. "What were you frightened of?"

Red-faced, Nicki glared at me. "The same thing I was frightened of the night I ran away from you during the rainstorm. Look at you. You may not be the biggest marine there is, but you are a man. We've all heard the stories of the Dumpster Killer. What girl wouldn't be a startled running into a stranger, late at night?"

We stood in silence.

It made sense.

Nicki continued. "I didn't get into the library that night. Ask that nice security guard. He was on patrol. We talked briefly while I was walking across the quad. He'll tell you he saw me try the door. He even saw you run into me. I've told the police all about this."

"And after you left, you went straight to your room?" Jill was not willing to halt her interrogation.

"No, I went straight for my car. I don't live on campus."

"Did anyone see you leave?"

She hesitated. Then spoke with great satisfaction in her voice. "Yes, as a matter of fact, Don Henderson walked me to my car." Nicki's eyes flashed with anger. "Now, if you don't mind, I'm leaving."

"Nicki," I pleaded.

"No, Jack." The muscles in her neck tightened. "We can get together another time. But I have better things to do than stand here and be accused of murder." She stomped down the stairs.

I turned to Jill. "You're something. Do you know that?"

"Me? What about you?"

"What did *I* do?"

"You promised you wouldn't tell anyone about the list."

"No." I raised my hand. "I promised I wouldn't tell the police. And I didn't."

She crossed her arms. "You are so aggravating."

"Thank you." With a triumphant smirk, I turned and headed out for my run.

"Sorry I can't have you over for lunch today." Mrs. Roberts approached me after the Sunday morning service. "It probably wouldn't be a good idea, with Pastor Roberts being under the weather and all."

"That's okay. I'll just have to live without your home cooking for one week."

"What did you think of Mr. Davis' message," she asked.

Mr. Davis, the Sunday school's superintendent, was a nice enough guy, but his message was a little dry for my taste. "It was fine." I tried to sound as diplomatic as possible. "I prefer Pastor Roberts though."

"I understand." She placed her arm around my shoulder and pulled me closer. "Maybe someday soon you'll fill in for the pastor."

I paused, waiting for the punch line. "Me?"

"Sure. Why not?"

"No thanks. I don't think preaching is in my future."

"You never know." She squeezed my arm, gently. "You need to be open to wherever God leads you."

"Yes, but preaching?" I shook my head. "I don't think God would use somebody like me."

She beamed. "Stranger things have happened. Look at Pastor Roberts. He had a very wild past."

"No way! Pastor Roberts?" The concept of my prim and proper pastor not being born with a Bible in one hand and a commentary in the other was more than I could fathom.

"The Lord got hold of him and changed all that. Jackson, God takes the worst people this world has to offer and uses them for the best. The apostle Paul said he was the chief of sinners. You can't get much worse than that. Look what God did with him."

I smirked. "So, you think I'm the worst this world has to offer?"

She began to walk away. "Just remember, let God do the leading. All right?"

"Uh-huh."

Just then, Jill trotted over. "Hi, Jack."

As soon as Mrs. Roberts saw her, she made a beeline back to me. "Good morning, Jill," she called out, all bubbly.

"Hey, Mrs. R., Good to see you." She turned to me. "Want a ride to campus?"

I wasn't sure whether this was a good idea or not. We hadn't parted on the best of terms this morning, but then again, things had been worse between us—much worse. "Okay."

Jill smiled. "I have a couple of things to take care of before we leave. See you outside in five." She was off.

"Well, I see you and Jill have patched things up. Maybe even become friends?" Mrs. Roberts eyes sparkled.

I nodded. "Nice girl."

"She certainly is. A nice *Christian* girl."

Jill disappeared through a door on the other side of the sanctuary.

"Sure," I said. "But I still think she's a bit of a nut."

The ride back to school was quick. Most of the way, we talked about the sermon and the church.

Once we'd reached the landing to Jill's floor, I brought up our early morning adventure. "Jill, I didn't mean to upset you today."

"It's all right. I'm fine." Jill leaned over the railing and gazed down the stairs. "But, did you notice how upset Nicki got when I brought up the list?"

"That's because you were badgering her."

"Asking questions is not badgering."

I shrugged. "It's all in the way you ask them."

Jill smirked. "Maybe I did come on a little hard."

"A little hard? Bulldozers are gentler." I laughed.

"But, she almost cried, she was so flustered." Jill tapped the side of her face, deep in thought. "She does have a pretty good alibi, though."

"Uh-huh." I turned to leave. "I gotta go. I'll see you later."

"Oh, by the way." Jill rummaged through her purse. "I have something for you." She handed me a sheet of paper.

Obediently I took it. Upon seeing what it was, I wished I hadn't.

"I made you a copy of the list." She closed her pocketbook.

"Why are you giving this to me?"

"I thought you'd like to help in my investigation."

"There is no investigation."

Again, she smirked. "We'll see."

"Jill, this list means nothing."

"If that's true, then why did Nicki get so upset when I brought it up?" She walked toward her room. "See you later."

Half dazed, I waved. Was I now Watson to Jill's Sherlock? I didn't know if I liked that.

Once in my room, I placed the paper on my desk and thought back to Jill's treatment of Nicki. I would never tell her this, but she was right. Nicki's actions had brought some questions to mind. First of all, why *had* she gotten so upset? Secondly, why had her story about searching for her necklace rung false?

I had to laugh. Jill must have learned her interrogating skills from her dad. The way she behaved this morning. I hesitated and sank into my desk chair. "This morning ..." Suddenly a third question came to mind, one I asked earlier, but never got an answer to.

What was Jill doing in the hallway at six o'clock?

Chapter Thirteen

Monday morning, I grabbed my breakfast at the Tank. That's a snack bar on campus. I don't know if it has an official name. Students simply refer to it as the Tank, because it's in the lower level of the Harrison F. Tank building. The variety of food is less formal than the dining hall. A little more burgers and fries.

Upon entering the building, I passed the student mailboxes. I hadn't checked mine in about a week, so I figured it was about time. I unlocked the tiny door and tons of flyers and letters poured out. I quickly gathered them all together.

How come they don't just email this junk?

I got a breakfast sandwich, found a table, and plopped the pile of letters in the center, figuring to wade through it as I ate.

Ultimate Frisbee ... Flag Football ... Hiking Club. There were a dozen or more flyers from various groups, all seeking new members. I was ready to bundle the whole lot together and dump it in the trash when an official-looking envelope caught my eye. It was on school stationery and the return address said, Dr. R. Spiner.

I ripped it open and read.

Dear Mr. Hill,

Would you please come by to see me at your earliest convenience?

Sincerely,

Roland   Spiner,   College   President

What have I done now?

To me, a college president was like a school principal. Being called to the office was never a good thing. I turned the envelope over, examining it, wondering how long it had been in my box. I needed to check my mail more often. My next class wasn't until ten o'clock, so I finished my food and hurried over to the president's office.

The administration building was a large stone structure situated on the north side of the quad. With its ivy-covered walls, large granite steps, and arched wooden doors, it looked like something from another century.

Once inside, there was no problem locating the president's office. It was the one all the screaming was coming from. I don't think its inhabitants noticed me as I pushed the door open and entered. Two women were having a standoff, glaring at each other. I recognized both.

One, tall with the looks of an aging Swedish beauty queen, stood guard behind a metal desk, arms folded. Ms. Fielding, the president's secretary. She leaned forward and pressed her fists into the desktop. "I'm telling you, you cannot have a rifle in here!"

"It's not a rifle," the other woman answered from her spot in the center of the office. She had a shotgun draped across her left arm, breeched open as if to reload. The lady with the No Trespassing signs.

I noted there were no cartridges in the chamber.

In contrast to the secretary, who was dressed sharply, this short and stocky woman looked like she'd just come from duck hunting in a swamp.

"It's a shotgun, and it's not loaded. Get your facts straight before you go causing chaos." She hoisted the weapon and rested it over her shoulder. "If it weren't for your confounded students traipsing through my woods, I wouldn't need it for protection."

"They're not your woods!"

"Yes, they are!"

The secretary's face shook with anger. "And what will you do if you come across one of the students out there? Shoot?"

The shotgun-toting woman went to speak but paused. Closing her lips tightly, her face turned red and swelled as she held in her breath. Finally, she exhaled with a large flare. "As I said, let me see the president, and we'll stop having this difficulty. Me and my rifle" —She exaggerated the word rifle— "will be off your silly little school's property."

"And as I told you, he's not here."

"He's never here," shotgun lady exploded. "It's a wonder the school can even run—"

"Caroline Webster!" The secretary marched from behind the desk. "You know that's not true. Don't you go spreading rumors."

Caroline closed the shotgun with a loud snap. "Would you please tell him to return one of my many calls or answer my emails." She waved her arms. "Send me a message by pony express if he'd like!"

The president's secretary straightened up. Her hands fairly shaking with rage, she patted down the front of her dress as she tried to compose herself. "I'll let him know."

Caroline Webster swung the door open and marched out.

Ms. Fielding took a deep breath and released it slowly. Then she turned and faced me. Her expression said, 'Here's another distraction for me to be bothered by'. "May I help you?"

"I found this note in my mailbox." I handed her the letter.

She read it carefully while peering at me over its top every few seconds.

"But if he's not—"

"Wait here." She glided to a door behind her desk and knocked before peeking inside. When she spoke, her voice was muffled by three inches of dark stained oak.

I smirked. *Looks like the doctor is in after all.*

She withdrew her head. "You may see him now."

Ms. Fielding remained in the doorway, her tall, statuesque frame blocking my way.

"Excuse me," I said.

She remained motionless for a moment, staring at me. Then, with a bit of a huff, she moved aside.

Dr. Spiner sat behind a large antique desk, speaking on the phone, anxiously running his hand through his thick, silvery hair. "No. I'm telling you to double the security." Barely glancing at me, he motioned toward a seat in front of him.

I dropped my jacket over the back of it and sat down.

"I don't care. The school will have to absorb it. Can you imagine the cost if we don't? Parents are removing their children left and right … That's correct … thirty-five this week." His eyes focused on me for a moment. "Listen, I have something to attend to … I'll talk to you later … Okay. Goodbye." He hung up. Then letting his head fall backward, he closed his eyes and sighed. "Foolish board members. They don't see the big picture."

Was he speaking to himself or to me? I wasn't sure.

He rubbed his temples and cleared his throat before leaning forward and extending his hand. "Sorry to keep you waiting. Jackson Hill, correct?"

"Yes, sir."

We shook.

"It's a pleasure to meet you. You're probably wondering what this is all about. Rest assured, you are not in any trouble. Frankly, the opposite is true. It's me who's been remiss." He strummed his fingers against the desktop. "From what I understand, you're the gentleman who found the poor unfortunate student the other morning."

"Yes, sir."

"I have to apologize for not contacting you sooner."

"I don't understand."

"To see if you're dealing with the situation in a … healthy way. After all, it must have been quite traumatic."

"I'm fine, sir."

"Good to hear, good to hear." He gave a sympathetic smile. "We have grief counselors in place if you need them."

"Honestly. I'm okay."

He glanced at the closed office door. "Would you like something to drink? Coffee? Tonic?"

Tonic is what old New Englanders call soft drinks.

"A glass of water," I answered.

"Of course. Excuse me." He stood and crossed the room.

I was surprised to see how tall he was. With his muscular-looking upper arms and shoulders, and a thin waist, it was obvious he took care of himself.

He stepped into the outer office and pulled the door shut.

During his absence, I perused the room. Behind his desk was a large bay window looking out over the mountains.

Nice view.

The wall to the left of his desk was covered with plaques, awards, and photos of what I could only assume were memories of his many years at the college. The wall to the right was lined with bookcases.

Under the window, a large model of a building sat on a table. Modern. Clean. Nice looking. A sign read—Roland P. Spiner Auditorium. A map next to it showed its future location.

The president returned. "Ms. Fielding will bring those refreshments right in." He sat on the desk's front edge, accidentally knocking over an eight-by-ten framed picture.

I lunged forward and caught it before it hit the floor.

"Good save." He took it from me.

It was a photo of him holding a fishing pole and dressed in the appropriate gear for the sport, including a bucket hat covered with lures. A large black dog, which looked more like a bear, was seated next to him.

"Nice dog."

"That's my baby." He stared at the picture, his face filled with pride. "He's a Newfie."

I chuckled. "Big baby!"

"Angus went for close to one hundred and forty pounds."

"Went for? You don't have him anymore?"

His jaw tightened. "Lost him about six months ago."

"I'm sorry. I know the death of a pet can really hurt."

"He didn't die." He choked. "Disappeared. One day he just disappeared." President Spiner's eyes flashed. "Someone took him. I know they did. Someone who's out to—" As if suddenly realizing I was seated there, he stopped, covered his mouth and coughed. "I'm so glad we've had this chance to talk. It would seem your time at our college has been … event filled." With a genial laugh, he replaced the picture on his desk, putting it next to a wooden nameplate which read R. Spiner—President.

I studied it for a moment. Something gnawed in the back of my mind.

Dr. Spiner fidgeted with a penholder. "And … er … the morning … when you found the poor girl, did you see anything? Anyone else?"

"No. Nothing," I answered absentmindedly, my eyes fixed on the plaque. Why did it feel so familiar?

Roland Spiner—President.

He continued. "I mean if you had seen something … a clue, I'm sure you would have told the police. Correct?"

Then it hit me. The name. His title. The initials.

"Correct?" He spoke louder.

PRS!

"Mr. Hill?"

"What? Oh yes." I pulled myself back to the conversation. "Correct. If I'd seen anything, I would have let the detective know."

"Good, good." He chuckled. "I want to assure you, things at our school are usually much quieter." The president stood and meandered toward a bookcase. As he fiddled with some of the memorabilia, he shared stories of their importance to him.

While he rambled, his mind focused elsewhere, I looked at the plaque. There it was. PRS, just like the initials of the list. President Roland Spiner.

Inwardly, I scolded myself. I'd allowed Jill's ideas to infect my brain. It had to be a coincidence.

"What do you think?" The president stared at me.

"Pardon?" I had no idea what he'd been talking about.

"I said, what do you think of the school?"

"Oh, it seems very nice." Right then he could have asked me what I thought of jumping a motorcycle off a thousand-foot cliff, and my answer would have been the same. All I could think about were his initials and the list.

Stupid Jill.

The president returned to the desk. "Do the police have any leads?"

"Leads?"

"They're pretty closed mouth with me." He leaned in. "But I noticed you were brought downtown as they say." He raised an eyebrow. "I wondered if you could shed any light on what they're thinking."

I shrugged. "I don't know any more than you."

All at once his cordial look was gone, replaced with an I-don't-believe-a-word-you're-saying expression. "You see, I'd like the school to return to normal operations as soon as possible. With this tragic murder, that's hard to do."

I hesitated. "Can I ask you a question?"

"Of course." He spread his hands in front of him as a sign of his openness.

"Did you know Emily Hamilton?"

His reply came in a split second. "No, not personally."

"Are you sure?"

His brow puckered. "Yes. I do my best to stay in touch with as many students as possible, but there's no way to know them all." His response seemed sincere.

"Do you know any reason why she might have your name on a list?"

"List?" His eyes narrowed. "What kind of a list?"

I tried to sound nonchalant. "I saw her going over a list of names and dollar amounts. I thought your name was on it."

He scratched his head. "I can't think of any reason. Maybe I pledged to some charity drive or fundraiser she was involved in." His chest swelled. "I always endeavor to support the student's charitable works." All at once, his attention diverted to something behind me. "Ms. Fielding, watch out!"

I turned around just in time to see the secretary almost drop a tray containing two glasses and a pitcher of water.

"Sorry," she said. "I'll have to be more careful." She crossed the room and placed them on the desk.

"Do you know Jackson Hill? He's the one who had the misfortune of finding that poor girl."

"Sad business." Ms. Fielding poured a glass and handed it to me.

"I was hoping our friend here could shed light on the police activity in this matter," Dr. Spiner said. "He seems to have the detective's ear." He stared at me with a look of anticipation.

Ms. Fielding stood transfixed. "Yes, I'm sure Mr. Hill is resourceful." She nodded, slowly. "Very resourceful indeed." Her green eyes stared at me, not moving, not blinking.

I looked away, hoping this would break the contact. But when I looked back, her eyes were still locked on me.

Creepy.

Staring back felt awkward, so I diverted my eyes, finding something else to look at. Finally, I focused on her necklace—a heart-shaped pendant, outlined in small diamonds. Unique and very expensive looking.

"That's pretty," I said.

Her gaze faltered. Her hand grasped the pendant as she backed off. "It—It was a gift." For a second, she looked at Dr. Spiner.

The room grew still. I sipped my water while they both watched. Was it just me or were things getting … weird? I wanted out. With one large gulp, I emptied the glass. "I'd like to help, but honestly I don't know anything."

"Are you sure?" Dr. Spiner said.

"Positive. I tell you what. If something comes up, I promise you'll be the first to know."

He considered my offer, then forced a smile. "I guess that's all I can hope for."

I jumped out of the seat. "If you don't mind, I have to get to class."

We shook hands, and the president slapped me on the back. "Now don't forget, if there's ever anything I can do for you, let me know."

"Yes, sir."

He held my hand in a tight grip. "And if there's new information about this investigation, you'll tell me. Right?"

"Right."

We stood there, him shaking my hand, and me trying to get away. Finally, when I was able to break free, I backed out of the office, leaving him gawking in my direction. Ms. Fielding took a position behind him. She wasn't gawking, though. Her look was more of a scowl.

I raced down the hall and exited the building.

Weird. I never wanted to go back there again.

The cold autumn air served as a quick reminder that I was missing something.

Where's my coat?

It took only a second to remember I'd tossed it over the back of the seat in the office. Heaving a deep sigh, I reentered the building.

Ms. Fielding's office was empty, and the door to the president's was ajar.

Just as I went to knock, Dr. Spiner spoke, agitation in his voice. "He knows more than he's letting on."

I held my breath and listened.

"You could be wrong," Ms. Fielding said.

"Stop doubting me," the president snapped. "He saw something. I tell you, he saw something!"

"What are you going to do?"

"I'm not sure. I'm starting to think he's dangerous. Might have to be dealt with."

"Do you know what I think?" Ms. Fielding said.

I leaned forward to hear better. In so doing, my shoulder nudged the door. It creaked open a couple more inches.

The conversation stopped.

I froze.

"Hello? Is someone there?" Dr. Spiner called.

I tiptoed at a double clip across the room and pulled open the door to the hall just as Ms. Fielding emerged from the president's office.

She eyed me, suspiciously. "Mr. Hill. Forget something?"

I closed the door as if I'd just entered. "My coat. It's in Dr. Spiner's office."

She backed into the room. A couple of seconds later she reemerged, holding my jacket. "Here you are."

When I took hold, she didn't let go.

"You should be more careful." Her eyes bore into mine. "You might catch your death of a cold."

After she released her grip, and I was leaving the building, I wondered … *Was it my imagination, or had she stressed the word death?*

Chapter Fourteen

It was nearly ten o'clock when I escaped from my meeting with Dr. Spiner. Was it really as strange as I thought or had Jill's list talk swayed my opinion? Her desire to have Emily's death be something other than a part of a serial killer's rampage had clouded her judgment. Now she was clouding mine.

My English Lit class was held in a large lecture hall. I climbed the steps to the stadium-type seating and found a spot about halfway back. Being swallowed up by the crowd to avoid questions from the professor was a benefit of sitting in a sea of students. We were studying Bacon. Up until now, I figured bacon was something you ate for breakfast.

Miss Hodgekins, our instructor, was a mousy-looking lady, whose large-framed glasses protruded beyond the sides of her narrow face. The lenses were so thick—probably from reading too much Bacon—they distorted her eyes. Don't get me wrong. She was a very nice lady. It was Bacon who was boring. I was bored, bored, bored.

When this happens, my mind usually wanders. I searched the room, trying to find something of interest to keep me from falling asleep. That's when I spotted her, three rows in front of me, over to the far left. Nicki. This was serendipity. Before I knew it, I'd somehow gotten her attention. She gave me a little wave. I waved back.

She mouthed the words, "I'm bored."

"Me too," I mouthed back.

Then I caught sight of another student in the row behind her, glowering at me. He was on the dorky side. Tall and thin.

Thin like a scarecrow after a windstorm. Black framed glasses hung on the tip of his nose. Several pimples appeared ready to erupt on his forehead. If eyes could throw knives, I'd have been punctured a dozen times over.

What had I done to him?

As I was wondering this, Nicki's lips curled up, and she stuck out her tongue.

Funny faces? What were we, kindergarten children?

She nodded at me as if to say, 'Your turn.'

No way.

She responded with crossed eyes.

Miss Hodgekin continued to lecture, but I had totally lost track of what she was saying. Instead, I was focused on the continual stream of faces Nicki was making. I had to admit, she was creative.

Once again, she nodded to me, 'Your turn.'

Was she serious? Not only were we college students, but I was also a marine.

Suddenly, I heard Jill's voice chastising me for being so pompous.

I'll show her pompous.

I contorted my face, stuck out my tongue, and crossed my eyes.

Nicki giggled, not too silently.

The dork glared at me.

Miss Hodgekin looked over at Nicki, semi-confused by the interruption. "Is everything all right?"

"Yes." Nicki's face reddened. "I—I just thought what you were saying was amusing."

The professor's brow wrinkled. She removed her glasses. "Francis Bacon … dying of pneumonia … That's amusing?"

Nicki cleared her throat. "It's—I think—" She sat up as if a brilliant idea had just come to her. "You know what? It's the word pneumonia. The way they spell it. Cracks me up every time."

Miss Hodgekin opened her mouth, but nothing came out.

After class Nicki rushed up to me as I was leaving. "You are such a bad boy, getting me in trouble the way you did."

"What about you?" I tried to mimic her voice. "Oh, Miss Hodgekins, you say the most amusing things. Pneumonia!"

"Stop it." She failed to conceal her smile.

As we walked out of the building, someone nudged me, hard, as he rushed by.

Mr. Dork.

"Hey!" I said.

His only response was a grunt as he continued down the sidewalk.

I wanted to chase after the guy, find out what his problem was, but Nicki touched my arm. "Don't mind him," she said. "So, what's next for you?"

After one more sneer at the shover, I pulled my attention back to her. "I'm done until after lunch. And you?"

"Chemistry." She frowned as she turned to leave. "I hate chemistry."

"Do you have a second? There's something I want to ask you. The other morning, with Jill—"

She moaned. "Why do you have to bring her up?"

I scratched the back of my head. "Jill said you made fun of Emily's Christianity."

"And?"

I swallowed hard. "You see, I'm a Christian. A military chaplain led me to the Lord."

An eyebrow raised. "Why are you telling me this?"

"Well, you mocked Emily's faith, and I'm ..." My words faded, letting her draw the implication.

Her eyes flashed with contempt. "Emily's supposed Christianity deserved to be mocked. Jack, there are things about her you don't know. Don't believe everything Miss High and Mighty Jill tells you."

I ignored the dig at Jill. "Let me ask you a question. Are you a Christian?"

"Sure. I was brought up in the church."

Typical response.

I pushed on. "Can I talk to you about—"

She looked at her watch. "I'm going to be late for class."

"Okay." Then I added, "Maybe you could go to church with me sometime?"

"Maybe." She picked up her pace as she moved down the sidewalk.

"There's a special service on Friday night," I called after her. "How about it?"

"I'll think about it and let you know." With that, she raced away.

I wished she'd have agreed to go to church right then and there, but I understood. No one wants to be late for class.

Before grabbing lunch, I headed to my room to swap my books—morning class for afternoon. I froze when I entered the residence hall.

Detective Thomas was chatting with Mrs. Oswald.

Wonderful.

This didn't bode well for me.

The woman gestured wildly with her hands as she spoke. "He said if he wanted to he could kill someone, and nobody would be able to stop him. He said there were hundreds of access points to the college and he could fade into the darkness and never be found."

Thankfully, Detective Thomas was facing away from me. I slowly backed to the door.

Mrs. Oswald continued. "He was complaining about a terrible headache. Kept rubbing his temple."

I was almost there.

"I hear he suffered a breakdown while serving overseas. He was in the marines, you know."

Oh, boy.

Quietly, I pushed the door open. As I did, a couple of students entered, bumping into me as they did.

"Sorry," one of them said.

"No problem." I spoke in a whisper.

"Something wrong with your voice, Jack?"

"Shh!"

Too late. Mrs. Oswald saw me. She pointed an accusing finger. "There he is now."

Busted.

"Good afternoon, Mr. Hill." Detective Thomas walked toward me. "I was wondering if I could have a word with you."

"Kind of busy. Can it wait?"

"No."

Mrs. Oswald tried to hide her pudgy frame behind a poster for the upcoming musical that someone had placed on the sign-in desk. "Be careful," she whispered. "He could be dangerous."

Double Oh, boy.

Detective Thomas did not look happy. "How about if we sit on the bench in front of the building?" He walked out the door, down the steps, and to a bench.

I followed reluctantly. The more I was seen with the police, the more accusing looks I received from my fellow students. But there was no way to avoid this. I braced myself, ready for the accusations. But instead of having to mount a defense, what he said took me by surprise.

"Jack, are you all right?"

"Yes. Why do you ask?"

He drew half circles in the air. "The dark circles under your eyes."

Feeling self-conscious, I tried to rub them away. "Not sleeping too well. That's all."

"Really?" It was a single word, but he packed a lot of meaning into it. "Tell me something. How long have you been in Springsbury?"

Why weren't we talking about Mrs. Oswald? "A few months, I guess. Ask Pastor or Mrs. Roberts if you need the exact date. I stayed with them for part of the summer."

Detective Thomas leaned back. He stared across the quad. "Visit here much before that?"

"No. Why?"

"Had you heard of the Dumpster Killer before you came here?"

"No, sir."

He scanned the sidewalk. "I guess if it turned out he was a local person … That would be hard to take. But if he were a stranger, someone we don't really know, that would be more palatable." He looked at me. "Someone like—"

"Detective Thomas, I am not the Dumpster Killer."

His voice became stern. "Then why do I have a witness who will swear that you said you were."

"Mrs. Oswald?"

"Jack, I—"

"It's Mrs. Oswald, isn't it? I can explain."

Without answering my question, or allowing me to explain, he continued. "My witness states you were bragging about being able to fool everyone."

"But—"

"That campus security was not enough to stop you."

"Now hold on." My mind raced.

Detective Thomas's eyes drilled into mine. "Well?"

I looked to the ground in surrender. "I—I said those things, but—"

"Oh, Jack. How could you be so stupid?"

"It happened after I left the library to get my card."

"I know *when* it happened. I simply need to know *why*."

I explained my relationship with our residence hall monitor, about the way she treated me. About my phobia of face pinching.

"That's no reason to tell her you were the serial killer."

"Please, let me tell you exactly what happened that night."

"Go ahead."

I proceded to tell Detective Thomas about my conversation with Mrs. Oswald the night of Emily's murder.

I went to my dorm to get my library card. Mrs. Oswald was there, manning her station. I was barely at her desk when she held up a pen between two pudgy fingers and waved it in the air. "Forget something?"

I pasted on a happy face. "Good evening, Mrs. Oswald."

She spoke as if chastising a five-year-old. "Did you forget to sign in?"

"No, ma'am. I just got here. You didn't give me a chance to—"

"We'll let it go this time. But, it's very important that we all follow the rules. I mean with a killer on the loose." She leaned in closer. I stepped back, fearing she was going for my cheeks. "A serial killer at that! We had best be careful."

"I'm not sure two killings make a serial killer."

Her eyes widened. "Are you serious?"

"Well—"

She huffed. "So far, two bodies have been found."

"I know, but—"

"Both girls were stabbed in the same manner."

"I know, but—"

"And both were found by trash receptacles."

"Yes, but—"

"Not a serial killer?"

"But, Mrs. Oswald." I practically shouted, which seemed like the only way I would get a word into the conversation. "For all we know the killer is long gone."

She clicked her tongue while giving me a you-naive-boy type of look. "I highly doubt that. Two killings. The first … When was it? About four months ago? And then another? No. These deranged killers don't just disappear. If anything, he's getting closer to us. You can't blame the parents for worrying about their daughters. Can you?"

"I know, but—"

"Extra security measures, like sign-in desks, give us some peace of mind. Knowing where the students are at night, and curfews, they're all important." She leaned back in her seat, a smug look on her face. This was her obvious way of letting me know she was done and believed I couldn't have any possible response to her supposed air-tight explanation.

That's when an idea hit me. In retrospect, it probably wasn't the right thing to do, but I decided to have a little fun.

I raised an eyebrow at my aunt's college counterpart. "Let me ask you a question, Mrs. Oswald."

Her plump face pulled into a big smile. "What, dear?"

"If the Dumpster Killer wanted to kill one of the girls on this campus—"

"God forbid!"

"Yes, God forbid. Do you think if the killer set his mind to it, these check-in desks would stop him?"

"Well …" The creases between her eyebrows deepened.

I lowered my voice to almost a whisper. "This campus has hundreds of entry points and scores of darkened pathways. The security is incompetent. It couldn't stop someone as intelligent as the Dumpster Killer. If I … er … I mean if this so-called Dumpster Killer wanted to kill … " I leaned in for added emphasis. "I …" I shook my head. "I mean, *he* would."

Her face soured.

I chuckled and spoke in a low guttural voice. "As a matter of fact, one of these sign-in sheets might have his name on it right now?"

"Wha—what on earth do you mean?"

In a melodramatic manner, I stabbed my finger into the paper. "He may be a student on this campus." My face darkened. "For all you know, I may be the Dumpster Killer." I stared deep into her eyes and tried to look as ominous as I could. "And Mrs. Oswald … You've just checked me in."

She gave a nervous laugh. "Oh, Jack. Stop that. You're just teasing me."

"Am I?" My lip curled in a half sneer. "Am I? Don't be deceived by looks. The Dumpster Killer may appear as normal as you or me. But who knows? Who knows?" Before she could say anything, I spun around and walked away, chuckling to myself.

Once I reached my room, it took me about ten or fifteen minutes to find my card and use the bathroom before returning to her station.

"Going somewhere?" Mrs. Oswald fidgeted with her glasses.

I grabbed the pen to sign out.

She watched my every move as I scratched my name on the page.

I glared at her. "Is there a problem?"

"No—no." Her eyes widened. "Jack … are you all right?"

With my eyes closed, I inhaled deeply through my nose, then exhaled long and hard. I gently rubbed my temple with three fingers. "I … have … these headaches. That's all."

"Headaches?"

I nodded. "Ever since … But never mind." I backed away from her, turned and slowly crossed the room. When I reached the door, without looking back, I added, "I have some business to attend to … personal business. No one can stop me."

As the door closed, I swear I heard Mrs. Oswald gasp.

I laughed out loud as I ran to the library.

Detective Thomas stared, somber-faced. "You laughed?"

"You gotta understand, this was before Emily was killed. Who'd have thought—" I shook my head. "And Mrs. Oswald drives me nuts. I was only kidding her!"

He remained calm. "If it was Mrs. Oswald who spoke to me, and I'm not saying it was, she didn't think you were kidding."

"But—"

"Can I give you some advice? Go see her. Be careful what you say. Clear things up. Whether you like it or not, you're a person of interest in this investigation."

"I'm a suspect?"

"A person of interest," he corrected. "You're new in the area. You found the body."

"I thought you didn't think I did it."

"I don't, but there might be some who do." He stood and brushed the front of his coat. "Be careful. Talk to Mrs. Oswald before she spreads the story any further."

"Do you have any other leads?"

"I can't really go into that."

"Your daughter still believes it wasn't the work of the serial killer."

He sighed. "I've told her several times when she offers firm proof, I'll consider it."

He removed his notebook from his shirt pocket and scribbled something. "This clears up one point."

"What?"

"Back at the station, it was obvious you were hiding something. The time it took from your room back to the library didn't make sense. Why didn't you come clean about your conversation with her?"

I shrugged. "Didn't think it would amount to anything. Besides, I knew how it would look and didn't want to put a bigger bullseye on my back."

"Your tomfoolery got you in trouble."

I shook my head. "You have to understand. This was before anyone was killed. A harmless prank. That's all."

His eyes stayed focused on mine. After an uncomfortable pause, he shifted his gaze slightly to the left. "I guess I'm done here. Thank you for your time." He rose and walked away.

I didn't go to my room to get my books. I was too embarrassed to face Mrs. Oswald. After class I spent time in the quad, tossing a frisbee with friends. Then I meandered around campus until I found a large oak tree and lounged under it, people watching and pondering the detective's words.

A person of interest.

It was only 3:30 and the trees' shadows stretched far across the grass as the sun dipped behind the pines. Soon dusk would give way to dark.

Just then, I spotted Boomer about fifty feet away, walking along the sidewalk like a man on a mission.

"Hey, Boomer!"

No response.

I hopped up and trotted after him, wondering how he was doing after the funeral. As I called again, he disappeared around the side of the library. I picked up my pace and rounded the back of the building just in time to see him skulk into the woods.

That's weird. Why'd he do that? There's nothing back there. Just woods.

I winced and reprimanded myself for sounding like Jill. He wasn't skulking. Sneaking, maybe, but not skulking. As I contemplated whether Boomer was skulking or sneaking, I suddenly realized I too was skulking into the woods. Come to think of it, maybe it was just sneaking. How had this happened? It was as if a little voice—sounding a lot like Jill's—whispered in my ear, *Follow him. Follow him.* And I did.

What was wrong with me?

On occasion, he'd glance back, forcing me to crouch behind a rock or a bush. We followed this pattern for a while. Then, after going through some heavy underbrush, Boomer paused by a large willow. As if sensing my presence, he turned and peered in my direction.

I ducked behind an old elm and counted to forty-five before peeking out. To my amazement, he was gone. But where? At first, I feared he was doubling back on me. Then I spotted him kneeling by the willow, quiet and still.

What's he doing?

I craned my neck for a better look. Boomer was staring at the ground, seeming transfixed on one spot. His mouth was moving, mumbled sounds coming out. For about ten minutes, I watched, motionless. Finally, Boomer climbed to his feet. Giving one last forlorn look, he turned and came in my direction.

I pressed against the tree as hard as I could and held my breath. Would he see me? His feet clomped against the forest floor as he went by and disappeared in the distance.

What had he been staring at?

Ungluing myself from my tree, I went to investigate. It was almost dark now, with the forest's canopy blocking the sky. Under the willow, a circular area had been cleared of fallen leaves and twigs. Sticking from a mound of soft dirt was a cross, crudely fashioned from two broken branches, about a foot and a half tall. It resembled a makeshift grave like you'd see in one of those old western movies.

I shivered and looked off to where Boomer had disappeared through the trees.

What are you up to?

A rustling, cold wind brought me to a more pressing concern. Where was I? How would I find my way out of the woods? Shadows and darkness covered everything. Maybe I should have followed Boomer. I fumbled around for about half an hour, tripping over tree roots and following paths that led to nowhere. Visions of my dead body being found, half picked clean by squirrels and chipmunks, filled my brain.

I made a mental note to pin a message to my chest before I died. "Jill, this is not a murder. It is the result of me being infected by your busy-bodyness."

Was busybodyness even a word?

Just then a branch snapped to my left. A light shone in my face. A husky female voice said, "What are you doing on my land?"

I used my hand to shield my eyes from the brightness. Caroline Webster stood there, holding a flashlight against the barrel of her shotgun. Both were pointed at me.

"Am I glad to see you," I said.

"Don't move or I'll take out your kneecaps." She aimed at the appropriate spot to do just that.

"Don't be afraid. I won't harm you."

She laughed. "Obviously, since I'm holding the weapon. And believe me, young man, I know how to use it. Served fifteen years in the army."

"I was in the marines."

She squinted. "Don't I know you?"

I took a tiny step forward. "I met you. At least I saw you in Dr. Spiner's office."

She spit on the ground. "Spiner? Hah! Should be Spineless!"

"I couldn't say. Don't know him that well."

She ran the light up and down me, ending back on my face. "You're the one who found that dead girl, aren't you?"

"Yes, ma'am."

"Don't call me ma'am. I worked for a living."

"Yes, ma'—I mean … okay."

She relaxed her aim and lowered the shotgun. "What are you doing here?"

"Went for a walk." I shrugged. "Got lost."

She harrumphed. "Not much of a marine, are you? I'll show you the way out. Next time I might not be so generous. Stay off my land."

"Sorry. Doesn't the college own this property?"

"No, I do!"

I thought back to Dr. Spiner's model and map. "Isn't this where Dr. Spiner's new building is going to be constructed?"

"Spiner! You mean the thief? Land grabber?"

"What did he—"

She wagged a finger in my face. "Mark my words. Be careful to have your wallet locked up when you meet with that weasel."

Ten minutes later, we emerged from the woods behind the library.

"Thank you."

She returned to the woods, muttering to herself. "Roland P. Spiner Auditorium, my foot. I'll kill before I let that happen."

Upon entering the residence hall, the first thing I did was stop to talk to Mrs. Oswald. It was time to face up to my stupidity. She reddened and looked away as I approached. Who could blame her? I explained my behavior and apologized for my actions.

"Oh, Jack." Her face showed a mix of scolding and sympathy. "I wondered if it was something like that. I hope you'll forgive me. I had to let the police know. Before the poor girl's murder, it was simply a joke. But after ..." Her voice trailed off. "After the murder, everything changed."

I nodded. Mrs. Oswald was correct. After the murder, everything *had* changed.

Chapter Fifteen

Tuesday. I overslept. Another nightmare.

I dressed and raced out of my room, hoping to keep my day on schedule. But when I entered the stairwell, I screeched to a halt. From down on the girl's side, a tiny sliver of light ran around the edge of Emily's door. It was open, just a crack. I moved to investigate but quickly stopped.

No. It's none of your business.

Instead, I began my descent, my feet dragging over the first stair as I leaned back to peer down the hallway. A couple more steps down and I had to lean so far backward to keep an eye on the door, I was almost lying on the stairs.

Yep. That door is definitely open. It's probably nothing, though.

Who was I kidding? With a grumble, I ascended the stairs and went to check it out.

I pushed the door open a few inches. The only thing inside was a clean and tidy room. The bed was made. Books and papers neatly stacked on a bookcase.

Not like Jill's.

But no one was there.

I shrugged. Maybe a cleaning crew or somebody left the door ajar. I was pulling it closed when a small sound, barely noticeable, came from inside the room.

My muscles tensed. My hand tightened on the knob. I shoved the door a couple of feet and barked in my most threatening voice, "No one is supposed to be in here." Would a knife-wielding maniac jump out? Or maybe just some thrill-seeking college kid looking for a souvenir from the dead girl's room?

I stepped in.

A meek voice, one I recognized, said, "Oh, it's you." Jill was plastered against the wall behind the door, holding a stapler, menacingly, over her head.

How could this possibly be happening? Doesn't this girl ever mind her own business? "What're you gonna do with that?" I pointed at her weapon. "Staple me to death?"

She looked up at the stapler, then frowned, and lowered her hand. "I didn't know who you were. This was the first thing I could find to defend myself." Placing the stapler back on the desk, she began rifling through its top drawer.

I closed the door to the hallway to conceal our presence. "What are you looking for?"

"I'm not exactly sure. Emily's family hasn't come to claim her stuff yet, and it occurred to me maybe there's a clue in this room that'll point to her killer. I mean, it's obvious Nicki was looking for something that morning you caught her breaking in."

"You realize, you're not supposed to be in here."

"Uh-huh." She continued her search.

"I don't want to throw cold water on this wonderful party, but I've recently been told I'm a person of interest." I looked around the room. "This is probably not a good idea."

"Then leave."

I should have, but somehow couldn't. It was insane. I had the oddest feeling if I walked out, I'd miss some big discovery. She'd find a signed confession from the killer or some fool thing like that. I was like a small child who didn't want to go to bed, knowing the good stuff happened after he did. I paced the room as she searched through the dresser, examined the closet, and checked under the bed. "Find anything?"

"Not yet."

"How did you get in here?"

"I picked the lock," she answered, not batting an eye.

"Are you crazy? This is a police investigation you're meddling in."

"Not really. This room was never a crime scene to begin with."

"I think you're taking this whole thing too far." I suddenly stopped pacing. "Hey, wait a minute. The other morning when I found Nicki here, you never explained why you were up and about so early."

With a slight smirk, she turned to the desk.

"Nicki wasn't the only one interested in getting in here, was she?"

The room grew quieter.

I raised my arms. "I can't believe it! You were going to break in that day, too! What's wrong with you?"

She stopped what she was doing and glanced at me, shaking her head. "You have no sense of adventure, do you?"

I sputtered for a second, then grabbed her by the arm. "Let's go."

She pulled away. "You go. I'm not done."

"I'm not leaving without you."

"Why not?"

I thought and thought, but for the life of me I couldn't come up with one good reason. Finally, I blurted out, "Because it doesn't seem right."

She touched my shoulder. "Relax, Jack. Everything is going to be fine." Leaning on the desk, she added, "You're too nervous. Tell you what? Think of something else. It'll help get your mind off this. Anything interesting happen since I saw you?"

Without thinking, I answered, "I went to Dr. Spiner's office."

Her face scrunched. "The president's office? Why?"

I explained about the note I'd received, not mentioning my discovery of Dr. Spiner's initials. There was no reason to feed her theories.

"What did he want?"

I shrugged. "To talk."

Jill's brow arched as she took a step toward me. "What's wrong?"

"Wrong?" I looked at the ceiling. "What makes you think anything is wrong?"

"Your face. It's obvious you're hiding something."

That was almost as annoying as her rolling her eyes at me. I always thought I had a good poker face. How could this girl—

"What is it?"

I shook my head. "You'll make a federal case out of it."

"No, I won't. Honest!"

I groaned. Why avoid the inevitable? So, I told her everything.

"PRS!" She pulled the list from her pocketbook.

"You know what? You've poisoned my mind to see evil and murderers everywhere."

"Of course! President Roland Spiner."

"Don't go jumping to conclusions—"

"I was wondering why there were three initials and not two like the others. His title." She squinted at the page. "Of course, it could be a DRS, but that fits, too. Doctor Roland Spiner!"

"I don't know about that, but I can tell you he was really pumping me for information about Emily's death."

She laughed. "He's not the only one."

"What do you mean?"

Before she could answer, someone knocked on the door.

Jill's face paled. She whispered, "Did you lock it?"

"I ... I don't remember."

She rolled her eyes. "Smart move."

I sneered. "You're the one who left it open in the first place."

Another knock sounded, this one louder and more determined.

"What do we do?" I whispered as I glanced around the room, frantic to find a way to either escape or hide. I dove for the desk. Jill did, too. In the process, we slammed together.

She grabbed my arm to steady herself. Quickly she regained her composure and pushed me toward the closet. "Move."

"We won't both fit," I said.

"Yes, we will."

"But—"

Jill opened the closet door and gave me a surprisingly hard shove. "I said move!"

My foot caught on the threshold, and I stumbled in, hitting my head against the back wall. Suddenly I found myself engulfed in dresses, blouses, skirts, and other unidentifiable items.

"You trip a lot, don't you?" Jill pressed against me and pulled the door closed. Light from the slatted vent at its top ran across her face.

"You're nuts."

"You're the one who didn't want to get caught. Person of interest and all."

"Now, you listen—"

"Shhh!"

The door from the hall squeaked. We stood there, engulfed in woman's clothing for what seemed like an eternity. There was shuffling of feet. Drawers opened and closed. Someone was looking for something. But who? And what? Next thing we knew, the door squeaked again.

"Fancy meeting you here," a girl's voice said.

Jill looked up at me and mouthed, "Nicki."

A male voice asked, "What are you doing here?"

"Don," Jill whispered.

"I followed you from outside. Why are *you* here?" Nicki answered.

"That's none of your business," Don snapped.

Nicki hesitated before replying. "All right."

There were a few seconds of silence. The two of us kept still, not even breathing.

"I'm sorry," Don finally said. "I didn't mean to sound so rough. Emily and I had some … personal business."

"Interesting. I promise you, mums the word. Any business you had with Emily is between you and her. However, I do have one little favor to ask."

I could almost hear Nicki smiling.

"Anything for you. You know that," Don said.

"If anyone asks, could you say you walked me to my car and watched me drive away the night of Emily's murder?"

Jill jabbed me in the ribs.

I almost yelped but caught myself. "Ow," I mouthed at her.

"Why?" Don paused. "Did you kill Emily?

"How could you say that? Of course, I didn't."

"Then why do you need an alibi?"

"Oh, come on, Don." There was sugar in her voice. "It's such a small thing."

Another pause. "Okay. No problem."

"Thank you, sweetie."

There was a long silence, maybe ten seconds. What were they doing?

Finally, Nicki spoke. "I have to go. I'm late for class."

Another squeak.

"I'll walk you out," Don said.

"Did you find what you were looking for?" Nicki asked.

"No. Probably not going to, either."

Their voices were cut off by the closing door.

Jill turned the knob, and the two of us tumbled out of the closet. "Did you hear that?" She pointed an accusing finger. "She lied to us!"

"I heard." I scratched the back of my head. "Still doesn't prove she's a killer."

"Then why is she worried about an alibi?"

"I'm not sure." I glanced around the room. "Interesting. Don was here looking for something."

"Hmmm." Jill stroked her chin.

The desk clock read 10:30.

"I've got to go. I'm so late for class, it's almost over." I walked to the door. Jill fell in step behind me. Before I could pull it open, someone pushed from the other side.

It was Detective Phillips. He stiffened, crossed his arms, and glared at me. "Mr. Hill."

Chapter Sixteen

"Detective Phillips. What are you doing here?" I asked.

His body filled the doorway. "That's funny. I was about to ask you the same thing. But a better question would be"— he placed his hands firmly on his sides— "how did you get in this room?"

Jill peeked out from behind me.

The detective's mouth dropped open. "Jill?"

"Uncle Henry," she answered with a sheepish grin.

"Uncle?" I asked. "Are you related to the whole police force?"

She blushed. "He's not really my uncle. Just been a close friend of the family for years."

Uncle Henry scanned the room. "What's going on here?"

"Nothing sir," I said.

Jill gripped my arm, trying to stop me from jiggling the change in my pocket.

"That doesn't answer my question." He looked from Jill to me, waiting.

My brain raced, trying to come up with a plausible answer. "Well, you see—"

Jill took a couple quick steps forward and interrupted me. "Jack saw the door to this room was open and—"

"Is that so?" Detective Phillips didn't sound like he was buying the story. "And you two decided you should just waltz right in?"

I answered with a little more confidence. "I was concerned that someone was in here." I glared at the top of Jill's head. "Someone who wasn't supposed to be. I figured it was worth checking out."

The detective turned to Jill. "Did you see anyone in here?"

"Besides each other?" She chuckled, nervously.

"Of course, besides each other."

"No," Jill said with conviction. "I can honestly say we saw no one else in here."

Detective Phillips raised a skeptical eyebrow. "I don't know what the two of you are up to, but—"

"Nothing." Jill smiled. "This only looks bad. That's all."

He continued blocking the exit, looking back and forth between the two of us.

"Can I leave now?" I asked. "I've got class."

He hesitated a second before stepping aside. "Next time don't go where you don't belong."

As I left the room, I heard the detective giving advice to Jill. "You better be careful who you associate with."

That stung. Was he implying I was a bad influence? It was the other way around. She was the one who broke into the room. She was the one who dangled from the sides of buildings. Not me! I had half a notion to march back and tell him so. But, what good would it do?

Jill caught up with me as I exited the building. "That was a close one, wasn't it?"

I hurried down the front steps. "Tell me something. Are you an escapee from a psych ward?"

She frowned. "What?"

Reaching the sidewalk, I turned to face her. "You just broke into a crime scene."

"As I've already told you, technically it's not a crime scene."

"You lied to a police detective. You said we didn't see anyone."

"No." She waved my objection away. "We may have heard Nicki and Don, but we never *saw* them. Besides, it was only Uncle Henry."

I shook my head. "Well, you didn't exactly tell him the whole truth."

"Jack, you worry too much. Relax."

My cheeks began to burn. I slowly exhaled through clenched teeth. "Jill. This isn't a game. Recently it's been brought to my attention how serious this is. I already told you, the police have me at the top of their suspect list."

"I'm sure my father doesn't believe you're guilty."

I looked back to the residence hall. "But others do."

"Uncle Henry?" She scoffed at the notion. "Don't worry about him. He's a teddy bear."

"That teddy bear would like to see me behind bars." I shook my head. This conversation was going nowhere. "I'm late for class." I walked away.

"Okay. See you later," she called out. "We can discuss what we've learned then."

I stopped. "Learned about what?"

"The case, of course. What else?" At a quick pace, she caught up to me. "Oh, come on Jack, you've got to admit something is going on here."

"No, I don't."

"You deny that Don and Nicki's actions are suspicious? They broke into Emily's room."

"So did you."

"That was different."

"No, it wasn't. They broke in. You broke in."

Flustered, she placed her hands on her hips. "Well, that's … that's just plain stupid."

"I'm stupid then."

"How can you—"

"Jill!" I hollered, perhaps louder than I should have, but it got the desired reaction. She fell silent. Of course, a few passing students also stopped to watch. A couple of sour looks from me and they quickly went on their way though. Having Jill's undivided attention, I continued, trying as hard as I could to keep my voice calm. "You've got to let this go. The list doesn't mean anything. Like the president said, maybe Emily was simply collecting money for a charity or something."

"With the heading, Blood Money?"

I raised a hand to silence her. "At first, I let you indulge in your little detective fantasy—"

"Fantasy?"

"Yes, fantasy," I said, sternly. "What you have is a piece of paper that has nothing to do with a serial killer. But," I immediately added before she could protest, "if you can give me some solid proof, then I will gladly join in your crusade."

It grew quiet. Jill looked up at me with sad, abandoned puppy, saucer eyes. When she finally spoke, it was in defeated submission. "All right then. I guess I'll be seeing you around." She turned to leave.

My heart sank. I hadn't meant to hurt her. "Jill, I—"

"I have to go." She walked away.

"I'll see you later," I called. There was no response.

My feet scuffed against the leaf-covered sidewalk. I hadn't meant for it to go like that.

But she's crazy.

Maybe this was her way of dealing with the grief, focusing her attention on some make-believe danger. I checked the time. I was almost forty minutes late for class.

Why even bother?

The library loomed large in front of me. I could always study. Then the notion of a snack at the Tank hit me. I really hadn't had any breakfast. I looked from one building to the other. *Library or the Tank? Library or Tank?* It didn't take long before I beelined it toward the Tank. My stomach had won over my brain.

By the time I got there and checked my mail, it was closer to lunchtime than breakfast. After finishing off a sandwich, fries, and a cola, I headed to my room to get the books for my afternoon class. Part way across the quad I spotted Nicki, along with six other girls. They were all dressed the same—jeans and green windbreakers with the word *cheerleader* printed on the back. Together they practiced their routines. A couple of boys watched. One of them joined in, or at least he tried to. But instead, he ended up flat on his back, laughing.

I considered making a detour to join them but thought better of it. After eavesdropping on Nicki and Don's conversation, I wasn't sure if I was ready to have a face to face with her. If I was as easy to read as Jill said, it could cause trouble.

As I entered my room, something crinkled under my foot. A letter lay on the floor. Someone must have shoved it under the door. I picked it up. A white envelope. Nothing written on the outside. I tore it open and read.

"Meet me in the administration parking lot. 10:30 p.m. Come alone."

It wasn't signed. Again, I checked the envelope. No marking ... Nothing.

Hmmm. That's odd.

Jill sat at a table in the library, staring out the window, wondering how Jack could be so thick-headed. After their last conversation, she was having trouble concentrating on her art project. Around 7:30 p.m. her stomach reminded her she'd missed dinner. So she abandoned her work in favor of food.

The Tank was busy. Jill spotted Don sitting all alone, munching on a plate of onion rings. Was he the Don H. on the list?

I'll prove this list means something.

As she approached, she debated how to bring up the subject. Should she just blurt it out? Beat around the bush? Maybe nonchalantly drop the list on the table and see how he reacted?

"Hi. Can I sit here?" She stood by the table, a smile on her face, her tray tightly gripped in her hands.

Don's eyes narrowed. "You want to sit with me?"

"Why not?" She took the seat across from him.

"Well ..." He smirked, taking a bite out of an onion ring. "I can think of several reasons. For one thing, we're not what anyone would call friends. For another, we run with, shall we say ... different crowds. You,"—he pointed a fork at Jill—

"run with the more religious type. Whereas I,"—he turned the fork on himself—"don't." He stirred his drink with his straw. "What has brought you down from your lofty tower to confer with a peasant like me?"

The muscles in Jill's neck tensed. "When was I ever in a lofty tower? When have I ever treated you with anything but respect?"

Don considered her remarks. "Good point. I hate those phony religious types who say one thing and yet do another." He leaned closer and smirked. "Do you know anyone like that?"

Jill met his stare. "No, I can't say I do. I wanted to ask you a question, that's all."

"Ask away." He'd finished his onion rings and ripped open a chocolate bar.

"What can you tell me about this?" She showed him the list.

His face reddened.

"It was Emily's," Jill said. "I noticed you're on it."

He shoved his seat back and jumped up. "I don't know what you're planning on doing with that, but you have no proof. It will be your word against mine!"

"Wait," she pleaded. "I don't think you understand. I'm not here to cause any trouble. I just want answers."

The crease between Don's eyes deepened. "Answers?"

From the beginning, Jill had had more than an inkling of what this list was all about. She took a deep breath and blurted out, "Why was Emily blackmailing you?"

Chapter Seventeen

Don sank into his seat, eyes narrowed, studying … assessing her. Finally, he spoke. "How do I know I can trust you? How do I know you won't take what I say, and use it to continue blackmailing me?"

"I guess you don't." She clenched her hands under the table, frantic to stop them from shaking with excitement. He admitted to being blackmailed.

"Then why should I trust you?"

"All I want to do is solve Emily's murder."

Again, he hesitated. His brow knit together. "And you think this list had something to do with her death?"

"Yes."

He struggled to make eye contact.

"It's either talk to me or the police." There was more pleading than intimidation in Jill's words.

Don's back stiffened. "The police?"

Jill nodded. "If I can't get answers, I'll be forced to turn it over to them." She patiently waited as Don mulled this over.

Finally, he slumped forward in his seat. "Okay."

Excited, she leaned forward. "So, Emily was blackmailing you?"

"Yes." His voice was drained of emotion.

"For how long?"

"Does it really matter?" Don shook his head in disgust. "About two months ago, I get this letter. *I know all about you. If you want me to keep quiet, you'll have to start paying.* It included a dollar amount and the drop off point. I went at the appointed time. Lo and behold, there was sweet Emily, holding out her greedy, little hand." He sneered. "Wasn't she supposed to be one of you? A Christian?"

Jill remained silent.

Don chuckled. "That's when I began to pay."

"Do you know anyone else she was blackmailing?"

"No idea. I knew there were other names on that." He pointed an agitated finger at the paper. "She always had it with her when she'd collect. I got the idea she had her claws into a few people."

"Why'd you pay so much more than the others?" Jill asked.

He shrugged. "I don't know. Maybe because my dad is wealthy."

"Your dad is well off?"

"No, he's not well off." His eyes widened. "He's wealthy!"

"Really?"

Don nodded. "He started a software company way back when. Made a fortune, invested well, and ta-da! The bad news is, somehow Emily found out about my large monthly allowance and has taken advantage of it."

"You were probably pretty angry about that."

His voice grew stern. "I didn't kill her if that's what you're implying. I can prove it."

"How?"

"I signed in to the residence hall that night and never left." He gave a defiant look. "Mother Superior will testify to that. She mans that main entrance like a prison warden. All the other doors are alarmed. No way out."

Jill tried not to smirk at Don's description of the woman on duty at the residence hall who had quite a reputation for being tough.

"So, I have an alibi."

Don stared at Jill as if waiting for her response. She remained silent, though.

"Are we done here?" He pushed his seat back.

She lowered her head, embarrassed. "Do you mind if I ask …"

"What was she blackmailing me for?"

"I guess I don't have to know."

Don sighed. Then he looked at Jill and shared his secret.

I left my room at 10:05 to meet with the mysterious note sender. Some would say I was a fool for going alone. At least I can think of one detective's daughter who would be of that opinion. But the way I figured it, up until now the killer's modus operandi was a knife. And facts are facts, I could handle a knife attack. But if he pulled a gun?

I didn't want to think about that.

Listen to me. I sounded like Jill! Falling for this whole notion that the killer was still on campus was ludicrous. He'd struck and was long gone. End of the story. Why someone had sent this note was beyond me. It was probably some silly prank. That's all.

Then why are you going?

I arrived a few minutes early to reconnoiter the area. I smirked. Reconnoitering was a military term. Jill wouldn't appreciate it. She'd say I was sounding too pompous again.

The parking lot was behind the administration building, secluded from the rest of the campus. Two streetlights were perched high on poles in its center. They did little to illumine the lot's outer edge or the dark woods beyond it. About a dozen cars sat in the shadows. I took a few cautious steps forward and peered into the black woods. The quiet night was occasionally interrupted by a passing car on the road. Besides that, it was dead.

"Good place to get killed," I chuckled.

About 10:25 I began wondering if the whole thing was a joke.

Just then headlights at the far end of the lot snapped on. An engine revved to life, a car shifted into drive and barreled toward me.

I shielded my eyes from the blinding lights, trying to see who was behind the wheel. A knife I can handle. A gun … maybe. But a car? I balanced my weight on the fronts of my feet, ready to dive to the left or the right, depending on which way the car swerved. Would my reflexes be fast enough to save me?

I never had a chance to find out. The car screeched to a stop right in front of me. The window opened, revealing the president's secretary behind the wheel.

"Ms. Fielding? What are you—"

"Here!" She tossed a manila envelope to the ground by my feet. Then, just as fast as she'd pulled up, she sped away, leaving me stunned.

I felt like someone who'd started watching a mystery halfway through. Very confused. "Well, at least I'm still alive," I muttered. I picked up the envelope, fumbled with the brass clasp and opened it. Money fell into my hand. My eyebrows raised. Fifty dollars. Two twenties and a ten. Something gnawed at me. I re-counted the bills. Fifty dollars. I dug into my pocket for my copy of the list. There next to the initials PRS. $50.00.

I have to call Jill.

I could picture Jill's face all scrunched together in a puzzled look as we talked on the phone. "Fifty dollars?" Is there anything else in the envelope?"

I stood in the parking lot, searching through the envelope again. "Nope. Just two twenties and a ten."

"I've been trying to call you." She sounded aggravated. "Where have you been?"

"I'm standing in a parking lot. I told you that."

"No, I've been trying to call you for a couple of hours now."

"Well," I hemmed and hawed. "I might have had my cell phone turned off."

She grunted. "Meet me in the residence hall's first-floor lounge."

By the time I got there, Jill was at the door, waiting. "Let's compare notes," she said.

The lounge was empty, so we could speak without being overheard. Its walls were lined with old couches and chairs. A box of leftover pizza sat open on the counter. A flat-screen television hung in one corner.

Jill reached out. "Let me see the envelope."

Obediently, I handed it over. She examined the contents. "Fifty dollars. Nothing else?"

"I already told you that," I said, irritated that she didn't trust me.

"I know." She checked over the outside of it. "There's no markings."

"I already told you that, too."

"Just making sure you didn't miss anything." She plopped down on an overstuffed couch that had seen better days.

I sat on a chair next to it. "What do you think it means?"

"Blackmail," Jill said, without missing a beat.

"What?" I scratched my head. "How would you know that?"

"Don told me that Emily was blackmailing him." She shared the gist of their conversation.

I leaned back, taking it all in. "Wow!"

"Uh-huh."

"Did he tell you why he was being blackmailed?"

Jill hesitated. Then she lowered her voice. "He told me he leads an alternative lifestyle."

For a second, I wasn't sure what she was getting at. But then it dawned on me. "What? He's gay?"

"No," she said sarcastically. "He's an alien from Mars. Of course, he's gay." She glanced around. "Could you be quiet. I promised I'd keep it a secret."

I smirked. "But you told *me*."

"That's different. You don't count."

I didn't bother asking why in the world I didn't count.

Jill stared at me, scrutinizing my face. "Why that look?"

"What look?" Again, I was aggravated by this girl's ability to read me.

"You look like ..." She scowled.

"I don't look like that."

She smiled. "Yes, you do."

I grumbled. "If you have to know, I don't like him."

"Don? Why not?"

"I don't know. Something about him bothers me." I shivered as if a hairy spider had crawled across my arm. "And his story doesn't add up. Who's blackmailed because they're gay? It doesn't happen today."

She shrugged. "He said his dad is an ultraconservative. Don's afraid if he finds out, he'll be cut off."

I rolled this around in my brain. "I guess. It still doesn't sit right with me."

Jill's expression changed as if something new had occurred to her; something that made her face beam like the proverbial cat who swallowed the canary. "You wanted proof the list means something. Here it is. Blackmail is a motive for murder. The list is important."

"Yeah, but it makes no sense. I can see killing for thousands of dollars, but for tens? Even Don, with his high amount, doesn't seem like a motive for murder. Sure, Emily was making a little extra cash, but I doubt this has anything to do with her death."

Jill shook her head. "It's not the dollar amount, it's the secret behind it."

"Don spilled his pretty quickly. Not much arm twisting there." I shrugged and smiled. "Either he's not the killer, or he'll have to kill you now to keep you quiet."

"Very funny."

"Besides, he and Boomer are roommates over at Simmon's. It'll be pretty easy to prove whether he could have done it. Boomer, too, for that matter. We can check to see when they signed in that night. That'll tell us if they had opportunity." I gave kind of a smug look, at the thought that I'd used an official term like opportunity.

"Not necessarily."

"Huh? If they signed in, they wouldn't be able to get to the library. Simmons is notorious for its warden."

"Well ..." Jill kind of stuttered, as if she wanted to say something, but it just wouldn't come out."

"What is it?"

She blushed. "Remember that night, behind Simmons?"

"Which night?"

"When I fell on you."

"Yes."

She paused. Her eyes twinkled. "I wasn't climbing up the building. I was climbing down."

"What?"

"Didn't you wonder why there were so many footprints on the bench? Someone or some group of people have discovered a way to get in and out without using the front door. I searched and found a window at the end of the third-floor corridor. It's tucked around a corner, out of sight. I almost made it all the way to the bench before I fell."

I gawked at her. "You're nuts."

She shrugged. "Maybe I am."

Arguing or further discussion was useless, so I glanced over the list. "I wonder what Emily had on Ms. Fielding."

"Don't you mean on Dr. Spiner?"

"No, Ms. Fielding. After all, he didn't give me the money. She did."

She pointed to the PRS on the list. "But they're his initials, not hers."

I had to admit, it made sense. "Maybe I'll pay a visit to the two of them tomorrow."

"Speaking of going to see people." She folded her arms and scowled at me. "Do you think it was wise of you to go off by yourself this evening?"

"I can take care of myself."

Jill's voice softened. "I don't want to see anything happen to you."

Before we could continue our conversation, a small group of students walked in. They sat around the television. One nabbed a piece of the leftover pizza. The television clicked on. This was our cue to leave.

We entered the stairwell and headed to our rooms. Our footsteps on the stairs echoed off the cement block walls. When we reached her floor, before I could say goodnight, she said, "Listen, I didn't mean to upset you earlier today. Sometimes I say things or do things without thinking them through."

"Like falling on top of me?" I quipped.

"Like that."

"Or pushing me into a closet?"

She laughed. "You get the general idea." Then her tone became more thoughtful. "I've been so upset. Deep down, I'm sure Emily's murder isn't as simple as the police are saying." She frowned. "I can't even imagine her being mixed up in blackmail. It's not like her." She paused. "You have to understand, you're the only one I can talk to."

My face flushed.

She reached her hand toward me. Her fingers were less than an inch away when she hesitated. "I'd really like to think of you as a friend."

I sighed. "And it's because we're friends that I have to warn you. This whole list thing is eating you up. Just give it to your dad."

"No!" She pulled her hand back.

"But—"

"Please, Jack," she begged. "You promised me you wouldn't tell him. I'm holding you to it."

"Okay," I surrendered. "I've always been a sucker for a pretty face."

She brightened and pushed a strand of hair behind her ear. "You think I have a pretty face?"

"Sure." I tapped my chin as I considered. "Let's see … Nice complexion, pretty blue eyes … Nose isn't too big." I gave it a gentle pinch.

"Very funny." With a playful hit, she slapped my hand away. "I thought you were being serious."

"I'm serious about one thing. You should consider talking to your dad. I'm not going to say a word to him. But for your own good, you should."

She lowered her voice. "Maybe soon." She turned to leave. "Not yet."

"Remember, as much as I think this list has nothing to do with the murder, blackmail is a nasty business. Please be careful."

"I'm not worried. I have a marine guarding me." She smiled and walked away.

Sure. When she needs me to be a marine, it's ok.

I had to admit she was right. This silly piece of paper meant something. I still wasn't convinced it had anything to do with Emily's murder. Who would kill for a few dollars? But I couldn't deny the money Ms. Fielding had tossed at me. Or Don's story. Maybe this was worth looking into.

I watched Jill as she retreated. "Well, Jill," I whispered. "Looks like you have a Watson for your Sherlock."

Chapter Eighteen

Wednesday morning, I scarfed down a bowl of cereal at the dining hall, then jogged across campus toward administration, anxious to take up the mantle of amateur sleuth.

Jill was right. Dr. Spiner's initials were on the list, not Ms. Fielding's. She may simply have been the deliverer of the envelope. Then again, that angry look that flashed through the car window said she was more than an errand girl.

So how did she figure into this? And was the *this* she figured into only blackmail or was it murder? Could Emily have been blackmailing both of them? It's possible. Maybe even for the same indiscretion. It was obvious they were close. Very close.

Is the president married?

As I approached my destination, I passed a group of students, including several cheerleaders, struggling to hang a large Welcome to Homecoming banner between two oak trees.

Preparations were well underway for this annual event. The groundskeepers were sprucing up the place. Special luncheons were planned for alumni and parents, concerts by our choral group and orchestra, lectures by some of our leading professors, plus more. All happening this coming weekend.

But the main event was the football game on Saturday between our team, the Wolves, and our rivals, the Chesterton Bulldogs, from Maine. Like most colleges, Springsbury loved its football. Though a small team in a small division— no one expected our games would be on any major television network—during homecoming our campus ate and drank, lived and breathed football.

There'd been talk about canceling everything because of the murder. As a matter of fact, the choice to go ahead with it was controversial. While some felt it was inappropriate, the president and other decision-makers had a different opinion.

Dr. Spiner issued a statement:

> Homecoming is a way to help our college return to its normal routine. Though we mourn the loss of Emily Hamilton, this weekend of festivities is a source of healing for those who have been wounded by the tragedy. Also, I am sure Emily would have wanted us to continue.

I scanned the banner hangers for Nicki, wanting to talk to her. I'd invited her to a special church event on Friday, before realizing it was homecoming. She probably wouldn't be joining me. Still, I'd like to hear it from her. She wasn't with the hangers, so I continued to administration.

The door to the president's office wouldn't open. I tried again. Nothing. It was locked.

I went to knock when someone from farther up the hall called, "May I help you?" A heavyset woman approached, her shoes clicking on the tiled floor.

As she grew closer, my eyes fixed on the hair above her lip. Not that it was a full-blown handlebar mustache or anything like that, but it was hard to ignore, especially with her standing smack dab in front of me, waiting for my answer.

"I'm looking for Ms. Fielding," I said.

She walked away. "She's not here."

"Is the president in?"

"He's not here either." She'd reached the next office.

"Do you know when they'll be back?"

"I'd say sometime this weekend." She added in a matter-of-fact voice, "That's how it usually works. About once a month they leave on a Wednesday night or Thursday morning, and come back sometime on Saturday." She placed a key in the door as she mumbled, "Kind of rude on homecoming weekend."

Before I had a chance to ask anything else, the woman entered the office and closed the door. I left, pondering this information.

A light mist was falling. Combined with the cold air, it created a chill. I shivered as I started across the quad to my biology class. I paused when an agitated female's voice called out, "Boomer, I thought you were going to help us?" The speaker was part of the group still trying to hang the banner—a cheerleader.

Boomer stood about thirty feet from her, tossing around a football with a friend. "You're doing such a good job, I'd probably only mess things up."

The girl, along with the others, groaned and grunted as they continued their struggle.

"We could really use your help." One of the other girls turned on the charm. "You're so tall and strong, you could tie up this thing without even using a ladder."

"Hold on." He spiraled the ball to his friend. "Two or three more throws and I'll be right there."

Again, the girls groaned. Something told me they'd heard that line before.

"Watch out," Boomer hollered.

I ducked just in time to avoid being whacked in the head by the approaching ball. It hit the ground and hopped along behind me.

"Sorry." Boomer ran over and scooped it up. "Bad throw. It's slippery from the drizzle. Hard to get a good grip."

"No problem." Since striking out with Ms. Fielding, I thought maybe I'd try my hand with Boomer. After all, his name was on the list, too. At least Jill thought it was.

I felt the best way to approach the subject was slowly and carefully, ask some easy questions. I wouldn't mention his skulking in the woods though. That would be a conversation for another day. "How've you been doing?"

Boomer sent the ball soaring to his friend. "Doing?"

"Yes. I mean with the funeral and everything, you were pretty upset."

The ball flew back in his direction. In one graceful move, Boomer one-handed the catch. "Okay, I guess. Trying not to think about it." He wiped the ball on his already wet sweatshirt, adjusted it in his hands and threw it again. A perfect spiral to his waiting receiver.

I continued. "From what I understand, you and Emily dated for a while."

"Uh-huh."

"If you don't mind me saying, I saw you that night in the library with Nicki and Don. There didn't seem to be any love lost between you then."

Boomer's step faltered, and he bobbled the incoming pass, finally pulling it in, in a less than perfect motion. Then he heaved it. The ball sailed past his friends and between the two buildings across the quad.

"Aw, come on!" The friend trotted after it.

Boomer stormed toward me. "Is there something you want to say to me?"

"No. Just making an observation."

"Listen, I know how that night looked. I regret what I said … what I did. Believe me!" The big man hung his head in silence.

"But why were you so—"

"None of your business!"

"But—"

"No! No buts!" His expression grew dark and ominous.

We stood there, squaring off, eyeball to eyeball. In our case, it was more like eyeball to chin. Boomer was trying to stare me down. Stubbornly, I refused to look away.

Finally, he blinked. "Look," he said. "That night in the library … Unfortunately, those will be my final memories of Emily."

"Five years is a long time to date. Why'd you break up?"

He grumbled as he walked away. "Things change."

I'd stuck my toes in, testing the waters with these simple questions. Now I decided to plunge headfirst. "Did the change have anything to do with the list?"

Boomer's foot scraped against the ground as he came to a stop. "List?"

I nodded. "With your name on it."

"I have no idea what you're talking about." He began to move away again.

I called after him. "Was Emily blackmailing you?"

The big man froze. His shoulders rose, making him appear even larger than he was. He took a few rapid steps away from me, toward the banner hangers. Then he seemed to change his mind and spun around. Red with rage, he opened his mouth, presumably to yell at me, but didn't get the chance.

"Watch out!"

The football soared toward us.

Boomer reached up high and pulled it tight against his gut. His enormous hands almost encased the entire ball, like a child's toy. He stood motionless, his knuckles turning white as he gripped it.

I wondered if he envisioned the ball was my head.

"Conversation is over," he said.

"Boomer, I—"

"I said the conversation is over!"

That's when I noticed just how big a man he was.

He lumbered toward the girls. "Okay, ladies. I'm ready to help."

"I'll see you around," I called to him. "And I'll be praying for you."

He stopped and turned a tortured face to me. "Pray?"

I stepped toward him. "I don't know what you're going through, my friend. But whatever it is, God is big enough to handle it. Believe me. I speak from personal experience."

He stood there, his chest heaving. When he spoke, it was in a halting, quiet voice. "Some things are so terrible, I wonder if even God can handle them." As he walked away, he added, "Or whether he'd even want to."

Chapter Nineteen

That next morning, the campus overflowed with people. I'd heard the local hotel swelled with alumni and parents invading for the weekend. By Friday, the commuting students struggled to find parking spots.

Throughout the day, things only grew more crowded as the visitors busied themselves with the planned activities. Several times, I saw groups taking pictures in front of buildings or with students, laughing and reminiscing as they toured their old haunts.

Homecoming had arrived.

A huge pep rally was planned for Friday night in preparation for Saturday's game. I couldn't go, though. Pastor Roberts had invited one of his old friends, a missionary from Haiti, to give a special presentation at the church, and I'd promised I'd be there. Hindsight says this was a bad time for a guest speaker. Because of homecoming there'd probably only be a handful of people in attendance.

I took consolation in a couple facts. First, I was assured the speaker was excellent, inspirational. Second, Mrs. Roberts' chocolate eclairs. I'll admit it, during the refreshment time at our church events, I would zero in on them. She may get take-out every Sunday, but she makes the best eclairs.

On my way into town, I passed the field at the edge of the campus where the rally was being held. A large crowd gathered around a burning dummy dressed like a Chesterton football player. People roasted hot dogs and marshmallows in the flames. The marching band, seated on the bleachers, blared the school song.

I continued through the parking lot. Just then, over in the corner, out of sight of the rally, a commotion broke out. A couple of security guards and a police officer were there. Whoever they were struggling with wasn't giving up easily. All I could see were flailing arms and kicking legs. One of the security guards jerked back like he'd been hit in the shins.

"Leave me alone! You have no right!" Caroline Webster swung a hammer at them. "It's my land! I can post these signs if I want to."

The officer managed to disarm her, but then she swung a handful of homemade No Trespassing signs at him. They scattered on the ground. He grabbed her arm and twisted it behind her back. "Assaulting a police officer is a crime. Maybe you need some time to cool off."

As they cuffed and escorted her to the cruiser, she kept fighting. "You can't do this." She twisted away from them and caught sight of me. "You there! Marine!"

I did a double take, then I pointed to myself. "Me?"

"Yes, you. Pick up my signs."

The officer took hold of her arm and gently guided her into the vehicle. They drove away.

Pick up the signs?

The small group of onlookers who'd stopped to watch, dispersed.

I did what she asked and went to scoop up her signs. I saw no reason to get the lady who carried a shotgun upset with me. As I gathered the papers together, one fell out. It was a letter. The heading read Connor and Howe, Attorneys at Law.

> Dear Mrs. Webster,
>
> Upon examination of the papers you submitted, it is our opinion that they contain enough verifiable information for you to move forward with your case. Though we cannot guarantee a favorable outcome, we believe there is a good possibility the court would

rule in your favor. Please see us at your earliest convenience.

It was signed by the lawyer.

Hmm. What's this all about?

"Hey, Jack!" A fellow student slapped me on the back as he raced by. "Awhooo!" He howled like a wolf. "Go Springsbury!"

I shoved the letter in my pocket and answered with as much enthusiasm as I could muster. "Go Springsbury."

I brought Caroline's signs to my room. Then I started for church.

Yup, Mrs. Roberts. There'd better be eclairs.

One problem with walking through town was that you passed Larry's Doughnut Shoppe. Something about the aroma and the trays of pastries on display in the front window acted like a magnet for me.

Maybe Jill's right. All I do is eat.

But then again, I'd skipped supper. A doughnut would tide me over until refreshment time. Besides, the pleasure of a fresh-made honey-dipped doughnut was worth a little extra running in the morning. I checked my watch. There was plenty of time before the service began.

The shop was nearly deserted, except for a couple who shared a booth on the side wall. The long counter was empty. I grabbed the end stool. A waitress, who didn't look old enough to be out beyond six o'clock, dragged herself over.

"Could I have a honey dip and milk," I said.

She crossed her arms and huffed in disgust. "Honey dip? What's a honey dip?"

Probably upset she has to work tonight.

"Glazed." I smiled. "They used to be called honey dip. I guess you're too young to remember that."

I don't think the girl appreciated my humor. She mumbled something about old people being weird, as she walked toward the display to retrieve my doughnut. She placed it on a paper plate and plunked it down in front of me.

Then without so much as a 'There you go,' she disappeared into the back room.

"Don't forget my milk," I called to the retreating figure. I wasn't sure whether she'd heard me.

A man approached and sat on the next stool. He looked a couple of years older than me, with sandy blond hair and a thin, likable face. "Teens today," he said. "They have no respect. Not like when we were young." He shook his head. "Courtesy. That's what they need to be taught."

I kind of resented that, not only had the waitress defined me as a weird old person, but now this man was categorizing me as a member of the good old days crowd. I gave a noncommittal nod.

The waitress returned with my milk. She looked at the newcomer as if to say, *Oh, no. Another one!* "Do you want something?"

"Yes, please. May I have a hot chocolate and a coffee roll?"

She walked away without answering.

"See what I mean." He sighed. "No training. And do you know what? It's not just here. A lot of people say we New Englanders are cold, but I just got back from California. The help there is the same." He extended his hand. "My name is Scott, by the way."

"Jack."

"Nice to meet you, Jack." He squinted. "I don't remember seeing you around here before."

"I'm pretty new to this area. I attend Springsbury." I took a sip of the milk. It was warm.

Blech.

"Oh." His attention was aroused. "I hear you people had some excitement over there. A murder?"

"Two weeks ago." I took a bite of my doughnut. Its taste made up for the milk.

"They say it's that serial killer. What do you think?"

Speaking through a mouth full of doughnut, I answered, "Oh, I don't know."

He raised an eyebrow. "Oh come on. You can give me more than that. I'm sure you have an opinion."

I forced another sip of milk. "I mean, the police say it was the Dumpster Killer. They know what they're doing."

He stared at the counter and mumbled, "Sometimes I wonder."

"Well, it resembled all the other killings."

"It resembled?" His eyes narrowed. "How would you know that? Did you see the body?"

The waitress returned with his order, plopped it down, and walked away.

"As a matter of fact, I did," I said. "I'm the guy who found her."

"Really?" He turned in his seat to face me. "And the young woman was stabbed?"

"Yes."

Scott peppered me with questions. "She was left by a Dumpster?"

"Uh-huh."

"Did you know the girl?"

"Briefly. I—"

"What was she like?"

"Oh, I don't know."

"I mean, they say all the others were ... bad woman. What about this one?"

A warning bell clanged inside me. Something wasn't right here. Scott was leaning forward, in eager anticipation of my responses ... Too eager.

"You're asking a lot of questions," I said. "Why?"

He turned toward the counter. "I'm just curious, that's all. Can't a fellow be curious?"

I stared at the side of his face. "I think it's more than curiosity."

"Sorry. I didn't mean to bother you. Just making conversation." He stood, grabbed his food, and stepped toward one of the empty booths.

Then a thought occurred to me. "Are you a reporter?"

His face beamed. "Guilty. You caught me."

"I thought so."

Hah! And Jill doesn't think I'm a Sherlock!

"I'm from the *Boston Globe*." He returned to the stool. "Got your name from the local boys and tracked you down."

"So it was no accident, you meeting me here?"

He shook his head. "Sorry. My paper wants an inside scoop. Kind of a story behind the story deal, and you're the man to talk to."

"I don't think so." I ran a napkin across my mouth.

"It won't take long," he coaxed.

I glanced at the clock on the wall. "I'm on my way to church."

He thought for a second. "Maybe later. I could meet you here. Or somewhere else if you'd like."

"Well ..." I wasn't keen on the notion of Emily's death being the main point of some sensational news article. Her parents had been through so much already. I couldn't imagine how they'd react to seeing her story plastered all over a Boston paper.

Scott must have sensed my qualms. "This is not some kind of a hatchet job. I promise. It's the *Boston Globe*, for crying out loud. If you don't like my questions, then don't answer them. All I'm asking is for you to give me a chance."

He waited for my decision.

"Okay." I grudgingly agreed.

"That's great." He grabbed my hand and shook it vigorously. "Listen, I have to get going now, but I'll be back. What time?"

"About nine?"

"Excuse me, dear." He turned to the waitress. "How late are you open?"

She frowned from her vantage point at the far end of the counter. "I'm stuck here 'til 10:30."

"I'll see you at nine," he said to me as he plunked a ten-dollar bill on the counter. "Let me pay for your doughnut." I went to protest, but he dismissed me with a wave of his hand. "No. I came to you under false pretenses. Please let me make amends." He walked to the door. "You can give me back any change at nine."

What a nice guy.

Anybody who pays for my doughnut had to be a nice guy. Scott exited the shop. As he did, he passed a figure on the sidewalk. The two nodded a greeting to each other and Scott continued on his way, walking by the large storefront window where all the goodies were on display. The other man followed him. I got a glimpse of his face.

Detective Thomas?

He quickly caught up with the reporter and tapped him on the shoulder. With a big grin, Scott turned. Did the two know each other? While words were being exchanged, Scott's smile changed to a look of shock and fear. Then without warning, he shoved the detective, knocking him to the ground, and bolted away.

I jumped to my feet and raced out. I got to Detective Thomas just in time to see two police officers emerge from the alley next to the building. They grabbed Scott and were wrestling him to the ground. A cruiser screeched to a stop beside them.

One of the officers spoke in a gruff voice as he handcuffed Scott. "You have the right to remain silent." He, with the help of his partner, lifted Scott to his feet and placed him in the back of the car as he continued reading him his rights.

I watched, bewildered. I felt like a television police drama was coming to life right in front of me.

"Jack!" Detective Thomas pulled himself off the ground.

"Sir, what's happening?"

"Just stay right there," he ordered. He turned to the cruiser. "Take him to the station, and get started. I'll be there soon." He pointed a finger at the officer, adding extra emphasis. "And remember—everything by the book."

The cruiser sped off.

"Jack, come with me." He hurried across the street to a car.

I followed and climbed in the passenger side. "What's going on?"

"Not now. Wait until we get to the police station."

"But—"

"We'll talk when we get there. Not before."

True to his word, he clammed up. When we arrived, I followed him into the building swarming with activity, much different than the other day. Officers rushed in a dozen different directions. The desk sergeant was barking orders and fielding questions. Something big was going on. I tried to make sense of it all as I was shown into the same side room I'd occupied before.

Detective Thomas went to leave, but at the last second turned to me. "Stay here and don't talk to anybody until I return."

"All right."

His voice was bordering on emotion. "I mean it. Don't talk to anyone!"

I gave a solemn nod.

He exited. I hustled to the door and opened it a crack. The room behind the main desk—the one I'd mistaken for the lunchroom the other day—was the hub of the action. Officers and plainclothesmen were coming and going at a swift pace. The door was barely able to stay closed for more than a couple of seconds before it sprang open again.

Detective Thomas strode up to the desk and issued commands to the sergeant on duty, who kept nodding and saying, "Yes, sir … Okay, sir … Yes, sir." He walked toward the back room but paused, turned back to the sergeant, and spoke once again. The sergeant glanced my way. I closed the door to the tiniest of cracks.

Am I in trouble?

About five more minutes went by with me waiting for someone to tell me what was happening. Just then, the door to the back room sprang open. The two officers who'd wrestled Scott to the ground appeared with him between them. Each held one of his arms, as they escorted him through a corridor at the back of the station.

Less than a minute later, Detective Thomas walked my way, followed by Detective Phillips. I returned to my seat.

Entering the room, Detective Thomas sat directly across from me. Detective Phillips didn't sit. He paced the floor, his hawk-like stare never leaving me. I have to say, it was disconcerting.

"Jack." Detective Thomas's voice was calm and even. "Why did you meet Scott Murphy at the doughnut shop?"

"I was on my way to church and wanted a doughnut. I guess he wanted one, too." I wasn't sure whether it would have been wise to tell them that Scott was a reporter.

"Did he really?" Detective Phillips sneered.

"Yes, sir. I don't understand. What—"

Detective Thomas interrupted. "How long have you known Mr. Murphy?"

"I just met him tonight."

Detective Phillips grunted his disapproval. "What did you talk about?"

"Different stuff."

"Jack, this is very important. Please." Detective Thomas spoke with a quiet intenseness in his voice. "Think. What were you talking about?"

My mouth went dry. "Do I need a lawyer?"

"Only guilty people need lawyers." Detective Phillips leaned against the table and looked squarely into my eyes. "You tell us. Do you need a lawyer?"

"No, sir." I matched his scowl. "I haven't done anything wrong."

"Calm down, Jack," Detective Thomas said. Then glancing toward the other detective, he said, "You too."

Detective Phillips responded with another grunt. Then he yanked out a chair at the end of the table and sat.

Detective Thomas spoke in those low even tones I'd heard him use before. "Why don't you start at the beginning and tell us everything."

What was he after? My mind raced through the evening's events. "Well, we talked about … courtesy."

The two detectives shared a dubious stare. Then Detective Phillips looked my way, an eyebrow arched. "Courtesy?"

"Yes." I related the story of the waitress and of how Scott had noticed discourteous behavior in California. Then I told them of his interest in the murder. I decided to come clean about his working for the *Globe*, and of how we were going to meet later that night. When I finished, I sat back and waited for their response.

Detective Phillips rose and paced again. "Do you want us to believe that this was a mere coincidence?"

"Sir, I don't see what the big deal is." I struggled to keep my temper in check. I didn't like being treated like a criminal. "I wanted a doughnut. A guy wanted a story. He followed me." I looked at Detective Thomas. "What's going on?"

He went to answer, but Detective Phillips interrupted. "And you're going to tell us, you never saw him before tonight?"

"No sir, I never saw him before tonight."

"All one big coincidence that the murderer and the fellow who found the body happened to end up in the same doughnut shop on a Friday night."

"Hank!" Detective Thomas glared at his partner.

"Oh, come on, Doug!" Detective Phillips pointed an accusing finger at me. "If he doesn't know already, then he's going to find out soon enough."

It took me a second to piece together what had just been divulged. "Hold on. Are you saying Scott is the Dumpster Killer?"

Detective Thomas looked from me to his fellow detective, seeming to wrestle with what to say. Finally, he came to a decision. "Fine." He took a deep breath and slowly released it. "We suspect that, yes, Scott Murphy is the Dumpster Killer. We've had a tail on him for several days now."

"How—How could someone as nice as Scott be the killer? Are you sure?"

"Yes, we're sure," they both answered.

"What proof do you have?"

"That not your concern," Detective Phillips said.

"But what did he want with me?"

Detective Phillips voice was thick with accusation. "Why don't you tell us."

"Calm down, Hank." Detective Thomas turned to me. "You say he wanted to meet you later tonight?"

"Yes, sir. He wanted to know about Emily and about the murder."

Detective Thomas scratched his head. "That doesn't make sense."

"Unless he was broadening his scope of victims, planning on taking Jack out too." Detective Phillips sounded like he wasn't sure of this but was tossing any possibility on the table.

"But it doesn't fit his MO. Why would he change?" Detective Thomas's eyes rapidly danced from left to right as he puzzled through this information.

"I can't believe Scott is a killer," I said. "He seemed so normal. So ..." I searched for the right word, settling on the one Scott himself had used that night. "So courteous."

Detective Thomas' face lit. "Yes." It was as if something clicked in his brain. "Courteous." Without warning, he jumped to his feet and marched out.

Detective Phillips watched, bewildered, as the door closed. Then he turned to me. "Look, kid, if there's something you're not telling us, then you should come clean."

I sat up straight. "Sir, I'm telling you everything."

"Are you sure?"

"Yes, sir."

Detective Thomas reentered the room. "Okay, Jack. We're done with you for now. You can go."

"What?" Detective Phillips' voice rose an octave.

"Do you need a ride back to the school?"

I looked at my watch. It was 8:30. Too late for church. I decided to accept the offer.

"Wait here." Detective Thomas went to leave again but paused at the door. "It would be better if you don't spread this around. There's nothing official yet. We've got a little more investigating to do. I'd hate for this to be leaked to the media, and then have him get off on some technicality."

"Can I at least tell Jill? This list thing is driving her nuts."

"List?" He asked.

I shook my head. "It's nothing. If I tell her, I'm sure she can keep it quiet."

He scowled.

"Listen," I said. "She's going to know something's up."

Detective Thomas's brow creased. "How?"

"Can't you keep your mouth shut?" Detective Phillips snapped.

"It's not that." I sighed. "She can read my face. It's really annoying. Then she'll badger me until I tell her."

The corners of Detective Thomas's mouth rose slightly. "Tell her to keep it under her hat."

Chapter Twenty

By the time an officer could drive me to the school, it was close to 9:15 p.m. It turned out to be Officer Grant. We were still a couple of blocks from campus when we ran into a small caravan of cars. Horns honked, and signs waved out many windows, declaring our team would be victorious.

We weaved through the road, lined with parked vehicles owned by the overflow of homecoming visitors.

"Must be tough on you guys," I said.

Officer Grant cast a charitable glance at the revelers. "We go a little more lenient during homecoming. Go Wolves!"

The school's main parking lot was jammed.

"Thank you," I said as I hopped out.

"No problem." He waved as he pulled away.

I watched as he maneuvered through a mob of shouting and cheering people, all excited for tomorrow's game. I was excited, too. But for a different reason. I pulled the phone from my pocket and punched in Jill's number.

She answered after a couple of rings. "Hi, Jack!"

Screams and cheers almost drowned her out.

"Jill. I have to talk to you."

"What?"

I raised my voice. "I have to talk to you!"

"I can't hear you. I'm on the field. It's pretty noisy here."

"Something very important has happened. I mean, this is really big!"

"What?"

It was no use. I was no match for the pep rally. I hung up and hoofed it over there in hopes of locating her.

By the time I reached the field, things were breaking up. Crowds packed the narrow road that led back to the main campus. I had to fight through a tide of people, all going in the opposite direction. Surprisingly, it didn't take long to locate Jill. She approached, walking with a small group of girls, all laughing and cheering.

Her eyes lit up when she saw me. "Hey, Jack. You hung up on me."

I pulled her to the side of the walkway. "We have to talk."

She waved to her friends to continue without her. Then she turned a cheerful face in my direction. "Did you see the donkey?"

People swarmed by, occasionally knocking into us or sharing a happy greeting.

"Donkey?" I absentmindedly shook my head.

"I can't believe they dressed it up in a Chesterton uniform." She laughed. "And they chased it around the field! It's a wonder some animal rights group doesn't sue them."

Though her story was intriguing, I focused on more important issues. "Listen. I have to talk to you."

"Well, here I am. Talk."

"Not here. We have to find somewhere private."

We made our way to the Tank, thinking it would be quieter. That was a mistake. The crowd from the rally appeared to have moved there, everyone anxious for a snack.

"Look. An empty table by the window," Jill said. It wasn't exactly what I had in mind, but she rushed across the room and claimed it as ours.

I tagged along.

"So what do we have to talk about?" she asked as she sat down.

I darted glances from left to right to make sure no one was listening.

"Boy, this must be important."

I leaned in very close and whispered. "They got him."

Jill followed my lead. With a silly grin, she leaned in and whispered back, "They got who?"

I tried again. "The police caught the Dumpster Killer."

Slowly the grin left her face. "I can't believe it. They caught him? They actually caught him?"

"Shh! Lower your voice. I told your dad we'd keep it under our hats."

Thankfully, the noise from the crowd was so loud she couldn't have been overheard.

Jill covered her mouth. Then, lowering her hands and her voice, she asked, "How? When?"

I recounted the events. When I finished, she gave a low whistle. "And you met the man? Wow."

My chest puffed with pride. "He bought me a doughnut."

"One thing doesn't make sense, though." The crease between her eyes deepened. "Why did he want to meet with you later on?"

"Does it matter?"

"Well, yes," she said as if stating the obvious.

"Why?"

"It doesn't fit." She scrunched up her face. "It just doesn't fit."

"Maybe you don't want it to because you're still hoping your list theory will pan out."

She shrank back. "Jack, list or no list, all I ever wanted was for the killer to be caught."

I nodded, not one hundred percent believing her.

Her brow puckered. "But it doesn't fit his MO."

"That's what your dad said."

"Really?" Her head tipped to the side, and she spoke louder. "Did he say anything else?"

"He said we shouldn't let it get around, so keep your voice down."

"Sorry." She pulled her seat closer to mine.

I continued. "He said there was more investigating the police had to do."

"Hmmm. I wonder what? What else happened?"

"Happened? Where? At the doughnut shop or at the police station?"

She considered, then shrugged. "Tell me everything."

Again, I related the account of my time at the station. It was all pretty standard, or so I thought. But Jill perked up when I mentioned her father suddenly leaving the room.

"Why did he do that?" she asked.

Privately, I replayed the scene. "I don't know. Detective Phillips seemed puzzled too."

"What were you talking about right before he walked out?"

"I was telling him about the waitress's rude behavior." I related the tale once again.

"You say Scott was recently in California?"

"That's what he said."

"Hmmm." She tapped the side of her nose.

"You do that a lot."

"What?"

I imitated her action and sound. "Hmmm."

"Sorry, but you've got me thinking. Why is Scott asking you questions about the murder?"

"Isn't it obvious? I found the body."

She shrugged. "So? If he were the killer, why would he need you to tell him anything? He was there."

I fumbled for an answer. "Well—I—"

"Also," She leaned in closer and spoke with more confidence in her voice. "Why did he wait almost two weeks to come find you?"

"I don't know."

She pointed in the air as if about to make some great declaration. "What if he wasn't here when the murder happened?"

"It would be awfully hard to kill someone if you're not there," I answered.

"Exactly. What if he didn't kill Emily?"

"Huh? Your dad was positive that Scott was the Dumpster Killer."

Jill smiled. "But what if the Dumpster Killer did not kill Emily?"

"Huh?"

"Let's say Scott is the Dumpster Killer. Sure, on the outside he seems like a normal, average person. But inside …" I could see Jill's mind whirling, as she created the image of the man. "Let's say he has some type of vendetta against women with loose morals. Maybe he's been jilted by a woman and wants to blame all of them. Maybe his mother abused him, and he's seeking vengeance."

I leaned back and folded my arms. "Maybe Jill Thomas is getting carried away."

She ignored me. "There's someone who wanted Emily dead. They knew about the Dumpster Killer, so they arranged the murder to look like one of his, to throw off the police."

"But—"

"No, listen," she calmly ordered. "There's only one problem. The real Dumpster Killer was out of the state when the murder happened. In California. Emily's true killer doesn't know this, of course. He figures everything is going to be okay and is betting the police won't ever catch the real Dumpster Killer. So, Emily's death will go down as part of his spree. But the police *do* catch him, much to the credit of a wonderful police detective who will go unnamed." She beamed with pride.

"Of course."

"Let's further say, the real Dumpster Killer is furious about the copycat. It's his moral obligation to clean up society, not somebody else's. He starts wondering, 'What if this murdered girl doesn't fit the profile? What if she didn't deserve to die?' It gnaws at him. He has to know. He decides to do some investigating of his own. Pretending to be a reporter, he seeks information from the person who found the body."

I chuckled. "That's a little farfetched."

"Is it? You told my dad that Scott had made a recent trip to California. I'll bet you anything he left the room to get someone to check into flights, to find Mr. Murphy's itinerary."

"Interesting theory. But what about this? What if Scott Murphy is the killer, and it's all over?"

She looked at me, eyes wide. "But what about the list?"

"What about it?"

"I think it's important."

"I agree. It's important for the whole blackmail thing. But is it the reason for Emily's murder? I don't think so."

"You're wrong. It is mixed up in the murder."

"Should we hand it over to the police then?"

With a violent shake of her head, she shouted, "No!"

"Why not?"

Jill's eyes glistened with tears.

I reached over the table and touched her hand to offer some comfort. It stiffened. I spoke softly. "Let it be, Jill. Please. They caught the guy. Accept it."

She placed her other hand on top of mine and closed her eyes. A tear rolled down her cheek. When she reopened them again, she looked from the table to our hands, to the people around us. Anywhere but me. "It's … It's so hard. I haven't been totally honest with you."

"What do you mean?"

"I have a confession to make." But before she could speak, something over my shoulder caused her grip to tighten. All the warmth drained from her face.

"Well, isn't this sweet," a female voice said. Nicki strolled up behind me, all decked out in her cheerleader uniform. She placed a warm hand on my shoulder and leaned into me. "Who would have thought that you two were an item? But I guess it only makes sense." She exaggerated our names as she pointed to each of us. "Jack and Jill! You were meant to be together."

"We're just good friends. Right, Jill?"

Jill didn't answer. She sat there, somber faced.

"You don't have to be shy," Nicki smirked. Then she hugged my neck. "I'm just sad that another of the good ones is taken. It leaves fewer for girls like me."

My face flushed.

Nicki giggled. "I'd join you, but you know what they say. Two's company, three's a crowd." She walked away.

"Can we get back to our conversation?" Jill cast a disgusted glance Nicki's way.

"Sure," I answered.

But before we could continue, I caught sight of that weird fellow from Lit class. Mr. Dork. The one who intentionally bumped into me. He made a beeline for Nicki, who was halfway across the room and stood square in front of her. He grabbed her wrist.

I jumped up.

"Jack? What—"

"Jill, I'll be right back."

Before she could protest, I shot across the room. I don't know if Dorky saw me coming or if it was coincidence, but before I got to the two of them, he turned and rushed away. I was going to pursue, but a group walked in front of me, blocking my path.

I rushed to Nicki's side. "Are you okay?"

She looked at me, puzzled. "Okay?"

I gestured toward the departing figure, about to leave the room. "I saw him grab you."

Nicki laughed. "Oh, him. He just wanted to know what the reading assignment was for class. That's all." She smiled, coyly. "Jack, were you coming to my rescue?"

"Well … I—"

She touched my arm. "That's so sweet. But you'd better get back to Jill. She doesn't look very happy."

Nicki was right. Jill was frowning.

"See you around." Nicki sauntered across the room to another table and joined the group there. Before she sat, she looked over her shoulder and waved.

I waved, then returned to Jill, who sat there with arms crossed and a sour look on her face.

"What?" I asked.

"Are you done?"

"Done what?"

"Chasing after Nicki."

I scowled. "What a silly thing to say. I wasn't—"

"The way your eyeballs were falling out of your head—"

"Are you serious? I thought she needed help. This weird guy grabbed her."

"Really, Jack!" Jill's voice overflowed with frustration. "You gawk at her like a love-sick puppy. Honestly. I would have thought spending a couple years in the military would have matured you beyond acting like high school boy."

I bristled. Why was she overreacting? I thought Nicki was in trouble and only went to see if I could help. "Well," I replied. "If it's any of your business, I do appreciate looking at things of beauty, and Nicki has a natural beauty that would attract the attention of any man."

Jill sat, openmouthed, staring at me. I thought my reply had silenced her, but I was wrong. She was only gathering momentum. Then an explosion of words came, slowly at first, but growing with intensity. A fire, in what I can only describe as Mount St. Jill, erupted. "Thank you very much for letting me know where you stand. Meeting with me tonight, but not able to take your eyes off that … that," she sneered, "natural beauty!"

I shrank down as best I could, as the people around us stared. "I—I—"

Jill jumped to her feet, almost knocking over her seat. "I guess if you call capped teeth, two pounds of makeup, and clothing too tight and revealing, natural beauty …" She sputtered and wound up to deliver more. "And who knows what else she's had done. If you call that natural beauty, well I guess the two of you deserve each other."

"Jill—"

"Oh, and by the way. You wouldn't know a beautiful woman if—if—if one were standing right in front of you!" Turning on her heels, she stormed out, with every eye in the place riveted on her.

Chapter Twenty-One

What in the world is wrong with that girl?

Though homecoming celebrations continued, I didn't feel much like partying. So, I slinked out of the Tank, red-faced from embarrassment, and made my way along the crowded sidewalk toward my room. It was only 10:30, but the lack of sleep had caught up with me. I was exhausted. Now that they'd caught the killer, maybe I'd get a good night's rest. Maybe tonight would be different.

I laid down, drifted off, and found myself wandering through a beautiful meadow on a bright summer day, surrounded by green grass and wildflowers. The sun warmed my face. Songbirds chirped as they flitted about.

But then the sound of crying invaded my dream. It came from a small grove of trees to the north. I figured I'd check it out and maybe find a nice shady spot to rest. I stumbled along the uneven ground. The tall grass swooshed against my pant legs.

Without warning, a flock of grouse sprang to flight in front of me and raced into the gray sky.

My throat tightened.

When had the sky turned gray?

The closer I drew to the tree line, the louder the noise grew. As I stepped between two birches, I spotted a small boy huddled on the ground by a tall elm. He was shivering and whimpering.

"What's wrong, son?"

He raised his head, and his thick, black hair fell to the sides of his face, revealing penetrating dark brown eyes. "I don't know," he sobbed. "I gotta get out of here, but I don't know why. I don't know how."

"Take my hand." I lifted him to his feet.

He pressed against my side. "I'm afraid."

"It's okay. Trust me." I gave a reassuring smile. "I won't let anything happen to you."

As we walked along, the sounds of the forest gradually changed. At first, I wasn't even aware it was happening. The birds' songs morphed into shouts of fear and anger, growing louder and louder. The color drained from the scene. Before I knew it, not only had the sky turned gray, everything around me was in shades of black and white.

The boy shivered. I patted the top of his head. When my attention returned to the path, it had disappeared. Everything was gone. The path, the birds, the trees. We stood in the middle of a vast desert.

I froze. My hand clamped tighter on the boy's.

The shouts and screams intensified. Deafening.

"What's going on?" My heart pounded.

"Help me!" The boy clung to my leg. Just then, the sand beneath his feet opened into a large gaping pit. He struggled to stop from falling in, clawing at its side. "Save me!"

The ground shifted and morphed. Large tendrils shot out, caught the boy's legs, and pulled him deeper into the black hole.

"Hold on!" I grabbed his arm and was pulled to my knees. Frantically I grasped at his thin hand. The sand whipped against my face, stinging my eyes, burning me.

The screams and shouts blared all around.

His weight increased. The pull of his body became too much for me. I was afraid his arm was going to rip off. I stumbled forward onto my belly. Horrified, I realized I was being sucked into the hole along with the boy.

"Don't let me die," he yelled.

Sweat dripped from my forehead and stung my eyes. "I won't!"

I blinked. In that instant, the boy changed. Now I was holding Emily's hand. She looked up at me with terror-filled eyes. "Don't let me die!"

I blinked again. The boy returned.

Suddenly, a sharp pain pierced my side. I clenched the boy's arm with my left hand, as my right hand instinctively reached for whatever had cut me. My hand came away, covered in blood.

"Hold me! Hold me!"

"I will," I cried.

But it was a lie. As hard as I tried, I couldn't. I watched, helpless, as the boy's arms dissolved and were carried away by the desert air. I grabbed fiercely at him, trying my hardest to hold on to something … anything at all. But it was no use. He slipped through my grip.

"Nooo!" His voice trailed off, as his neck … face … and mouth turned to dust. The last thing I saw were those huge brown eyes, looking up, pleading with me.

"No! I can save you!"

In vain, I grasped at nothing.

The air was charged with screams, explosions, angry cries.

I lay in the sand, screaming back.

The noise grew louder and louder. It went on and on, never-ending.

Then I became aware of a different sound. A banging. It was more intense, more real somehow.

My eyes snapped open. I bolted up. The scene changed. "Where … What?" I struggled to focus. Self-awareness slowly returned.

My room at college.

I rubbed my eyes, trying to clear my brain. The cold, sweat-covered sheets clung to me.

Things returned to normal, except for the banging. It continued.

"Jack," someone called out. "Are you okay? Jack!"

"Hold on!" The sound of my own voice, plus the solidness of the floor as I jumped off the bed, jolted me back to the land of the living. The banging came from my door. I stumbled across the room and opened it. I shielded my eyes from the corridor's blinding light. My vision quickly focused.

Several students had gathered, probably wondering, who was the crazy man doing all the yelling? But that wasn't the worst of it. In the center of the group stood Jill, gawking at me.

Chapter Twenty-Two

Jill stepped toward me, away from the group, her eyes wide, her face etched with genuine concern. "Are you all right?"

Half hidden behind the door, I grasped its edge. "Sure. Why do you ask?"

"You were yelling." She peeked in. "Or at least someone was yelling. Maybe your roommate?"

"Don't have a roommate. He left mid-September. Got homesick." I had a nightmare. That's all."

With this revealed, the rest of the group broke up, going their different ways, some mumbling their disappointment that it wasn't anything more major.

Jill remained, gazing at the floor and shuffling her feet.

"Do you want to come in?" I forced half a smile. "Make sure I'm not murdering someone?"

"Maybe for a minute," she said in a quiet voice.

I flipped on the light switch and crossed to the mirror hanging over the dresser. I was a sight—wearing only pajama bottoms, my hair plastered with sweat, my face white as chalk.

Jill stepped in and closed the door. "Are you sure you're okay?"

"I'm fine."

I could tell by her wary look that she didn't believe it. Who could blame her?

"You're shaking." She sounded like a mother concerned for her hurting child.

I turned to face her. "Everything is all right. Just one of my nightmares."

"One of? You have them often?"

I didn't answer.

"I—I was walking by when I heard … That must have been quite a—" Her eyes shifted off my face and froze on my exposed right side. "Oh." She covered her mouth.

What a dummy I'd been. Being caught off guard by a crowd at your door while having a terrible nightmare, can make you forget your cardinal rule: Never let anyone see you with your shirt off.

I hurried to my dresser to rectify the situation.

"I'm—I'm sorry." She blushed, took a couple of steps toward the window, and turned away from me. "I didn't know."

"That's okay." I fumbled with the folds of my shirt, trying to cover the sweat-soaked scars that ran from my underarm to below my waist. Once done I placed a hand on her shoulder and slowly turned her to face me. "Really. It's okay."

Even though she tried to not look, Jill's eyes were still drawn to the spot. "Can I ask … What happened?"

"A small gift from my time in the service, that's all."

She gasped. "The marines did that to you?"

"No, no," I chuckled. "I mean I got it while serving in the Middle East."

Jill's mouth remained open. "How?"

A bit nosey, isn't she?

And yet, something in me wanted to tell her, yearned to tell her. I bit my lip and pulled those feelings back inside. "I don't want to talk about it."

"Are you sure?"

Was she reading my mind? Was my face giving me away again?

"Sometimes talking helps," she said.

The feeling resurfaced. Where to start? How much to tell? "There was an explosion in a med unit. I got hit by some shrapnel. Broke some bones. Did some damage." I hesitated. "But I'm all healed now."

"But what caused the explosion? Was anyone else hurt? How did—"

"Can we just leave it alone?" I closed my eyes. For a brief second my world erupted in flames. "Just leave it alone. I'm okay. That's all that matters."

"I—I don't think so."

"No. Really. The doctors removed the metal and wood. Stitched me up. I'm—"

"I'm not talking physically." She said. "Jack, no one goes through something like this without getting some emotional scars. If you ever want to talk about it, I'm here for you." Then she did something unexpected. She reached out and gently ran her hand along my side.

I flinched.

She yanked her hand away. "Did I hurt you?"

"No. Just a little sensitive. That's all. The doctors say over time it will get better." I gave a quizzical look. "What are you doing here? You couldn't just be walking by my room. You're not on this floor. Besides, aren't you mad at me or something?"

She hesitated. "I wanted to apologize."

"Really?"

"I acted childish, stomping off like that."

I sighed. "Why don't you like Nicki?"

She sank down at my desk. "My feelings about Nicki have nothing to do with it. We were in a private conversation. There was something important I wanted to tell you and ..." She looked away. "It's been eating at me. When Nicki interrupted ... And then you raced after her ... I lost it."

"And I ignored you." Again, I sighed. "I didn't mean to. I'm the one who should apologize." I crossed the room and sat on the edge of the bed. "You have my undivided attention. What was it you wanted to tell me?"

She fidgeted with a pencil sharpener on my desk. "It's about the list."

I shook my head. "I don't know what else you can say. I mean, we've been checking into every single name on it."

"Not everyone." She spoke so softly that I almost didn't hear.

"I don't understand."

She closed her eyes.

"Jill?"

She winced as if whatever she was about to reveal was causing her pain. "We haven't looked into everyone on the list."

"What do you mean?" I grabbed my copy off the desk. "We've checked everyone."

"No, you don't understand. There's another name."

I scanned the page. "No there isn't."

"Under the line." She pointed to the thick black line that ran across the page, under the words, Blood Money. "There's another name there. I blacked it out."

"What? Why would you do that?"

She took a deep breath. "It's mine."

Chapter Twenty-Three

I sat speechless.

Jill pointed to the paper. "If you look carefully you can see this line isn't quite even with the thick line at the bottom of the page. I did a pretty good job of matching it, trying to make it look like a pattern. But it's not perfect. Besides," she pulled out her copy of the list, "mine's the original. Run your finger over the area. You can feel the indentations of the writing."

I examined it more closely. "Why would you do such a thing?"

She rose and crossed to the window. With a faraway look, she gazed at the campus below. "I knew right away what this list was. At least I suspected."

"But why was Emily blackmailing you?"

"That's just it. She wasn't." Jill turned and leaned against the sill. "The Wednesday before Emily's death, I got this anonymous letter, telling me they knew all about my problem. It instructed me to meet them at the back of the library the following Tuesday night with ten dollars. I never dreamt it was Emily who sent the letter. Imagine my surprise when I found this stupid list in her pocket, and there it was— Jill T—$10. Though hard for me to believe, it seemed my letter came from Emily. I even kept the Tuesday meeting, hoping someone else would show up and prove my theory wrong." She sighed. "No one did."

"Why didn't you tell me?"

"I wanted to, but I wasn't sure if I could trust you."

"Not trust me?"

"Not at first. Think about it. I barely knew you."

"Do you trust me now?"

"Yes."

"Enough to tell me why she was blackmailing you?"

Jill paused. She took slow and deliberate steps toward my desk and sat. After a moment to gather herself, she continued. "I told you that my mother passed away?"

I nodded.

"It was a car accident. We were coming home from shopping … She and I. She died instantly. I was pretty banged up. Three breaks in my left leg."

"I'm sorry." I felt my side. "I know how painful that can be."

She gave a small nod. "My rehab took weeks. I kind of … got used to the pain pills." Her head dropped into her hands. "I got real used to them. You have to understand, it wasn't just physical. There was the emotional pain. My mother's death." She wiped the tears from her eyes. "I had to take a year off from school. Get my head together. My dad was a rock. So helpful."

"Is this why you didn't want the list to go to the police?"

Jill nodded. "We kept my problem pretty much hushed up. Not because of what it would do to his career, but because he was concerned for what it would do to me. I'm over it now. I promise. No drugs. No pills. I know it sounds stupid, and I'm sure my dad could handle it, but it wouldn't take long for the police to determine what was below that black line. Imagine the headlines—*Detective in Charge of Investigation has Drug Crazed Daughter Mixed up in Blackmail.*"

I crossed my arms. "I think your dad is made of stronger stuff than you give him credit for."

Her shoulders slumped. "I know, I know."

I scratched the back of my head. "And Emily knew about your problem?"

She nodded. "I confided in her last fall. She was so supportive." Jill looked away and spoke softly. "Even when I found the list and saw my name on it, I couldn't imagine her doing something like this. It's just not her." Her forehead puckered. "It's a strange thing … I never gave her a cent, yet my name was marked as paid."

"Maybe it's another Jill T."

She considered this. "But I got the blackmail letter."

Again, I scratched my head. "I don't get it."

She perked up. "While we're talking about letters, you told my dad you saw Emily working on some the night she was killed. Where'd they go?"

I shrugged. "Either she mailed them, or they were taken by the police or the killer. Do you think they were more blackmail letters?"

She chewed on the tip of her finger as she thought. "Were they regular writing?"

"What do you mean?"

"My blackmail note was in big block letters like someone was trying to disguise their handwriting."

I shook my head. "Looked like just plain, cursive writing to me."

Jill closed her eyes. "Hmmm."

"What?"

"Oh, nothing. If you could only remember who the letters were to."

"Why?"

"Think about it. Her last letters before ... before ... Well, you know."

I did. "Honestly, I haven't given them much thought. Didn't see any reason."

"Well, now you do."

I shrugged. "I don't remember."

"Have you really tried? Think back. Visualize the desk at the library. Imagine you're standing right there."

I smirked. "Should I close my eyes and go into a trance?"

Her brow knit. "You don't need to go into a trance, but closing your eyes might help."

I obliged.

Jill spoke in a soothing voice. "Think back to that night. You're approaching the desk."

"Is it me or my astral projection."

"I'm serious!"

"Sorry."

"Try again." She spoke, soft and slow. "Take a deep breath. Relax."

I closed my eyes and exhaled. My shoulders slumped.

"As you walk up to Emily, she's working on something," Jill said. "You scan the desk. What do you see?"

I concentrated. "Letters."

"More than one?"

"Yes … Some are crumpled. Some … are torn."

"As you stand there, you notice a name."

In my mind, I tried to pull in for a closer look. "Dear someone or other." I opened my eyes. "I don't remember."

Jill rested a hand on my arm. "Slow down. Pretend it's like the movies. A slow-motion shot. Now close your eyes again."

It wasn't going to work, but I did it anyway, just to avoid a fight.

She spoke in a soothing voice. "You look … and … what … do … you … see?"

I thought this was all a bunch of hooey, but I tried.

Slow the camera down … Look.

My eyes popped open. "Well, I'll be!"

"What?"

"It was you!"

She drew back in surprise. "Huh?"

"One of the letters said, 'Dear Jill.'"

"But—but I didn't get a letter."

"Maybe she was getting another blackmail letter ready to send."

"But you said they weren't done in block letter form."

I shrugged. "Then the police must have them."

She shook her head. "My father would have told me."

"Then the murderer took them."

"But why?"

That was a good question.

Saturday morning, Jill rushed to the dining hall early, figuring she'd beat the breakfast crowd. She was wrong. The long line of hungry people snaked all the way to the entrance of the building. It took almost twenty minutes to get her pancakes. That was only half the battle. The dining area itself was mobbed. People holding food-laden trays circled the room like vultures just waiting to pounce on any empty seat.

"Excuse me, young lady," an older woman called to Jill. She and a gentleman were at a four-person table, enjoying some scrambled eggs. "We have an empty seat over here if you don't mind sharing a table with a couple of old-timers." She waved a happy hand at the chair.

"Thank you." Jill made her way to the seat. "I love pancakes, but they're not too good when they're cold."

"Well, dive right in," the man said. "Don't mind us." He picked up a copy of the local newspaper, fluttered it open, and began to read.

"Is that today's?" Jill craned her neck to catch a glimpse of the headline.

"Sure is."

Do you mind if I check the front page?"

The man ruffled through his paper until he found the front section. Then he dropped it on the table for all to see.

Wolves Favored to Win was the big news.

"Problem?" The woman's brow creased.

"No. Just curious about the news."

There was nothing about the arrest. Of course, it may have happened too late to make the paper. The *Springsbury Gazette* was no great metropolitan newspaper and was probably sent to print early. Besides that, Jill knew her father was extremely cautious. He wouldn't release any unreliable information.

After polishing off the pancakes and thanking the couple—Martha and Walter—for their company, Jill headed off. She called Jack's cell phone to see how he was doing. No answer.

That figures. He always has it shut off.

She wandered around the campus in the bright sunshine, perfect for a football game.

Speaking of which ...

A steady stream of people headed toward the stadium. Remembering how crowded breakfast was, Jill figured getting an early start would be the smart thing to do. Several times along the way she called Jack. Each time, her call went to voice mail.

"He never answers his phone," she grumbled.

The crowd moved smoothly until it bottlenecked at the tunnel-like entryway that led into the cement bleachers. Finally, emerging from the tunnel's other end, Jill discovered three-quarters of the seats were filled.

"Jill!" Donna, one of her friends, called from over on the far left side.

With a bit of maneuvering, Jill made her way there.

Soon it was standing room only for the howling Wolves' fans. Jill's face darkened. There was Nicki on the field with all the other cheerleaders, doing some flips and tosses.

"What's wrong?" Donna asked while munching on a hot dog.

"Nothing. Just wishing the game would start."

An older gentleman walked to the middle of the field, carrying a microphone and dragging its long, unwieldy cord behind him. "Welcome everyone! My name is Jonathan Turner. I'm President Spiner's assistant. He was called away on some family business and asked me to share his warmest thanks to all the alumni and special visitors who've come to celebrate our homecoming events."

The crowd cheered.

Someone behind Jill grumbled, "Family business? Ha!"

Jill looked over her left shoulder. It was an older woman, a little on the heavy side with a slight mustache. Jill tried not to stare but couldn't help herself.

Why doesn't she bleach that thing?

"He must have regularly scheduled family business every month," the woman murmured to the man seated next to her.

"Shhh," he scolded. The two shared a throw blanket, covering their laps. "Keep your opinions to yourself."

She ignored him. "Interesting that his secretary always goes with him on his *family* business." Suddenly the mustache lady caught sight of Jill and glared. "What are you looking at?"

"Nothing." Jill flushed and spun forward.

"On a more somber note." Mr. Turner's voice echoed through the speakers. "We had an unfortunate tragedy on campus a couple of weeks ago. Emily Hamilton, one of our students, was killed. At this time, we'd like to have a moment of silence in her memory."

The noise died down. Some individuals bowed their heads. The wind whistled through the stands. After an appropriate pause, Mr. Turner broke the silence. "Once again, thank you all for coming, and,"—he shot his arm into the air— "Go Wolves!"

The crowd erupted with wolf cheers and yells.

Jill's stomach ached. *A quick, silent prayer, then we continue with our lives and Emily is forgotten.*

I spotted Jill during the game but didn't get a chance to talk to her. Boomer was great—fantastic running and receiving. In the end, we won! Final Score—Wolves 21, Bull Dogs 13.

Students, parents, and alumni gathered that evening for a victory celebration around a large bonfire. My cold fingers wrapped around a cup of hot cocoa. The smoke from the fire billowed into the dark sky. I smiled, satisfied about a different victory—Scott's arrest. Yet, the police were taking their own sweet time in letting people know. I would have thought they'd want to get the news out, calm people's fears.

Across the fire from me, some alumni broke out in a loud song. The youngest of them looked to be in his late 50s. Between the singing of old school fight songs and their laughter, it was obvious they were having a great time.

"Escapees from a nursing home," a voice to my right grumbled. "Kind of a nuisance, aren't they?" The newcomer tore open a candy bar and bit off a chunk. "Why don't they stay where they belong?" Don tossed the candy wrapper at the bonfire and pulled a can of beer from his pocket. He cracked it open and took a long drink. Then offered it to me.

"No, thank you."

He smirked. "Your loss." He swirled the can as he stared at the fire. "I think we have a mutual friend. Jill Thomas."

I didn't reply.

"You know her, right?" he said. "I've seen the two of you hanging around together."

"Yes, we're friends."

He glanced at me through the corner of his eye. "How good of friends?"

I took a page out of Detective Thomas's playbook and remained stoic. "Like I said, we're friends."

The right side of his mouth curled up. "Interesting girl. Filled with curiosity. Almost too much."

A cold wind blew, but I didn't move to turn my collar up or tighten my coat. Instead, I stood rigidly.

"You know what they say? Curiosity killed the cat." He took another swig, then tossed the can into the flames. "Well, I'll be seeing you around." He walked away.

If they hadn't arrested Scott, Don's the kind of person I'd have suspected of being the Dumpster Killer.

Nope. I don't like him at all.

Chapter Twenty-Four

"I feel honored that you came home for breakfast." Jill's dad looked across the kitchen table at her as she munched on cereal and bananas. "Nice surprise. Any particular reason?"

"Do I need a reason to stop by and see my dad?" She smiled.

Usually, her visits home were accompanied by a request for some necessity of life, like cash.

"I suppose not." Detective Thomas, smirked at his daughter's innocent motive as he sipped his coffee.

"How's everything going?"

"Good."

Jill twirled a stray banana around in her bowl. "And the investigation?"

The detective eyed her over the top of his mug. "What investigation?"

"You know what investigation. How come word hasn't been released about the arrest?"

In response, her father spread the Sunday newspaper on the table in front of her. The headline read, Dumpster Killer Caught.

"So, that's it?" She shrugged. "You're not going to look for Emily's real killer?"

Detective Thomas remained silent.

"Daddy?"

He sighed. "You know I can't discuss the case."

Her eyes narrowed. "You don't think Scott did it, do you?"

"Like I said, I can't talk about it." He took another sip of coffee.

Jill huffed. Another line of questioning came to mind. "What can you tell me about Jack?"

His brow puckered. "What do you mean?"

She rose, crossed to the counter and leaned on it, trying to appear nonchalant. "Jack was in the Middle East, wasn't he? Do you know anything about what happened to him over there?"

"Ah, so that's what this is all about. Jack?"

Jill sometimes wished her father would stick with the stone-faced facade he used at work. She didn't feel like taking his teasing. Her eyes widened. "I'm shocked at you! Can't a girl come home to enjoy breakfast with her father?" She sat back down. "I want to help him. That's all. He has these nightmares, and these—" Jill quickly shut her mouth. How would she explain being in Jack's room late at night and seeing the scars? A father might not understand.

"Honey. I wish I could help you, but I can't."

"But—"

"I'm not trying to be obstinate," he said. "From what I understand, Jack's been through quite a bit. But you can't force him to talk about it. Give him time."

Jill folded her arms. How much time did she have to give him?

"Now if you don't mind, I have to get going." He rose from his seat and took his dishes to the kitchen sink. "For once, I have Sunday morning off, and I'm going to church. You coming?"

"I've got some stuff to take care of." Before he could chastise her for missing morning worship, she added, "But I'm going to the evening service. Pastor Roberts' friend is speaking."

"Okay." He kissed the top of her head. "You have a nice day." Halfway to the door, he stopped. "I'm running late. Could you put the kitchen trash out before you go? Make sure you secure the lid. Bob's been digging for scraps lately." He grumbled, "Makes me want to shoot him."

"Daddy!"

"I'm only kidding … Kind of." He stared off into space, an odd expression on his face. "Maybe I could Taser him."

"Daddy!"

"Just kidding, just kidding." He chuckled. "Goodbye, sweetheart. Thanks for coming by." The detective was out the door.

Jill folded her arms.

Give Jack time?

All she wanted to do was help him. She startled at a loud ringing. The culprit sat on the counter—her dad's cell phone. She crossed over and picked it up, shaking her head.

What is it with men and their cellphones?

She let the call go to voicemail, not wanting to get caught in a long, drawn-out conversation with anyone. *Best to see who's calling first.* After a minute, the voicemail message chimed. Jill thought nothing of listening to it. Her father had asked her to do this on several occasions. If the call were important, she'd get in touch with him and let him know.

"Hello, Detective Thomas," the message began. "This is Chaplain Evans. I'm following up to make sure the information you requested on Corporal Hill came through."

Corporal Hill? That must be Jack.

"If there's anything else you need, please let me know." Chaplain Evans ended the message with his telephone number.

Jill, being a resourceful girl, copied it down. "Well, Dad, if you won't give me the information I want, maybe there's someone else who will." She strolled out of the house, much happier than when she'd gone in. The door was about to slam shut when she was stopped by the neighbor's chihuahua barking next to the trash cans.

Whoops!

Jill went back into the house to retrieve the plastic bag from under the sink. She brought it out. "Sorry, Bob. No trash for you today." She dropped it in and secured the lid, pulling the side handles up to lock it in place.

Bob, the chihuahua, smacked his lips and sniffed the base of the barrel.

Jill raised an eyebrow. "How does a tiny fella like you get in there anyway?" She leaned over and patted him. "Go home, boy. Before you get shot by a certain police detective."

As if he knew what she was saying, Bob skittered away and disappeared through the hedge.

Jill climbed behind Matilda's steering wheel and started the car. She looked back at the house and smiled. Yes, she'd come home today under false pretenses, but it was always good to be here.

She started backing down the driveway. About halfway, she came to an abrupt stop. "Hmmm." Her forehead furrowed as she stared at the trash barrels.

Sunday.

I skipped morning worship. Barring any unforeseen run-ins with murderers, I'd be able to go to the night service and hear the missionary speak. So, I decided to sleep in, then have a private devotional time and spend the rest of the morning on homework.

At noon I walked across the quad toward the dining hall. The campus was quiet compared to yesterday's activities. Many of the visitors had gone home, and a lot of the students were sleeping in after last night's celebration.

A crowd gathered at the bottom of the dining hall stairs, engaged in an excited conversation.

"Hey, Jack." David, a classmate from Philosophy 101, was waving a newspaper in the air. "Did you hear? They caught Emily's killer." He held up the paper for me to see. Sure enough, there on the front page was a big picture of Scott Murphy. Dumpster Killer Caught, it read.

"Oh, that."

"What do you mean, 'Oh, that'? Another student eyed me. "You sound like it's old news."

I shrugged. "I was there when they arrested him."

"Get out of town!"

"No way!"

"What happened?"

I probably should have kept my mouth shut. Maybe I wanted another fifteen minutes of fame. I made a mental note to be careful, or I'd become a fifteen-minute junkie. A small group followed me into the dining hall. Some stayed while I ate, hanging on my every word as I recounted the story. Eventually, the crowd dispersed.

"Sounds like you had an exciting Friday night," Nicki said. She and Don approached the table.

"Sure did. Have you two eaten yet?"

"We're all done," Don answered.

Nicki beamed with excitement. "You met the killer."

I nodded.

"I'm glad they caught him." Don chuckled derisively. "I was starting to wonder if it was you."

"Oh, don't be silly," Nicki said as she and Don sat. "Jack couldn't kill anyone. Could you, Jack?"

I bit into a french fry.

"How about it, Hill?" Don's face hardened. "You kill anyone when you were in the army?"

"Marines," I corrected.

He scoffed. "Is there a difference?"

"Sure. You could make it in one,"—I took a sip of my root beer, placed the glass on the table and looked Don square in the eyes—"but not in the other."

Nicki laughed.

Don wasn't amused. "The question is, what's Jill going to do with that list?"

I was surprised he was willing to bring the subject up in public.

"Don't know," was my noncommittal answer.

"List?" Nicki's face paled.

Maybe Jill was right. Nicki seemed unusually concerned for someone who didn't have anything to hide.

"She could destroy it," Don said. "Talk to her. You have some influence."

I snickered at the thought of me having any influence over Jill.

Don's face tensed. "They caught the killer. The list had nothing to do with it. Why shouldn't she just destroy the fool thing?"

"Yes ..." Nicki hesitated as if realizing her sudden interest confirmed her guilt. "Why not?"

I searched her face for the pounds of makeup Jill had mentioned.

"If the police investigation is over," Don continued, "why not help a few people out?"

I shrugged. "I'll ask her. Meanwhile,"—I turned my attention to Nicki— "what are you doing tonight?"

"Why?" She gave a provocative smile. "What did you have in mind?"

"Church."

The smile disappeared.

"There's a missionary speaking. I thought maybe you could join me."

"What's this?" Don steepled his fingers. "Is our Nicki getting religion?"

She glared at him. "Don't be a jerk."

Ignoring the exchange between the two, I continued to push. "I've asked you a couple of times now. You said you'd think about it. So?"

"Yes, Nicki. Tell us," Don teased. "What do you think?"

Nicki's eyes darted nervously from me to Don. "Jack, I never said I'd go. I just said I'd think about it. That's all. The fact is, I have other plans for the evening."

"I see."

Don smirked.

"Don't worry." She patted my hand. "Maybe next time."

"Sure. Maybe next time." I didn't believe a word of it.

Chapter Twenty-Five

Don and Nicki left as I finished my meal. With that done, I ambled across the quad. It was a beautiful day. Indian summer. The sun felt especially warm on my face. The lawn was lightly peppered with students enjoying a variety of activities from football to sunbathing, behaving more like it was spring than fall.

Out beyond where a couple of people were playing bocce, Jill strode along the sidewalk. I waved, but she didn't see me. She approached the library, but instead of going up the steps she went around its side.

I hurried after her. When I rounded the back of the building, she was gone. No one in sight. This was becoming a bad habit. First Boomer, now Jill. I looked up, half expecting to see her scaling the walls. Nothing. I peered into the woods. Nope.

Grunting sounded from the far side of the Dumpster. I crept forward, expecting to find a raccoon or some other wild animal foraging for some scraps. It was a wild animal, all right … of the female persuasion. Jill balanced on the edge of the receptacle, struggling to reach inside.

"What are you doing?" I asked.

She jolted, hit her head against the hard rubber lid which hung precariously above her, and fell to the ground. She pulled herself up from the walkway. "Warn someone before you come sneaking up on them!"

"Sorry. The next time I see you Dumpster diving, I'll call from a distance. Now, do you mind telling me, what's going on? Didn't you have enough for breakfast?"

She turned up her nose at me. "As a matter of fact, I had a nice breakfast with my father. That's where I came up with this idea. He asked me to put out the trash. I guess the neighbor's dog, Bob, has been getting into it." She frowned. "I think my father wants to shoot him—"

"Hold on!" I held up a hand. Then with dramatic flair, I said, "Your neighbor's dog is named Bob?"

"Yes."

I slapped my forehead. "No imagination."

"Very funny."

"So what does Bob have to do with you Dumpster diving?"

Jill took a deep breath and continued. "You said Emily was writing letters that night in the library. They weren't found on her. The police don't have them. The only other explanation we could come up with was that the murderer took them. But then I thought, what about all the crumpled or torn pages? Seeing the garbage cans at my house jogged my memory." She pulled herself up on the Dumpster's side.

"Jill, the morning paper confirmed it. Scott Murphy has been declared the Dumpster Killer."

"Maybe, but he's not Emily's killer."

Stubborn to the end.

"What's the big deal?" I said. "The letters are probably just … letters."

"Then why can't we find them? It's a long shot, I know, but what if she wrote several drafts? I could just see her doing that, starting one, not liking what she said, crumpling it and tossing it aside."

"Don't you think they've emptied the trash since then?"

"I checked. It's only emptied once a month. Not much stuff builds up in it. It was emptied two days before Emily's death."

I peered inside. "This is gross."

"Don't be a baby. It's not like it's the garbage from the dining hall. It's the library for heaven's sake. Mostly paper."

She reached farther and farther into the belly of the beast, mumbling as she tossed scraps aside. "You know, this would go a lot faster if you helped me."

Gazing at the refuse, I frowned. "Probably a wild goose chase."

With her stomach balancing on the edge, she said, "Grab hold of my legs."

"Huh?" I stepped back.

"Those pages on the bottom look promising. I can't quite reach them though." She grunted as she stretched her arm as far as it possibly could go. Failing this last attempt, she turned to me. "Grab my legs!"

I hesitated.

She smiled. "Unless you want to go in there for me."

"Fine!" I took hold of her legs and lowered her part way into the Dumpster. "You're insane, do you know that?"

"Easy. You're hurting my ankles."

"Sorry." I felt like a kid, fishing the storm drain with a stick and a piece of chewing gum.

"Almost there," she said. "A little more ... a little more."

Out of nowhere, a voice called out. "Hey, you! Stop that!"

I turned. Dr. Spiner stood openmouthed at the edge of the woods.

Surprised, I dropped Jill. She yelped and crashed to the bottom of the Dumpster.

Dr. Spiner marched toward me. "What are you doing?"

I froze. "Me, sir? Doing? Nothing."

Thuds and clunks rose from the trash receptacle. Jill's face popped up above the rim, pieces of paper and goo protruded from her hair.

Dr. Spiner raced to her. "Are you all right, young lady? What has he done to you?"

Why is it whenever Jill does something totally crazy, she's the innocent one, and I'm the big bad wolf? "I didn't do anything."

"I'm all right," Jill said as she pulled herself onto the rim. "I accidentally threw away an important paper. Jack was helping me find it. That's all."

Amazing how easily she comes up with these little white lies.

I offered her a hand.

She scowled. "Do you think you can hold me this time?"

"Very funny." I hoisted her out.

"Are you sure you're all right?" Dr. Spiner cast a distrustful glance my way.

"I'm fine." Jill brushed some dirt off her pants. "Thank you for asking." She looked at the president, concerned. "What about you? Are you okay?"

"I'm—I'm fine," he answered, somewhat flustered. "Why do you ask?"

I hadn't noticed it at first, but on closer examination, President Spiner's clothes were covered in dirt. He had a small abrasion across his forehead.

"Are you sure you're okay?" I said.

Before he could answer, Ms. Fielding came rushing up the road. "There you are! I've been looking everywhere for you."

"Well, here I am." With a nervous laugh, he gingerly touched his bruise. "I think I fell … or something."

Fell or something?

Wide-eyed, Ms. Fielding hovered over him, inspecting the cut. "That doesn't look too bad. We'll take care of it when we get you home."

"Yes, home." Dr. Spiner gave his secretary a vague stare. "I went for a walk."

I took a step toward them. "Excuse me, sir."

Up until now, Ms. Fielding had been so focused on the president I don't think she recognized me. Now that she did, her face turned bitter.

"We missed you at the homecoming events," I said.

His brow knit. "Homecoming?"

"Yes. The football game, the—"

Like a mother bear, Ms. Fielding stepped between me and her cub and glared. "The president had more pressing matters."

"Ms. Fielding, I think there's been some kind of misunderstanding," I said. "You gave me an envelope."

She quickly turned to Dr. Spiner. "Let's go, Roland. It's time for lunch."

"Lunch? Of course." He scratched his head as they walked away. "It must have slipped my mind."

"Wait." I walked after them. "The money."

She kept walking. "Not now."

"When?"

"Come see me in the office, sometime during the week."

"But—"

"During the week!"

That message was clear enough.

The president looked back at Jill. "Are you sure you're all right?"

She nodded. "I'm fine."

Ms. Fielding eyed the Dumpster. Then she glanced over at a disheveled Jill. Finally, at me. "Funny place to take a date." She wrapped an arm around Dr. Spiner. "Let's go."

I stepped toward them. "One more thing, Dr. Spiner. What's going on between you and Caroline Webster?"

He slowly turned, his fingers stroking his chin. "Caroline Webster? I don't think I know that name."

I pointed to the woods. "She said the college doesn't own this land. Land, I assume you need to build—"

"Let's go." Ms. Fielding gently pulled at his arm until he followed.

After they were out of earshot, my attention turned to Jill. "That was weird."

"You're telling me."

"Sorry about dropping you."

"I'm all right." She pulled a sticky glob off the top of her head. "Looks like someone spilled a drink on this one." Handing me the soggy bits of folded paper, she continued removing debris from her hair.

I was about to toss it when something caught my eye.

Jill sighed. "I'm going to have to shower for a couple of hours before I feel clean again."

"Dear Jill ..."

"Oh, cut it out."

"No. It says, 'Dear Jill.'" I held up the scrap of paper for her to see.

She flicked her fingers, trying to get an unknown substance to detach itself. Then she took the paper from me. It was covered in what I assumed was cola stains. Only the edge of the sheet had survived. But two words could be seen clearly. Dear Jill.

She almost jumped off the ground. "That's Emily's handwriting. Where'd you find that?"

I pointed to the goo in her hair.

She reached for the top of her head. "Do you see anything else up there?"

We looked like two monkeys in the zoo, as Jill leaned forward allowing me to pick through her hair. "Nothing."

She peered over the Dumpster's edge and started pointing. "Look! On the edge of the gunk I fell in! Do you see it?"

Sticking out of the ooze was a torn off chunk of paper that appeared to match ours.

"Go get it," she said.

"What? Me?"

"Yes."

I shook my head. "You go."

"But I think I hurt myself when I fell." She whimpered and rubbed a spot on her leg. Her acting wouldn't even get her a spot in a grammar school production. "Besides, this is a job for a brave marine."

"More like a job for the army."

"Come on, Jack. Please." She whined that last word, stretching it out for what felt like fifteen seconds.

I surrendered and climbed up the side of the Dumpster, grumbling as I did. "I can't believe this."

"You're such a good friend."

"Stop trying to butter me up." Speaking of butter, that's what the puddle on the Dumpster's rim felt like. My foot slid across it, and I went tumbling in.

After a pause, a quiet voice from up above asked, "Are you okay?"

"Just ducky." I searched the ooze and the surrounding area for any matching pieces of the paper, knowing full well if I didn't get every scrap, Jill would send me back in.

"I appreciate this so much. You are such a good friend."

"You already said that."

After picking the spot clean, I climbed out. Carefully, we placed our treasures on the loading dock, letting the sun dry them as much as possible. It wasn't easy. The ooze had taken its toll, leaving very little that was legible. What we could decipher said, Dear Jill ... Sorry ... erson ... oomer ... away ... my fault.

"Not much."

"I know," Jill said. "But at least it tells us Emily wrote letters."

"Why throw them away?"

Her face scrunched in concentration. "I think I was correct earlier when I said these were rough drafts. Maybe she rewrote them." The scraps had sufficiently dried, and Jill carefully gathered them together. She flashed me a mischievous smile. "You should have seen the look on your face when Dr. Spiner showed up."

I smirked. "When you popped out of the Dumpster, I thought he was going to have a heart attack."

Jill's head tipped to the side. "I wonder what he was doing back here?"

I shrugged. "Going for a walk, I guess. Stop looking for trouble."

She ignored me. "And wasn't Ms. Fielding acting odd? Kind of like she was hiding something?"

"They were both acting odd."

"You were like a bulldog, asking questions." Jill pulled bits of gunk from her hair and winced. "I need a shower."

"Good idea. I think I'll join you."

"What?"

"I mean—" My face warmed. "I'll join you taking a shower," I flustered. "Not *with* you. I mean ... Oh. You know what I mean!"

Jill laughed. "Yes. I know what you mean."

Two things about the Sunday evening service made it special. Number one—Pastor Roberts' friend was a wonderful speaker, who shared many inspiring stories from his mission experience. Number Two—Chocolate Eclairs. Mrs. Roberts had saved me some from Friday.

When everything was over, I started the trek back to the school. The night air had a faint odor of burning wood from a nearby fireplace or wood stove. I'd barely gone twenty yards from the church when hurried footsteps approached from behind me.

"Jack, wait for me." It was Jill. "Can I walk with you?"

"Sure." I waited until she caught up. "I see you got all the gunk out."

She laughed. "You clean up pretty good, too."

"Where's Matilda?"

"I gave her the night off. Thought I'd walk."

We discussed the missionary's talk as we continued.

After a couple of minutes, Jill shivered.

"Where's your coat?" I asked.

"In Matilda."

"Here." I removed my jacket and draped it around her shoulders.

"No, I couldn't." She tried to push it off, but I stopped her.

"Of course, you can."

The coat hung to her knees. I almost made a comment about her looking like a little girl but feared verbal or physical retribution.

She pulled it around her. "Aren't you cold?"

"No. I'm—"

"I know." The corners of her mouth rose. "You're a marine."

I smiled. "I was going to say I'm kind of warm."

"Oh …" She looked at the ground.

We walked on, neither of us speaking very much. There was a lonely stretch of country road between the town and the campus. It bordered a large open field. The stars filled the sky like a blanket, reaching from horizon to horizon.

"Be still and know that I am God," Jill murmured.

"What?"

She flustered. "Psalm 46:10. Whenever I'm faced with the awesomeness of God's creation, I think of that verse." She raised an open palm to the sky. "'Be still and know that I am God.'"

I looked up at the stars and nodded. "It's a nice verse."

Again, we fell silent and kept walking. Jill kicked through the piles of fallen leaves along the side of the road, sending them sailing into the air. We approached what appeared to be an almost deserted campus—very still, very quiet.

"Everyone's recovering from homecoming overload," I joked.

She laughed.

Behind our residence hall, light from the rear windows streaked across our path and into the narrow strip of woods that separated the building from the parking lot.

I slowed my pace.

"Something wrong?" Jill asked.

I swallowed hard. "Jill? I've been thinking about us."

She stopped. The color in her cheeks rose. "You have?"

"Yes. I've noticed, whenever we get into an argument, it's usually you who apologizes."

"Oh?" She hung her head and continued to walk. "Is that what you've been thinking about?"

"Yeah. Why?"

"Nothing. Go on."

"It's not right. I mean, you always apologizing, always saying you're sorry. Maybe you were right when you said I was pompous. If we're going to be friends, then I have to be man enough, to be Christian enough, to admit when I'm wrong."

A cool breeze whipped across the parking lot.

"I'm sorry I called you pompous," Jill said.

"There you go again! Apologizing."

"Sorry."

"Again!"

She covered her mouth. "Bad habit."

We laughed.

I rubbed my stomach. "I'm kind of hungry."

"Are you serious? We just had refreshments at the church. You ate four eclairs."

"You counted?" I smirked. "You spying on me or something?"

"What? No, I—"

"Just kidding. I can't help being hungry. The eclairs were kind of like an appetizer. Now I want more. Maybe a couple candy bars from the Tank's vending machines will do the trick."

"Want company?"

"Sure."

We'd just started toward the Tank when Jill stopped short. "Hold on." She raced into the parking lot.

"Where are you going?"

"To get my coat."

"Want me to get it?"

"No. I'll only be a minute."

Matilda, the old Ford Pinto, was parked at the far end of the lot. Probably to hide it, it being so ugly and all. I dare not say that to Jill, though. She took about forty-five seconds to get there. The car was a couple of feet beyond the ring of illumination from the security lights. I could just make out Jill fiddling with the key in the lock and was about to ask if she needed help when the door opened. As Jill reached inside, a shadow behind the car took form. It leaped out and ripped Jill's pocketbook from her shoulder.

"Jill!" I raced toward her. "Jill!"

It only took a couple of seconds for the mugger to gain his prize, toss Jill against the car like a rag doll, and bolt for the woods at the edge of the lot. I was halfway there when, much to my surprise, Jill produced a baseball bat from the open car door.

"Jill, no!"

It was no use. She chased after her mugger, disappearing into the woods.

What does she think she's doing?

I stormed past Matilda and plunged through the trees. I could never live with myself if something happened to that fool of a girl. Almost immediately the light from the parking lot was blocked by the thick tree line. I paused, struggling to hear anything over my heavy breathing.

There were footfalls on the forest floor up ahead.

I bolted toward them.

Things grew quiet.

I stood perfectly still, listening.

A thud and a yelp came from somewhere up and to the left. I fought through the bushes, arms in front of me, blocking the branches from slapping my face.

Where is she? If anything—

I tripped over a lump on the ground. My arms smashed against the earth, cushioning my fall. Something—I assume a stick—jabbed at my forearm. Twisting to my side, I went to push off the ground. But instead of landing on dirt, my hand hit the lump I'd tripped over.

My throat tightened. The lump was soft.

I gasped.

No. No. Jill.

Chapter Twenty-Six

The body was still warm. In the darkness, I felt around for a wrist. I located an arm and slid down toward the hand. No pulse.

Why couldn't she wait for me? Why did she have to go traipsing into the woods?

On the side of her neck, my hand landed in something wet and sticky.

My chest tightened. My head sank low. "Oh, Jill ..."

"What?"

I startled at the female voice. A light flashed in my eyes. A small figure stood about ten feet away.

"Jill?"

"Yes. Who'd you think it was?" She waved her light in the air. "See. If you kept your phone with you, you'd always be prepared for the dark."

"Stay where you are!"

Of course, she did the exact opposite of what I said and stepped forward, her light dancing along the ground. "Why?" When it landed on the dead body, the dancing stopped. "Who—Who?"

"Bring that phone closer."

The body was facedown, legs tangled together. A shotgun lay by its side. The head rested in a field of stones, blood oozing from a large gash in the back of the skull. I rolled the body over on its back to get a better look.

"Oh, no," Jill moaned.

Caroline Webster was dead.

After taking a moment to recover, Jill punched some numbers in her phone. "Calling the police." She placed it against her ear and listened. Then she grunted. "No signal. I'd better go to the parking lot and call from there."

"I'll go with you."

"No, you stay here." She dismissed me with a wave of her hand.

My jaw tightened. "You're not going alone."

I got the distinct impression she wanted to argue the point, but instead, she marched away. I followed.

The walk back to the parking lot was not as pleasant as our recent stroll from the church.

"Jill, what in the world did you think you were doing, rushing into the woods like that?"

"I was fine." As if to prove her point, she raised her baseball bat in the air.

"No!"

The force of my voice made her jump. It surprised even me.

"Never do that again," I said. "Do you hear me?"

She picked up her pace. "You're not my father."

"No, I'm your friend. I'm sorry, Jill, but what you did was careless. Foolish."

"I can take care of myself."

"No, you can't." I grabbed her shoulder and spun her around. "You're a little bit of a thing. A girl."

She placed her hands on her hips. "So now, not only are you anti short people, you're a male chauvinist."

"You are so pig-headed." I'd had enough. She needed a demonstration. So, I gently backed her into a tree and held her there.

"Hey! What are doing?"

"Proving a point." My hands grasped tightly on her upper arms.

"Stop it!" She struggled. The bat fell from her hand and clunked to the ground.

"I thought you could take care of yourself."

"I can."

The more she fought, the tighter I held. As a last-ditch effort for freedom, she kicked me in the shin. It hurt, but I refused to let go, at least not right away. Finally, I released her.

She pushed away.

"And I'm not even trying to hurt you. Imagine if I was." I ran my hand through my hair. That's when I realized I was shaking. "Jill, please. I couldn't bear to lose another—" My voice cracked.

"Another what?"

"Never mind."

She stepped toward me. "Tell me!"

"Let's go." I turned to leave.

"Do you feel responsible for Emily?"

"Drop it!"

We reached the parking lot, and Jill checked her cell phone. "I have a signal."

I looked at her, and my breath caught in my throat. Now that we'd stepped out of the dark woods, I saw the large lump above her eye and a couple of small cuts and scrapes running along her cheek. "You're hurt."

"What?" Wide-eyed, Jill touched her forehead and quickly pulled her hand away. "I'm—I'm all right."

"But—"

"I'll call the police and wait in my car until they get here." She stepped away from me. "You go back to the body."

The parking lot looked deserted, but I wasn't going to take the chance. "I'll wait with you."

"But—"

"Jill, please."

We stood, staring at each other.

"Fine," she finally said.

She made the call, and we waited. A police car and an ambulance arrived within five minutes. They'd kept the lights and sirens off, which was good. We didn't need a crowd of spectators.

Even though there was an ambulance with EMT's, upon seeing his daughter's condition, Detective Thomas wanted to take her to the hospital. Despite her protests, he loaded her in his car, and they left.

The police took half the night with their crime scene procedure. Several times I suggested I'd come to the station in the morning to give my report, but Detective Phillips insisted I wait and return with him.

I think this was a tactic to rattle me.

After they finished, we drove into town. I spent over an hour in my favorite interrogation room before the detective appeared. Question after question was thrown at me, many times the same one being repeated in a slightly different way.

"Tell me, Mr. Hill." Detective Phillips leaned on the table. "Why is it whenever we find a dead body, you're there?"

I shrugged. "This is only my second one. It's not like there's a whole truckload or anything."

"Funny guy. So why were you in the woods?"

"I already told you, four or five times. Jill was attacked. She ran into the woods after the guy. I followed. That's all."

"Where was Jill when she was attacked?"

"At her car, getting her coat."

"Why didn't you get it for her?" He smiled. "You're a gentleman, aren't you?"

"She ran off before I knew what she was doing."

"When she was by the car, did she look back at you?"

I frowned. "What?"

"Wave at you?"

"No ... I ... What are you getting at?"

"Tell me something? Would she have known if you were trotting along behind her as she ran? Would she have known if you pulled on a hoodie? Would she—"

"You're out of line!"

He stood up and straightened the collar of his shirt. "Maybe. But I have to look at all possibilities."

"So now, not only are you insinuating I killed Caroline Webster, but I also stole Jill's pocketbook along the way?" I soured my face and shook my head. "I must have super speed or something to accomplish all that. Is Detective Thomas back yet?"

He sneered. "No friendly face to buy everything you say?"

"Do I need a lawyer?"

"No lawyers yet." He walked across the room. "As for Detective Thomas, he's still at the hospital with Jill."

I paused. "Is she okay?"

He opened the door. "You're free to go but remember what I said."

I raised my voice. "Is she okay?"

Detective Phillips softened a bit. "Sheesh. Relax. As far as I know, she's fine."

"What hospital is she in?"

"The General."

"Thank you." I was out the door.

It was 7:30 a.m. The sky was heavy with rain clouds. The hospital was in the next town, a good seven miles away and I was exhausted. How was I going to get to there? Hitchhike? I looked up and down the street. Not a cab in sight.

Does this town even have cabs?

Then, I gave in to the inevitable. Slowly walking along the edge of the road, I extended my thumb to every passing car.

After ten minutes with no takers, I was growing impatient and was about to give up, call the pastor and see if he could give me a ride. But then, an older model Toyota drove by. It slowed and pulled to a stop about twenty feet beyond me. The driver's window lowered. A hand came out, waving at me. I trotted up the side of the vehicle to discover Nicki behind the wheel.

I hoped my face didn't show the surprise I felt. For some reason, I always envisioned her in something flashier.

"What are you doing?" she asked.

"Considering the benefits of thumbing."

She grimaced. "You look awful."

"Thanks. Been up all night. I'm trying to get the hospital to see Jill."

"Is she all right?"

I explained about last night's activities.

When I finished, Nicki tossed some schoolbooks from the front seat to the back. "Jump in. I'll drive you."

"Are you sure? You'll miss classes."

"No problem."

I climbed in. "That's nice of you."

"Don't sound so shocked. I'm not the ogre that some people make me out to be."

"I don't think you're an ogre."

Nicki remained somber. "And Jill? What does she think?"

I fidgeted with my seatbelt. "You'd have to ask her."

"Uh-huh." She put the car in drive and pulled onto the road. "I know Jill and I aren't the best of friends, or any type of friend, but ..." Nicki shook her head. Her features tightened. "I wouldn't wish a mugging on anyone. Not even my worst enemy."

"I'm glad to hear that. And I'm sure you can relate, considering what happened to you that night in the quad." I thought back to that rainy evening when I rescued her from a mugger.

"Huh?"

"You remember. That night in the rain."

"Oh ... Oh, yes." She was quiet for several seconds. "That area of the parking lot where you say Jill was attacked ... those woods ..." She shivered. "They've always frightened me."

We arrived at our destination, parked the car, and hopped out. Nicki walked toward the entrance, but after a couple of seconds stopped and looked back at me. "What's the matter? You're as white as a ghost."

With my feet stuck to the ground, I stared up at the steel and cement structure with its rows of shiny clean windows.

They try to tell you hospitals are good for you, with their antiseptic walls, volunteers delivering newspapers and smiles, cheery-faced staff members taking your food order. But I know different. A lot of grief happens in hospitals. Grief and pain. Some people carry memories of the pain when they leave.

I lowered my head. "I don't like hospitals."

Nicki slid her hand into mine and pulled me along. "Come on."

It took us ten minutes to make our way through the halls and find Jill in the ER.

"Jack." Her face brightened when I appeared in her doorway. There was a bandage on her forehead. Her right cheek sported a large bruise.

"How're you doing?"

She tried to smile, but it ended with a wince. "I'm all right. This is all really silly, but my dad insisted that I get checked out. I spent half the night in the waiting room. I'm so happy you came to see me."

I shrugged. "We weren't sure we'd be allowed in."

"We?"

Nicki peeked around the door frame. "Hi there."

"Oh."

An icy chill filled the room.

I motioned for Nicki to take the single chair pushed up against the wall.

"I saw Jack hitchhiking." Nicki lifted some folded sheets off the chair, placed them on the edge of Jill's bed, and sat down. "Thought I'd pick him up and come see how you were doing."

"That's ... nice."

I chose to ignore Jill's self-imposed chill and asked, "So, are you going to be okay?"

She shrugged. "Couple cuts and bruises. My ankle hurts. Nothing broken, though. Jack, you don't have to stand." She patted the side of the bed. Then with some effort, shifted over.

"Poor dear." Nicki almost sounded sympathetic.

I looked for the nurse's call button. "Do you need help?"

"I'm not an invalid. Just a little stiff." She slid enough to make room for me. "Sit here."

I settled on the edge of the bed.

Nicki asked, "Did you see your attacker's face?"

Jill shivered and held the hospital gown tightly around her neck. "No. I thought I heard a noise when I was unlocking the door but didn't think anything of it." She nodded in my direction. "I wondered if you'd followed me."

"Don't tell Uncle Henry that."

"What?"

"Nothing."

"Next thing I knew," Jill continued, "someone was grabbing for my pocketbook. I tried to fight, but—"

"It's all right." I went to pat her shoulder, but pulled back, afraid I'd touch an injured area. "You don't have to go on if it's too painful."

"No," she said with marked determination. "The only thing painful about it was my stupidity." She sighed. "To let someone get away with my bag like that!"

"Brave girl." Nicki shook her head. "And to think, I almost witnessed it."

"Witnessed it?" I asked.

"Yes. I'd been on a date."

"Oh?" I said.

"Now, Jack." She gave a coy smile. "Don't be jealous."

I rolled my eyes. "I'm not jealous. Just curious as to who you were with. Maybe he saw something."

"No, Donny and I went out to eat. When we came back, he went straight to his room. I headed to the library to return an overdue book. But honestly, by what you told me on the ride over here, we'd just parked the car and left the lot."

"Wait," Jill snapped. "Donny?"

Nicki nodded. "You know. Don Henderson."

"Don Henderson?" Jill's tone was doubt-filled.

"Yes."

"You went out on a date with Don Henderson?"

"Yes."

Jill leaned in and peered at Nicki. "A date date?"

Nicki looked amused. "Yes, a date date."

"Impossible," Jill said. "He's gay."

"What?" Nicki laughed. "Believe me, Donald Henderson is not gay."

"But he told me—"

"I don't care what he told you. We've gone on maybe ten dates over the past year. You can trust me when I tell you,"—Nicki grinned—"he likes girls."

The crease between Jill's eyebrow deepened. "He lied to me." She was speaking to herself more than to us, having trouble accepting it.

"Boys do, sweetie," Nicki said.

"I can't believe it. Unless"—she turned an accusing glare on Nicki—"unless you're lying?"

Nicki laughed. "What possible reason would I have to lie to you?"

Before Jill could answer, a voice called from the doorway. "Am I interrupting?" A semi-frazzled Detective Thomas stepped in.

"Good morning, sir," I said.

"Jack." He nodded in my direction.

"Jack and Nicki stopped by to see how I was doing. Wasn't that nice?"

"Very nice." He was trying his best to keep the emotionless, detective facade in place, but a night of fretting over his daughter had taken its toll.

Nicki stood. "If you don't mind, Jack, I have to get to class. Are you ready to leave?"

Detective Thomas answered. "That won't be necessary. I'll make sure Mr. Hill gets back to campus."

"That's okay. I can leave with Nicki—"

"You should wait for me." Detective Thomas said, his tone leaving no room for debate. "I'd like to talk to you."

Nicki went to leave. "I hope you're feeling better, Jill."

"Thank you."

"See you on campus." She strolled out.

Before we could continue our conversation, the detective's phone rang. "Excuse me." He sought privacy in the hallway.

The room grew quiet. I hung my head.

"What's the matter?" Jill asked.

"It's my fault."

"What?"

"If I'd gone to your car, you'd have never been attacked. He'd never have hurt you."

"Hurt me?" Jill touched her bandage and turned red. With an embarrassed laugh, she said, "Actually … these bruises aren't from the mugger. I tripped over something in the woods, fell and smashed into a tree."

Though it wasn't humorous, I couldn't stop myself from chuckling. "Well, I guess that's good to know. Better it was only a common thief."

She scoffed. "Common thief?"

"Yes."

"Anything but common. The thief wanted the list."

"What?"

"Think about it. First, someone broke into my room—"

I raised a finger. "Er … That's up for debate."

"When the intruder didn't get what they wanted, they came after me."

"Now hold on! Are you saying—"

"Excuse me? Am I interrupting something?" A stout nurse, whose name tag read Betty, stood in the doorway, hands on her hips. "Could you please keep your voices down?"

"Sorry," I said, not even realizing we'd been talking so loudly.

Nurse Betty focused her hall-monitor glare on me. "Do I need to escort you out of here?" She took one menacing step into the room.

"The detective asked him to stay here until he returns," Jill quickly offered. "He'll only be a couple more minutes."

"All right then, but please talk quietly. This is a hospital, after all." With a disapproving huff, she marched away.

"And once again," I whispered, "the fast thinking Jill Thomas comes to Jack's rescue."

"Glad I was here." She mustered a weak laugh.

"Hurt?"

"A little. Listen, whoever did this wanted the list. Luckily, it was back in my room."

I wasn't going to argue with her. Maybe she was right. But I had to wonder, did everything that happened to her have to do with the list? I changed the subject. "It's too bad Don and Nicki weren't in the parking lot when it happened. Maybe they'd have seen who it was."

"Seen who it was?" Jill gave a contemptuous snicker. "It was Nicki."

Chapter Twenty-Seven

Jill and Nicki got along like two cats with their tails tied together and slung over a clothesline. I had to wonder if her point of view was a bit tainted. One thing was for sure, she had my attention. "I thought you said you didn't see your attacker. How could you know it was Nicki?"

"I couldn't see her." She tapped the side of her nose, "I could smell her."

"Smell her?"

"Nicki wears a very distinct perfume. Haven't you noticed?" Jill snorted in disgust. "Of course, you have. I can tell from that silly grin on your face."

Amused, I covered my mouth.

"When she tore the purse from me, that perfume's scent came through loud and clear."

Not quite swallowing her testimony as solid evidence, I said, "I'm sure other girls wear that scent."

Jill crossed her arms. "You're awfully quick to defend her."

"You're awfully quick to condemn her," I countered. I let a few seconds pass before continuing. When I did, I tried to speak in a calm voice, not wanting to get into an argument. "Jill, I'm not denying what you say could be true. However, I don't want you making accusations that may be partially based on your dislike of Nicki. Isn't it possible that someone else wears the same perfume?"

She didn't answer.

"Think about it. She told us she was near the parking lot. Would a guilty person do that? For crying out loud, she offered me a ride this morning. Look, I know you and Nicki don't get along—"

"Don't get along? Hah! That's an understatement. I'll admit I lost my temper the other night at the Tank, but you don't see Nicki for what kind of girl she is." Jill began to count on her fingers. "Rubbing against you when she talks, hanging on your every word." She grew more and more flustered. "Batting her big brown eyes at you."

I smirked. "It's okay."

"No, it's not! I don't want to see you—"

"You don't understand. I'm admitting it."

"Huh?"

"You're right about Nicki. After our discussion the other evening, I've been doing a lot of soul-searching."

She quieted, which I was thankful for. I didn't need the big bad nurse kicking me out.

"And?" she said.

"You made some valid points." I chuckled. "Of course, now when I look at her, I find myself trying to see the two pounds of makeup you say she's wearing."

Jill never cracked a smile. "So, you see her for what she is?"

I nodded. "Yes, I see her for what she is."

"Good."

I continued in a matter of fact tone. "She's a sinner in need of a Savior."

Jill's mouth dropped open.

Since I had her undivided attention, I pushed forward. "You expected me to focus on her bad qualities? Maybe mention her loose morals. Her flirtatious attitude. Here's the truth. People like Nicki will attract attention as long as they have their good looks. And let there be no doubt about it, she has her good looks."

"Yes, she does," Jill was forced to quietly agree.

"But when those are gone, where is she going to be?"

Jill answered harshly. "She'll be where she deserves to be."

I ignored her. "Jesus died for her sins. He loves her. The question is, what are you doing to show her His love? As Christians, it's not our job to condemn her, but to be a light to her. Who knows what kind of past Nicki has had, what kind of an upbringing, why she is the way she is? All I can tell you is this. I too was once lost in my sins, but somebody cared enough to show me Jesus."

Jill stared straight at the wall, sulking. "She won't listen. She doesn't want to listen."

"Maybe not. But then again, maybe we've been talking the wrong language. We need to tell her about Jesus, not just with our words, but with our actions." I looked at Jill for any signs that I was getting through to her.

Detective Thomas entered, and the discussion ended.

"Who was on the phone?" Jill asked.

"If you have to know, it was the coroner. They're saying Ms. Webster's death was accidental."

"Accidental?" I said. "How could they think that?"

"The body was found in a grouping of large, sharp rocks. It appears that she tripped and hit her head."

Jill frowned. "But why was she in the woods to begin with?"

"From what we've been told, she was frequently seen wandering around in there." He turned to me. "Are you ready to go, Mr. Hill?"

I nodded.

"What about me?" Jill attempted to rise from the bed.

Her father placed a hand on her shoulder to stop her. "The doctor wants to do another couple tests."

She rolled her eyes. "I wonder whose idea that was?"

"That's a nasty looking bump. Better safe than sorry." He kissed the top of her head.

Jill grumbled. "Oh, Daddy. I'm fine."

"In the meantime, Officer Collins is in the hall if you need anything."

A young police officer peeked into the room.

Jill groaned. "I don't think he's necessary. It was just a … simple mugging. I'm sure they happen all the time."

Detective Thomas ignored her protests. "I'll be back in a bit."

As we exited, he nodded toward Officer Collins. "Stay alert."

"Yes, sir."

I called to Jill. "See you later."

Once we were on the road, the detective said, "Very nice of you and Miss Foster to visit."

"It was the least we could do."

"You've been associating with my daughter quite a bit lately."

I hesitated. Should I tell him that Jill had pulled me into her personal private investigation? Probably wouldn't be a good thing to bring up, with her being in the hospital and all. Instead, I simply said, "We're friends."

"Do you know anyone who would have a reason to attack her?"

Don't lie to him. He's trained to know when people are lying.

"No," I said.

He took quick glances from the road to me. "What is it?"

My vision fixed on some distant point through the windshield. "Nothing. Really."

"Are you sure?" His eyes bore holes in the side of my head.

I gave a nervous shrug. "Just a bit tense with everything going on. I mean with Emily's death. Now Caroline Webster."

"That was an accident."

"Of course. Besides, the killer's been caught."

An awkward silence fell over the car.

"Jack, I'm going to share something with you. It's not public knowledge yet, but it'll be out there soon enough. Scott Murphy *is* the Dumpster Killer, but he didn't kill Emily."

"What?"

He nodded. "Airtight alibi. He was in California."

I stared at him, my mouth hanging open. "Jill was right. That crazy girl was right. I mean—" My voice faltered, realizing I'd just called Jill crazy in front of her dad.

"She usually is," he mumbled. "Right, I mean ... Not crazy. But don't tell her I said that."

"But—but why did Scott want to meet with me?"

"He was angry over the copycat killing. Thought you did it. As a vengeance thing, he planned to kill you. So again, I ask, do you know any reason someone would attack my daughter?"

I should tell him about the list. That was obvious. But I'd made a promise to Jill. I didn't want her to be caught off guard by an irate father. It would be better to talk to her first. "I—I know someone broke into Jill's room, but—"

With a quick cut of the wheel, the car swerved to the curb. Detective Thomas slammed on the brakes. "Broke into her room?" Anxious eyes focused on me.

"Maybe. Maybe not. Jill's not sure. Her proof was the room's messiness, but it's always messy." I tried to sound reassuring. "I'm sure there's nothing to it."

I could almost see the gears turning as he tried to figure where this piece of the puzzle fit in, if at all. His eyes skittered from left to right. "This has the potential of all connecting. Remember that. Scott Murphy's not our man." He sighed. "Maybe I'm just being paranoid, but there's a possibility that whoever stole my daughter's pocketbook, also killed Emily, as far-fetched as that might sound."

"What makes you think the two are connected?"

His head slowly shook. "I don't know ... Just a feeling."

"Jill has those all the time."

"Her feelings are usually correct. After all, she knew Scott wasn't the killer." He pinched the bridge of his nose. "She's going to be impossible to live with now. The question is, why would Emily's killer want to steal my daughter's pocketbook?"

I could taste the lies I'd told like bile in the back of my throat. But because of my promise, I remained silent ... for the time being. However, Jill had to be kept safe. While in the hospital the police would protect her. When she got back to campus, that would be my job. And as soon as we could, we'd have a talk about giving the list to her dad. Funny thing, though. If the mugger wanted Jill dead, there was plenty of opportunity in the woods.

Unless I scared him off.

When Detective Thomas dropped me at school, I went to my room to grab some sleep. I had trouble settling down though. After tossing and turning for a couple hours, I gave up. It was around noon when I went to the administration building to see Dr. Spiner. Or his secretary. Though Jill wouldn't admit it, I had some pretty powerful deductive muscles of my own. Regarding the president and his secretary, I'd already figured it out. They'd been, what some would call, fraternizing.

Ms. Fielding's desk was empty, but voices sounded from Dr. Spiner's office. I knocked. Ms. Fielding opened the door a few inches, not much, but enough for me to see Dr. Spiner seated behind his desk. He had a glass of water and a bottle of pills in front of him.

Ms. Fielding's slender face and high cheekbones darkened. She motioned toward a seat by her desk. "Sit there."

The door slammed shut.

With a shrug, I crossed the room and sat.

After a moment she stepped out, still speaking to the president, "I'll be here if you need me." The door closed. Her tall figure stood, back to me. With her hand still holding the knob, her head bent forward and rested against the wooden frame. She heaved a sigh. The room grew quiet. Then she turned and scowled. "What do you want?"

"I think there's been a misunderstanding." I pulled the rolled up manila envelope out of my pocket and tossed it on her desk. "Why did you give me that?"

"Shh!" She rushed over and sat next to me. Grabbing the envelope of money, she tried to shove it back in my hands. "What's the problem? Isn't it enough?"

"Enough? It's too much."

She looked baffled. "I don't understand. It's the same amount I always paid that … that witch."

"Emily?"

"Yes, Emily." She spit out the name. "Now you're telling me it's too much?"

I took the envelope from her and placed it back on the desk. "I'll tell you what I know. Emily Hamilton was blackmailing the president, correct?"

She remained rigid.

"Why?"

"Why?" A look of hope crossed her face. "Weren't you working with her? Don't you know?"

"The answer to both questions is no."

She turned up her nose. "Then why should I tell you?"

"First of all, I'm not interested in blackmail. I'm only interested in truth. Jill Thomas found this list—"

She paled. "She has the list?"

I nodded. "She's convinced it has something to do with Emily's murder."

Ms. Fielding jumped out of her seat. "Are you accusing me of murder?"

"No, ma'am. I'm accusing you of being a … person of interest." I chuckled inwardly at how I sounded like Detective Thomas. "Dr. Spiner, too. By the way, since he's involved shouldn't he be out here?"

"Leave him alone." The fire grew in her eyes. "He knows nothing about the list or the blackmail. I've been taking care of everything."

The reason for the president's blackmail seemed obvious, so I decided to chance a guess. "You love him. Don't you?"

"Of course, I love him."

"Enough to kill for him?"

"Yes." Her answer came without hesitation, but she was quick to add, "But I did not kill Emily Hamilton. I'm not sorry she's dead, nor will I pretend to be." She crossed to the coffeemaker in the corner of the room and poured herself a cup. "She was a source of grief and pain. Thankfully, I open all of Roland's mail. When I found that letter saying she knew everything and wanted money, I knew I'd have to protect his reputation." Her face turned cold and hard. "At all costs."

"So, Emily was blackmailing Dr. Spiner because he was having an affair with you?"

Ms. Fielding almost did a spit take with the coffee. She laughed.

Not the reaction I expected

"What?" she said. "No!"

"You just admitted you love him."

"Of course, I love him. Any sister would love her brother. Wouldn't they?"

It took a couple of seconds for this to sink in. "He's your brother?"

"We don't advertise it." She bristled. "You know how some people are about nepotism. When my husband died, I had nowhere to go. Roland was gracious enough to offer me a job. I've been with him for twenty-five years now." She added as an afterthought. "I'm a very good secretary. Over the years, people have taken my Ms. to mean Miss. I've never bothered to correct them. Frankly, back then, we didn't hide the fact we were related. But as time went by the faculty changed, and people forgot."

"Why was Emily blackmailing him?"

A stone wall went up. "That's none of your business."

"But—"

"Mr. Hill, why should I tell you? You seem like a nice man, but if truth be known, Emily seemed like a nice girl. How do I know what you're planning on—"

Just then, the door to Dr. Spiner's office opened, and he stumbled out. "Where? What's ... I don't ..." He looked around, confused and dazed.

Ms. Fielding raced to his side. "It's okay, Roland." She gently guided him toward the door. "Come on. Let's go back into your office."

I took a step in their direction. "Can I help?"

"No." Her answer came in a calm voice. "We're going to be all right, aren't we Roland?"

"Roland," he muttered as if hearing the name for the first time. All at once, his eyes lit up. "Yes, Roland." Then a sudden look of resentment took the place of the light, and he turned to his sister. "Leave me alone. Why are you bothering me? I can do this myself." He pushed her aside and stomped back into his office. She chased after him. The door closed.

A pill bottle lay on the floor between me and his office. I was pretty sure it wasn't there a minute ago. I picked it up and read the label. Donepezil. Pocketing it, I returned to my seat just before Ms. Fielding returned.

"He's all right." She sat and began tapping her fingers on her knees. "He'd just woke from a nap and was ... confused. That's all."

"A nap?" I settled back and folded my hands in my lap. "The college president takes naps?"

"Well, I—"

"Tell me something, Ms. Fielding. How long has your brother suffered from dementia?"

"What?" She looked away. "I don't know what you're talking about."

My heart suddenly ached for this poor woman. My late uncle had suffered from dementia. I remember the torture that not only he, but also my aunt went through. "Trust me. I've spent some time around dementia patients. I recognize the symptoms. I'm not here to hurt Dr. Spiner. I'm only interested in the truth." I removed the pill bottle from my pocket and handed it to her. "I know what this medication is used for. Sorry."

Ms. Fielding's beautiful face contorted in anguish. Finally, the resistance drained from her. "He's in the early stages of Alzheimer's." Her head collapsed into her hands. Her long graying hair fell forward and covered her face.

"I'm so sorry."

"Once a month, I take him for a new experimental treatment in Concord. That's where we were this past weekend. The doctors are guardedly hopeful."

"I don't mean to sound callous, but under these circumstances, shouldn't he resign?"

"You don't understand." Tears streamed from her eyes. "It's his pension. The way it was written up, if he resigns now, he loses everything. I think trying to get his auditorium built has added extra stress. Of course, now that Caroline Webster is out of the picture—"

"How convenient."

"Now hold on! You don't think …" She sputtered. "That's foolish! Caroline was aggravating, but she wasn't going to stop Roland from building. She didn't have a leg to stand on."

Suddenly the letter from the lawyers to Caroline made sense. I didn't mention it though. No reason.

"Even his health insurance will be canceled if he resigns," she said. "I, along with a couple of other faculty members, have been covering for him. Carrying him." Pleading eyes looked into mine. "He just needs to make it to the end of this year, then he can retire."

"That must be a heavy burden for you to bear. Is that why Emily was blackmailing him?"

She nodded. "Somehow she found out. Threatened to expose him if he didn't pay." She took a tissue from a box on the desk and dabbed her green eyes. "Usually he's fine. Honestly. You saw him the other day in his office. It's only occasionally that he gets confused."

"Speaking of the other day in the office. I overheard the two of you talking. What did Dr, Spiner mean when he said I'd have to be dealt with?"

She shook her head. "You have to understand. One of the symptoms of his illness is paranoia. He loves this school so much, the stress of the murder was more than he could take. He was sure you were hiding something." She stared at me, anticipating a response.

I shrugged. "I didn't know any more than he did."

"The question is, now that you know about his condition, are you going to tell the police about the blackmail?"

I waited four beats before answering. "No. At least not at the present time."

Ms. Fielding raised a dubious eyebrow.

"I have my reasons for remaining silent. Let me ask you another question. What was he doing the night of the murder?"

A measure of coldness returned to her voice. "Are you looking for alibis?"

"Yes, ma'am."

"Roland was at home. I was there, also. Since his … condition, I've moved in with him."

I didn't bother to ask if anyone else could verify this. "I appreciate your time." I stood to leave. "I'll be keeping Dr. Spiner and you in my prayers."

She followed me to the door. "When I said I wasn't sorry Emily was dead, I may have spoken in haste." She sighed. "I'll never understand how she could do such a thing. She seemed like such a nice girl."

"People change."

The door clicked shut as I walked down the corridor. I paused and looked back. "People change."

Chapter Twenty-Eight

Jill had been discharged from the hospital around noon. After a quick lunch with her father, which included a stern warning to be more careful, she went to the college library to do some work on a research paper. Set far in the back of the building were old oak tables nestled between tall bookshelves. This created private areas, little cubbies, her favorite spot to study.

But today there wasn't much studying going on. Books and papers were scattered across the table in front of her. But she couldn't stop thinking about the mugging, why it had happened, who did it, and why she was so foolish as to let her guard down? The idea of using her trauma as an excuse to get an extension on this paper was percolating in her brain. Maybe she could get a couple more days out of it.

Might work.

She was about to call it quits when a familiar voice yelled from the next cubby over. "You lied."

That sounded like Jack. Who's he accusing of lying?

Curiosity got the better of her, so Jill tiptoed to the bookcase that separated her from the voices, quietly pushed aside some big volumes and peeked through.

There was Jack, on the other side of the table's sole occupant, Don. "You lied." There was intensity in Jack's voice. "Why?"

Don sat there, a dumbfounded expression on his face, a chocolate bar in his hand.

Jack raised his voice. "Homosexual, my foot!"

"Quiet!" Don cast a wary glance around him. "What are you talking about?"

"You told Jill you were gay."

"So what?" He laughed. "A little white lie to shut her up. No one was hurt."

Jill's face turned hot.

"The truth," Jack said. "I want to know the truth. Why was your name on the list?"

Don snickered and returned his attention to the book propped on the table in front of him. "Does it really matter?"

"Maybe not to you, but it's important to her."

Jill's heart rate quickened.

Don bit off a chunk of chocolate bar and dismissed Jack with a shrug. "Why should I tell you?"

Jack went to reply, but Don cut him off.

"Nope." A smug look spread across his face. "You took too long to answer. That mouse of a girl will have to deal with not knowing. Life's tough. I told you she's too nosey for her own good. Serves her right, butting in where she doesn't belong."

Jack's hands clenched into fists and white-knuckled the table as he leaned forward. He spoke softly through gritted teeth. "I don't think so. She wants to know the truth, and you're going to tell me what that is."

"And what if I don't?" Don wisecracked. "Is the big, bad marine going to beat me up?"

Jill covered her mouth. *Oh no! Jack's going to punch him!* She suddenly felt a smidge of guilt. Somehow the idea of Jack decking Don pleased her immensely.

Jack looked at his clenched fists. His face reddened from embarrassment and he straightened up. "Don't be an idiot." He pulled out the seat across from Don, sat and folded his hands on the table. "I'm sure we can come to an agreement."

"Agreement?"

"Tell me what I want to know, and the police won't get the list."

Don's face paled. "What?"

"You heard me." Jack shrugged. "You're not leaving me much of a choice. I guess I'll have to let the police straighten things out."

"But—but Jill promised she wouldn't—"

"Jill promised. Not me." Jack leaned back and smiled. "She made me a copy. I'd gladly hand it over to the authorities."

Their eyes locked.

Jill's fingers dug into the bookshelf.

Finally, Don threw his hands up. "Fine! I'll tell you, but you have to promise—" He pointed a finger at Jack. "No! You have to swear that you won't tell the authorities or anyone else."

Jack nodded.

"Not good enough. Swear!" Don was emphatic. "Give me your word."

"I give you my word."

With a loud thump, Don closed his book. He leaned forward. His voice dropped to an almost a whisper. "This isn't going to be easy. I could get kicked out of school … or worse." He took a deep breath. "One night last spring, me and a friend got wicked drunk." He chuckled quietly, remembering the incident. "It was a good time. While in our … our uninhibited state, we decided to go into the woods for some target practice with my friend's .22. We had the common sense to go way off so no one would get hurt." Don ran his fingers through his hair. "We'd shot a few rounds at some tin cans when suddenly the bushes behind us rustled. Two eyes glowed in the moonlight, and something big and black moved through the branches, toward us. I don't mind admitting, we were freaked out. Thinking it was a bear, I grabbed the rifle and fired. One, two, three shots. There was a howl and a thud as it hit the ground. Scared out of our wits, we crept toward the brush." He sighed. "It wasn't a bear. It was Angus."

"What?" Jill exclaimed a bit too loudly. Right away she realized her mistake. Jack's head jerked toward the bookshelves. Jill jumped back.

"What was that?" Don asked.

She froze. Her heart jumped when a chair scraped against the floor. Someone was coming her way. There was no time to escape. It wasn't like she was doing something illegal. But Jack was doing so well with Don she didn't want to ruin it.

Quickly she sunk under the table.

Footsteps approached. Two legs moved around her cubby.

Jill held her breath.

Whoever it was—Jack or Don— paused for an uncomfortable moment right by the table.

Go away!

As if in answer to her plea, the legs left.

She could barely make out what the muffled voices were saying until she hopped up and positioned herself back at her listening post.

"It was nothing. Nobody there," Jack said. He sat down again. "You were saying you killed someone named Angus?"

"Don't be stupid. I couldn't kill anyone."

"Then who's Angus?"

Don winced. "The President's dog. That goofy Newfie. It was dark! I'm telling you, he looked like a bear. President Spiner loved that stupid mutt, I think more than he loves his students. If he found out, chances are I'd face criminal charges."

"What happened to Angus' body?"

"We buried it, there in the woods."

"Buried it?" For some reason, Jack's face wrinkled.

"What is it?" Don asked.

"Nothing … Thinking, that's all."

Jill smiled. *That boy must be a lousy poker player.*

"Who was the friend?" Jack asked.

Don shook his head. "Nope. I'm not going to get somebody else in trouble. The rest of the story is basically what I've already told you. I got a note from Emily. Somehow she'd found out about the incident." He glared. "You satisfied?"

Jack ignored the question. "Some friendly advice. Tell Dr. Spiner what happened."

By the stunned look on Don's face, Jill would have thought Jack had suggested he eat maggots.

"Are you a moron?" Don asked.

"The guy's got a lot going on right now. He deserves closure."

"Well, I'm not going to tell him. And neither are you."

Jack waved a hand at Don. "I gave you my word."

"Lot of good that is." Don sneered. "Now leave me alone. I have work to do." He buried his face in his book.

Jack waited a moment before he left the cubby.

Jill's heart warmed. Jack had handled the situation well. On top of that, he'd defended her.

I strolled around the library, perusing the various books. Waiting. Finally, my cell phone buzzed. I whispered into the receiver, "You know you're not supposed to use your cell phone in the library."

There was a pause before Jill answered. "I'm not in the library. I'm sitting out front."

"I'll be right there." I hung up and exited the building. Jill was on the bench at the bottom of the stairs. "Fancy meeting you here," I said.

She patted the space next to her. "Join me?"

I obliged and filled her in on all the details of my meeting with Ms. Fielding.

"Alzheimer's." She raised an eyebrow. "Pretty clever of you to pick up on that."

"I have my moments."

She cocked her head to the side and squinted. "Brother and sister? You know what? I can see it. Especially around the nose."

During our conversation, the shade from a nearby elm tree moved across us. A chilly wind blew. Jill vigorously rubbed the goosebumps on her arms.

"You cold?"

She smiled, sheepishly. "A little. Let's walk in the sunlight."

We did. The warm rays were a happy relief.

Jill hobbled a bit.

"How's the foot?" I asked.

"Not too bad. It's stiff, that's all. So," she said in a mischievous voice, "anything else you want to share?"

I thought for a second, then answered nonchalantly, "No."

"Nothing?"

"Not that I can think of."

We continued for a few more yards.

She asked. "Anything happen recently?"

"Nope."

She sighed. "Maybe in the library. Did anything interesting happen in the library?"

I came to a stop and slapped my forehead. "How could I forget. Of course, something happened in the library!"

"What?"

I looked from left to right. Then I leaned in so close that my lips almost touched her ear. "I saw someone."

She pulled back. Her brow wrinkled. "Who?"

"A crazy girl hiding under a table." I grinned. "Anybody you know?"

She hit me in the shoulder. "You brat! You knew I was there all the time."

"You may be small, but you're not that small. Besides, you left papers all over the table, some with your name on them. Why didn't you join us?"

She shrugged. "You seemed to be handling the situation. I didn't want to interfere. Didn't want to stop him from talking. By the way, thanks for sticking up for me."

"What are friends for?"

We cut across the grass.

"Do you believe Don?" I asked.

Jill's answer was measured and cautious. "I don't know. He's lied to us once already."

"Heads up!" Boomer raced over, flew in the air and fielded the well-thrown pass, just before it hit Jill. Then he turned to us. "Hey, you two."

"Hi," Jill said.

With his head tipped low, he scratched at the back of his neck. "Jack, I uh … I want to apologize for the other day. I was kind of being a jerk.

"No problem."

"As long as there are no hard feelings." He heaved the ball back at his two friends situated farther down the quad and stuck out his hand for me to shake.

Suddenly I found my hand engulfed in his huge paw.

"See you around." He trotted back to his game.

We continued our walk.

"That was nice of him. Don't you think?" Jill had gotten about five feet away from me when she stopped and looked back. "What's the matter? Aren't you coming?"

"What? Oh, sorry." Engrossed in thought, I hadn't realized I'd stopped walking. I gazed over at Boomer as he and his friends lobbed the ball back and forth. In a flash, I made up my mind. "Listen, Jill. I have to talk to him about something. I'll catch up with you later." I turned and walked away.

Jill came up behind me. "What do you have to talk to him about?"

"It's nothing. Just something I'd like to clear up."

"What?"

"If you must know, Don said he was drinking with a friend the night he shot the dog. I kind of wonder if that friend was Boomer. After all, they're roommates. On top of that, I saw Boomer off in the woods, visiting a makeshift grave."

"A grave?"

I nodded.

Jill looked dubious. "I don't think Boomer drinks."

"There's only one way to find out." I marched toward the big guy.

"Seriously, Jack." Jill tagged after me. "I don't think this is a good idea."

"Then you stay here," I snapped. "I didn't ask for your help anyway.

Jill gave a sarcastic smile. "Of course, I'm coming with you. I wouldn't miss this for anything." She pushed past me and continued across the field.

Boomer caught sight of us. "Did you two see the homecoming game?"

"It was great," I answered.

Jill added, "You're really good."

"Thanks." He faded back to grab a pass that had been thrown over his head.

"Well?" Jill whispered to me. "What now? Are we going to stand here all day or are you going to say something?"

"Hold on." I rubbed my chin. "I'm thinking of the best way to phrase my questions." How was I going to handle this? Should I beat around the bush? Mention Angus and see how he would react? Finally, I settled on the direct approach, or at least my version of it, which I'd call Shock and Awe. If he were caught off guard, maybe he'd reveal something. I took a deep breath and walked toward him, "Hey Boomer, what's this I hear about you being involved in a killing?"

Jill's eyes bugged out. "Jack!"

Instantly, Boomer's face fell. "Where did you hear that?"

I shrugged. "News gets around, you know."

His face paled. "Gets around?"

The ball came flying in Boomer's direction and whacked him in the side.

"What are you doin'?" the friend called out. "Sleepin'?"

The two at the other end of the field laughed.

Boomer retrieved the ball and tossed it back, calling to them, "I'm taking a break." He walked over and slumped under a large tree as his friends put space between themselves and continued their game of catch.

Boomer glanced in my direction. His face said it all. Grief. Remorse. Sadness.

Jill and I approached and sat with him.

"I can't believe you said that," he sputtered. "I can't believe people know. How?" He grabbed his hair. "Oh man!"

"Listen. Accidents happen," I said.

"Some accident." His face contorted with pain.

Jill touched his arm. "Do you want to talk about it?"

"To be honest, Jill." His guilt-filled eyes quickly shifted to the ground. "I do want to talk about it, but not with you."

"What?"

"It's not something ... it's not easy ... I mean ..." Boomer sighed. "I'd like to talk to just Jack." Without looking up, he pleaded, "Please."

"All right." Confused, Jill got to her feet. "I guess I'll go sit by that tree." She pointed to a large oak, about forty feet away.

I was perplexed. Why didn't he want to talk in front of her? The two had known each other a lot longer than he and I. In the grand scheme of things, I was almost a stranger.

Boomer waited until Jill was well out of earshot. "I hope she understands. This is hard for me to talk about, especially in front of her. Do you know what I mean?"

I nodded, even though I had no idea what he was talking about.

"I haven't shared this with anyone. But the other day, when you said you'd pray for me ... It kind of hit home. Maybe I need prayer. Maybe you're the guy I can talk to." He shook his head. "This whole thing has been killing me! I don't even know if I can find forgiveness for what I did."

I didn't want to trivialize his crime, but a dog's a dog, and it was an accident. He shouldn't have to go through life with this kind of guilt hanging over him. "Look, Boomer. Let's face it. We're young. Sometimes we do stupid things. But the Lord will always forgive. I know it looks bad, but people have done a lot worse."

His mouth dropped open. "Are you serious?"

"Sure." I patted him on the back. "So, you got drunk one night and were a little careless. I mean, it wasn't even your fault. You were just there, weren't you? The wrong place at the wrong time."

His eyes narrowed. "Just there?"

"Sure. From what I understand, there was someone else who was more to blame." Don had said he'd taken the fatal shot. "Somebody else who was a lot more careless. That's the person who should be held accountable."

Boomer erupted with rage. In one rapid motion, he was on his feet and had me hoisted in the air and pinned against the tree. His iron-like grip clutched my neck.

Chapter Twenty-Nine

Boomer's sudden attack took me by surprise. From my vantage point, high against the tree, I saw Jill jump to her feet. Wide-eyed, her hands covered her mouth. She probably figured I was about to be broken in two pieces.

I wanted to say, "Don't worry, Jill. I got him right where I want him."

Frankly, I wasn't too concerned. Boomer might have been strong, but he wasn't a fighter. His stance left him wide open for my counterattack. As I gazed down at him, though, I saw the pain in his eyes. This man was suffering. I hesitated before striking.

With one hand gripping at his hold on me, I waved the other at Jill, who was rushing toward us, signaling her to wait.

She stopped.

"How can you talk like that." Boomer's nostrils flared. "I don't care if you were in the marines. It's not going to stop me ... to stop me ... from pounding you, if you—" His words cut short. Choking back emotions, he growled in frustration and dropped me.

I landed on my feet. "I'm sorry."

"You make it sound like it was nothing." He slid his back down the tree until he came to rest on the ground, dejected and miserable. "All life is important."

I rubbed my sore throat. Was he a member of some animal rights movement or something?

"Sure, it was an accident, but—" Boomer's voice cracked. "It was wrong."

My heart broke. For some reason, the death of a dog weighed heavy on him. I wanted to help alleviate his pain. "Are you sorry for what you did?"

"Of course! I feel responsible for not one, but two deaths."

My brow puckered. *Two deaths?* I shot Jill a perplexed look. Not having heard our conversation, her only response was to raise her hands, palms up, as if to say, 'What are you looking at me for?'

"Well," I turned back to Boomer, "if you feel guilty, then ask forgiveness."

He grunted. "It's not as easy as you think."

"I know admitting you're wrong is never easy. But just go to the president and—"

"The president?"

I nodded. "Dr. Spiner."

He squinted. "What's he got to do with this?"

I don't know who looked more bewildered. One of us was really confused. I had a sinking feeling it was me. "Maybe you should start at the beginning. Tell me everything that happened."

"It's so hard. I've never told anyone."

"Maybe you need to. And I promise I'll do whatever I can to help you get through this."

Leaning back until he rested on the tree, he stared across the quad. "You know Emily and I were dating for a while."

"Emily?" Now I was totally lost. Not only was I on the wrong street, I wasn't even in the right town. "What does Emily—"

He raised a hand. "You're the one who told me to start from the beginning."

"Sorry. Go ahead."

He continued. "We actually knew each other a long time. My dad had been her pastor since we were in the third grade. Of course, back then I didn't look at girls much. But in high school, Emily caught my eye." He gave a sad chuckle. "That's the expression my mom used for what happened. 'Bernard,' she'd say. 'That girl has really caught your eye.'

My parents were happy too because Emily was a Christian girl." For a moment, he sat in silence, nodding. "They were also happy that we were going to the same college, figured I could look after her ... Make sure she didn't get into any trouble." He flinched as if someone had struck him.

"Go on," I encouraged. "You're doing fine."

"Everything was going well. We both got involved in a good church." He took a deep breath and slowly released it. "There was no doubt in anyone's mind that someday Emily and I were gonna get married. But last winter. That's when the ... that's when ..." He struggled to come up with the right words. "That's when it happened. Emily and I ... we had never ... had never before." He looked at me and blurted out, "I swear it. That was the first time."

It hit me like a falling boulder. We weren't talking about the president's dog.

"It was in early April when she told me she was pregnant. I was scared to death. She was, too."

"Pregnant." I spoke a bit too loud, and Jill perked up.

"We didn't know what to do. She was three months along. It meant the end of our college life. That was for sure. And what would I tell my mom and dad? What would his church think if the pastor's son got a girl from the church pregnant? This would kill him."

Suddenly, I realized that my previous comments about accidents happening were way off. So foolish. No wonder he thought I'd trivialized his problem.

"Emily and I met one Thursday afternoon to try and figure out what to do." He clenched his teeth. "I'll remember that miserable day for the rest of my life. Flippantly, I said that ending the pregnancy would solve all our problems. I didn't mean it. I was scared!" His jaw tightened. "We had a big fight, and she left, hysterical. I chased after her. Just as I exited the building, she tumbled down the front stairs." He grew very quiet. "She fell hard. I'll never forget that image, her lying on the sidewalk. That night she lost the baby."

The air around us grew very still as I absorbed all he was saying. Boomer, himself, sat in silence, staring at the ground in front of him. A formation of geese broke the mood, as they flew overhead, honking loudly.

He moaned. "I blame myself. If I hadn't started the fight … if I hadn't mentioned abortion!" He broke down. "That's when we started to drift apart." He hammered his fist into the ground. "What kind of a Christian am I?"

I put my hand on his shoulder. "I'm sorry."

"I really loved her."

"I'm sure you did. And she loved you."

"Yeah, sure. Then how do you explain the blackmail?"

I hadn't thought about that.

Boomer continued. "It was the beginning of the semester when I received a note in my mailbox. 'I know what you've done. There's blood on your hands. Meet me behind the gym, tonight at ten. Be prepared to pay.' I was stumped. Who could have known about the baby? It was a nightmare" He wiped the tears from his face. "And the nightmare got worse when I saw Emily waiting there to take my money."

I finally understood Boomer's pain. "But wouldn't revealing this have hurt her too?"

"She didn't seem to care anymore. And all I could think of was how it would affect my dad."

"Have you told your parents?"

"No … I don't know what to say."

I thought this through. "So, Emily was blackmailing you about the baby."

Puzzled, he turned to me. "I thought you knew that. You said I was involved in killing someone."

"Dr. Spiner's dog." It sounded so stupid to say now. So trivial.

"Angus?" He was mystified. "What are you talking about?"

"You don't know anything about the president's dog?"

"He's missing." He shrugged. "That's all I know."

"Then what's that cross in the woods?" Embarrassed, I explained how I'd followed him that day. "After I'd heard about the dog being buried, I put two and two together. Figured it was his grave."

"Grave?" Boomer frowned for a moment, but then his face brightened. "Emily and I used to take long walks in the woods. We put that cross there. We'd sit and talk for hours. That was one of our favorite spots." He sighed. "I still don't understand how she could do such a thing. She always looked so sad when we'd meet for my payments. I'd give her the money, then she'd check off my name on that stupid list."

"I can't give you an answer to that. What I can tell you is this—God forgives."

Boomer glanced at the cloudless sky. "Maybe that's what I need. Some forgiveness."

"I'd be happy to pray with you. I mean, I know I'm not a pastor or anything. But I'd be glad to do what I can."

"Yes," he said without hesitation. "Please."

We bowed our heads and prayed.

"You know," I said after we'd finished. "There's one other thing you could do."

"What?"

"Tell your mom and dad."

Boomer froze.

"Hear me out. I know it won't be easy. But this guilt is killing you. They'd be able to help you. Support you."

"You don't know what you're asking."

"I think I do. Give it some thought, okay? If you'd like, I'd go with you when you talk to them."

Boomer mulled over my suggestion. "I'll think about it." The two of us got to our feet. "Man, was I afraid the other day when you mentioned that list. I figured I was going to be a murder suspect." His expression hardened. "I'd never hurt Emily. I loved her. What you saw that night at the library was my frustration." He sighed. "It still doesn't make sense. Emily and blackmail. The two don't go together."

Speaking of two. "You said you felt responsible for two deaths?"

He nodded. "The baby's ... and Emily's. If I hadn't been so cruel ... if we hadn't broken up ... Somehow I can't shake the feeling she'd still be alive." He shook his head. "Oh,

Emily. Why? Why did you get involved in …?" His voice trailed off.

"Losing a baby can change a person," I said. "Maybe it was her way of getting even with you."

"And the other people on the list? Was she trying to get even with them, too?"

Our conversation ended with my promise to keep him in my prayers and assurance that if he ever needed to talk, I'd be there.

He walked toward the residence hall, and I crossed the quad, lost in thought. *Boomer definitely has motive. But is he a murderer?* I rubbed my sore neck. *Would he have used a knife … or just his bare hands?*

After going about fifty feet, I stopped. I'd forgotten something. Or to be more precise someone. I turned on my heels.

"Sorry, Jill!" I raced back to where she was standing under the tree, tapping her foot against the ground and shaking her head.

Chapter Thirty

For the rest of the week, the college was shrouded in a proverbial dark cloud. We thought death was behind us, but with Caroline's, and the startling news that the real Dumpster Killer was not a suspect in Emily's murder, it came to the forefront again. Panicked parents swamped the office with concerned calls. Who could blame them?

By Friday, the whole school breathed a collective sigh of relief. We'd made it through the week. The following Monday was Columbus Day. Usually, most students went home for the long weekend, so the campus practically closed down. I imagine Dr. Spiner was thankful for the few days of respite. The general feeling was, we'd come back on Tuesday to a new beginning as if over the weekend the cleaning crew could sanitize the whole campus of death.

I pulled up the collar of my jacket and sat on the library's cold, concrete steps. Jill said she'd meet me here at six o'clock. I checked my watch—6:15.

Is that girl always late?

We'd argued, off and on, throughout the week about the list. She'd always come up with one excuse or another not to hand it over to the police. But the time for excuses was done. I'd made a decision. It wasn't going to be easy, but I had to convince her to give the list to her dad. And if she wouldn't, I would.

The quad was empty, deathly quiet.

A bad choice of words.

Though the day had been cold, over the last couple of hours the temperature had risen, and a light fog rolled across the lawn. Streaks of light from the lamposts permeated the mild haze. It reminded me of one of those old mysteries set in London. I half expected to hear a horse-drawn carriage clip-clopping down the walkway.

Just then, two figures emerged from the mist, coming toward me.

"Hey, marine!" Don's contempt-filled voice echoed.

I ignored him and turned my attention to his companion. "Well, look who's here. How come you haven't gone home yet?"

"That's where I'm going now." Nicki glanced around and shivered. "It's kind of weird here."

Don scoffed. "Just your imagination."

"An empty campus is an eerie campus," I joked.

"What about you?" Don popped a hand full of what appeared to be dry roasted peanuts into his mouth. "Why are you hanging around a closed library?"

"Just waiting for Jill to show up."

"Oh." Nicki frowned. "What do you want with her?"

"Uh-oh. Watch out, Nicki. Your claws are showing," Don laughed. "Meow!"

She scowled at him. "Oh, shut up."

"So, you're leaving for the weekend?" I asked, speaking to neither in particular, simply trying to change the subject.

Nicki shook her head. "I'm on my way home to check in with my mom. She worries about me. I might come back later. One of the other cheerleaders, Michelle, isn't going home until tomorrow. She's invited a few of us to stay over."

"Sounds like fun," I said.

Nicki shrugged. "I'm thinking about it. My mom's nervous, though."

Somehow, I hadn't pictured Nicki as the type of individual who had a concerned mom.

"Michelle promises we'll be safe. When I arrive, I'm supposed to call her. The whole group of them will come to the parking lot and escort me to the room." Nicki laughed. "I don't think we'll even go to the bathroom by ourselves."

I chuckled. "Kind of like mob security." I turned my attention to Don. "How about you?"

"Oh, I don't know. I wasn't invited to the slumber party." He feigned a crestfallen look.

I ignored his juvenile attempt at humor. "You going home?"

"I was thinking about it." He glanced around. "But there's something about being here for a long weekend, practically alone. It's very peaceful."

"Creepy, if you ask me." Nicki surveyed the quad. As her eyes passed behind me a mischievous smile curled her lips.

"What are you looking—"

Before I could finish the sentence or turn to see what she was looking at, Nicki threw her arms around my neck. "Oh, Jack," she giggled as she spoke in a loud voice. "You always know the right thing to say."

"Huh?"

"You're so smart."

"What are you—"

My words were blocked by Nicki's lips. She pressed her mouth tight against mine. I have to admit, there were times when I'd wondered what it would be like to kiss her. This was nothing like I'd anticipated. Cold and hard was how I'd describe it. I tried to push away, but she held on with all her might.

Finally, she released her grip. "Jack! You are such a naughty boy. Try to control yourself." Though she spoke to me, her eyes were directed at a spot over my left shoulder.

I turned to see what had caught her attention. There was Jill, about twenty feet away from us. Maria, another RA from the building, was standing with her.

"Jill, I've been waiting for you," I said. "We have to talk."

Jill backed away. "Maybe another time."

"But—"

"No, no." Her voice cracked. "I'm on my way home."

"It's important that we—"

It was no use. She disappeared into the fog.

"Jill?" I stepped in her direction.

"No," Maria said to me. "You look busy." She gave Nicki a contemptuous look. "I'll take care of Jill."

"Maria, I—"

"Honest, Jack. I'll make sure she's okay." She darted into the fog.

"Let her go." Nicki laughed.

Don clicked his tongue. "You can be so cruel."

Nicki pointed to herself in mock surprise. "Who me? What did I do?"

"You know what you did," Don answered, a slight grin on his face.

"Oh well." She smiled. Then, turning to us, she said, "Now, who'd like the privilege of walking me to my car?"

"I suppose that would be my job." Don stepped forward.

I stood, staring after Jill. My face burned. "No, let me do it." I looked at Nicki. "We have a couple of things to discuss."

Don glanced at me. "It's all right with me if it's all right with Nicki."

Her eyes shown with cautious curiosity. "I suppose so."

"Let's go." I headed toward the parking lot as Nicki and Don shared a quick goodbye.

Then she caught up to me. "It was very nice of you to volunteer to walk me out."

"No problem."

At the end of the administration building, Nicki pointed to the dirt path which ran along its side—a shortcut created by students anxious to get to their cars. It had been used so many times the grass had died long ago, and the ground was trampled rock hard. "Let's take the shortcut."

"You sure?" I asked. The path was much quicker, but darker and dangerous at night as it curved around the side of the building over gnarled tree roots and rocks.

She wrapped her arm around mine, grinned and pulled me toward it. "Why not? You'll protect me."

Before I knew it, we were in the shadows. One side of the path was a wall of bushes and trees. The other, the cold stone building. The ground in front of us was impossible to see.

A twig snapped somewhere to our right.

"What was that?" Nicki asked, her voice trembling.

Before I could answer she tripped over something.

I caught her. "I got you."

She steadied herself. "It's so dark. I'm not sure this was a good idea."

We plodded forward. Soon light filtered in from the parking lot, enough for us to feel more secure in our movements.

Another twig snapped.

I stopped.

"What's wrong?" Nicki's grip on my arm tightened.

I leaned closer and whispered. "Someone is watching us."

"Stop trying to scare me."

But I wasn't trying to scare her. Those twig snaps had to be a human ... or a really overweight squirrel. I raised a finger to my lips. We listened.

There was a sudden scuffling against the leaf-covered ground. A shadow moved behind the trees. I jumped into the woods and grabbed at it. He or she was smaller than me. Wrapping my arm around its neck, I yanked it from its hiding place.

"Hey!" It was a male voice.

In the dim light, I recognized our would-be attacker. That strange kid from Lit class, the one who kept giving me those looks.

"Hold still!" I spun him around, shoved his arm into his back, and pressed his face against the tree.

"Don't hurt him." Nicki's voice verged on hysteria.

"Don't worry. I have him," I said.

The kid squirmed. "Let me go."

"You're not going anywhere," I said. "Hiding in the woods. Stalking us." I pushed his arm farther up his back.

He yelped.

"Could it be I caught Nicki's attacker or Jill's mugger? Maybe Emily's murderer?"

"What?" He froze. "No. I—"

"I said, don't hurt him!"

"I'm okay, Nicki. Everything's under con—"

Suddenly, she started slapping the top of my head. "Let him go! He wasn't doing anything wrong."

"Nicki?"

She jumped on my back and pulled at my arms. It was like trying to fend off a wild animal. To be honest, the she-wolf on my back was giving me a harder time then the dork in front of me.

"You're hurting him," she cried.

"Hurting him? You're hurting me!" Confused, I released my captive. He crumpled to the ground.

Nicki rushed to his side. "Are you all right?"

He croaked in a small, high-pitched voice. "Yes. I was waiting to talk to you. Saw you walking away with him."

Nicki stroked the side of his face. "Now, now. There's no reason for you to be upset. Jack's a friend. That's all. He was just walking me to my car."

"And the other one?"

"Don?"

"Yes, Don." His lip curled. "I don't trust him."

The dork's a good judge of character. I'll give him that.

Nicki helped him to his feet. "Jack, this is Benson."

Benson looked like he was on the verge of tears. "I was waiting for you to be alone. To talk to you. I have those papers—"

"Don't worry about it now," Nicki blurted out.

"But I thought you wanted them before you went home for the weekend."

Her voice hardened. "It can wait."

"I have them here." Benson reached under his shirt and removed a large manila envelope.

Nicki grabbed for it. The two fumbled for control, resulting in the envelope ripping and its contents falling to the ground and sprawling across the path.

"Now look what you've done." She dropped to her knees to collect the pages.

I crouched next to her, wanting to help.

"I'm fine." She pushed my hand away.

That wasn't the response I expected. Then again, ever since whats-his-name showed up, Nicki had been acting peculiar. On edge. Before I stood, I quietly picked up one of the sheets of paper and hid it behind my back. "Sorry. Just trying to be useful, that's all."

"I know," she said, her voice strained. "I've got this under control." She turned to the newcomer. "Benson, why don't you run along. I'll see you later."

With a look of total distrust thrown my way, he spoke to Nicki. "Are you sure you're okay?"

"I'm sure."

He didn't appear happy as he slinked off into the darkness toward the quad. Part of me wondered if he'd planned on doubling back and lurking in the shadows, watching.

"Admirer?" I asked.

"What can I say?" Nicki did her best to shove the remaining papers into the ripped envelope. "He's wild about me."

By the time we entered the safety of the well-lit parking lot, Nicki had regained her composure. A handful of cars were scattered about. Hers wasn't too far away.

"Where'd you learn to go all savage like that?" I asked.

"Mom told me if I was ever attacked, to act as crazy as I could. Try to scare off the attacker."

We'd reached her car. She opened the door and tossed the envelope on the front seat.

"Oh, wait." I revealed the sheet I'd picked up. In so doing, I caught the heading. Midterm Answer Key. "What have we here?"

"Jack!" She tried to snatch it from my hand, but I lifted it out of her reach.

"Now, why would you have this?"

"Give me that." Her eyes flashed with anger. "It doesn't belong to you."

"It doesn't belong to you either."

She pouted. "Please."

"I'll give you this on one condition. Tell me why your name is on the list."

"What?"

"That's why I volunteered to walk you to your car. I want information."

"But, Jack—"

Still holding the page above my head, I gave it a casual glance. "I could return this to its proper owner. Of course, a lot of questions would be asked, I assume."

After a couple failed attempts to reach the prize, Nicki huffed and folded her arms. "Fine! But you can't tell anyone else."

"That depends."

"On what?"

"On what you say. If you killed somebody, or—"

"Jack!" Her mouth fell open. Then the old Nicki returned, and she batted her big brown eyes at me. "What a thing to say. Me? A killer? Isn't it obvious why my name is on that blasted list?" She leaned on the driver's door and took a moment to collect her thoughts. "It all started last semester." She smiled, coyly. "You may have noticed I like to have fun."

I remained stern-faced and quiet.

She continued. "I like parties. I'll admit it. And I do enjoy being in the company of a good-looking guy like you."

I think she added this last part to try and sway my sympathies.

"I guess I kind of fell behind in my studies and grew dangerously close to failing a couple subjects. If that had happened, I might have lost my scholarships."

"So, what did you do?"

She shrugged. "I got hold of a copy of my psych final ahead time."

"How did you do that? Wait. Let me guess. Benson ... or someone like him?"

"Well ..." She twirled a strand of her hair. "Let's just say, a little attention from a pretty girl can go along way."

"Nicki!"

She rolled her eyes. "Don't go getting all high and moral on me. It's not what you think. I didn't sleep with him or anything like that." She grunted. "He did get ... frisky the other night. You saw it. During the rainstorm. I had to put him in his place."

I rethought what I'd seen by the maintenance shed, with this new information in mind. "So that's why you didn't want to report it?"

She nodded. "Sorry to pretend to faint. I couldn't have you chasing after him." Then she flashed her pearly whites, as she ran her finger along my arm. "Simply put, there are always some guys who want to do nice things for pretty girls. That's all. Last spring went so well," she looked at the envelope in her car, "I thought I'd try it again."

Suddenly, I was able to see the two pounds of makeup.

"I thought I'd gotten away with it, too. But then, right after this semester began, I received a blackmail note. Frankly, I don't know how Emily found out and I don't care." She sighed. "Do you know what? The night of Emily's murder, I went back to the library hoping to talk to her ... to beg her to stop this foolishness."

"What did she say?"

"I knocked on the door." She shrugged. "I saw her standing toward the far end of the room. I figured she must have seen me and refused to open up. Then the lights went out."

"But you saw her alive?"

Nicki nodded.

"And your real reason for trying to break into her room that morning?"

"Evidence of the blackmail, silly. I didn't want to be implicated in a murder investigation. How many times had I seen that list? Whenever she collected, she had a copy."

"Hmmm."

"What?"

"What you said. Emily made a list every time she collected. I wonder what she did with all the old ones?"

"Beats me. Of course, little Miss Perfect has a copy."

The hair on the back of my neck bristled. "That's another thing. What do you have against Jill?"

"How can you ask that?" Nicki grew indignant. "You were there. Don't you remember?"

"Where?"

"The Tank. The other night. I heard the things she said to you about me. Cruel things." With a disapproving shake to her head, she continued. "Jack, I have to be honest with you. You talk about Christianity. Well, the two examples I've seen are Emily and Jill. Not the best pictures painted there if you know what I mean."

Unfortunately, I did. "Please remember, Jill and Emily didn't die for your sins. Jesus did. We are all imperfect. We're all sinners. Jill … Emily … me … and you. Jesus loves you so much he took your sins to the cross."

She tipped her head to the side and peered at me through squinted eyes. "You really believe that stuff?" There was no mocking or teasing in her voice. She was genuinely asking.

"I do, with all my heart. You know how you said there are always some guys who will do nice things for pretty girls, especially if the pretty girls show them attention? Tell me something. Is that true love? Is that real friendship?" I didn't wait for her response. "I don't think so. Jesus loves you. You don't have to do nice things for him. He loves you just the way you are."

Nicki raised an eyebrow. "Well, you tell me this. Would you have been my friend or done anything nice for me if I hadn't flirted with you?"

"Yes," I said without hesitation. "I'd like to think I'm not so shallow that the only thing which matters to me are your looks. Of course, I'd be lying if I said I didn't like your flirting." I smiled. "Let's face it. You're extremely beautiful."

"Thank you." She blushed, turned, and unlocked the car door.

"That's not the basis of our friendship, though."

"You *are* my friend, aren't you?" The words were spoken as if they were a new thought to her. "Oh, Jack." She groaned. "I'm sorry that I kissed you."

I stiffened. "That's an odd thing to say."

"I guess Don was right. I was just being cruel."

"I don't understand."

She looked at me, a twinkle in her eye. "You don't, do you?" Then giggling, she hopped into her car. "Sometimes boys can be so thick-headed."

"Huh?"

"Oh, nothing. I have to go."

I pushed the door shut.

The window rolled down. "Oh, by the way." Nicki smiled. "Back on the path. That was a very gallant of you, protecting me from Benson."

I grinned. "What can I say? I'm a regular knight in shining armor." I steered the conversation back to a more serious note. "Would you at least think about the things I've told you? I'm not trying to be preachy or anything. But Jesus does love you."

Her face lit up. "For you, Jack, I'll think about it." Nicki put the car in gear and drove away.

Chapter Thirty-One

My footsteps sounded especially loud in the empty quad. No one in sight. So lonely. I know it was my imagination getting the better of me, but I sensed a coldness, a hollow feeling hanging over the campus. What a difference one week makes. Last weekend was alive with homecoming. Now …

Wisps of fog danced along the ground.

I was thankful people like Nicki had the common sense to travel in packs and Jill was going home.

My phone rang. I answered it.

"Jack. Come up here, quick."

"Jill? Up where?"

"I'm in my room."

"I thought you'd be on your way home by now."

"Hurry!"

I quickstepped in the direction of the residence hall while continuing our conversation. "By the way you acted outside the library, I figured you were mad at me."

She grumbled. "Not you. Nicki. Never mind that. Get over here as fast as you can."

Less than two minutes later, out of breath, I was knocking on her door.

She flung it open. "Get in here!"

Her room was a mess. Not much different from the night it was supposedly ransacked. One addition had been made though. A large white chart, constructed of several sheets of poster board, hung on the wall. Scribbled across its top were the words Murder Suspects. Jill had pictures of the people from the list. Large thick lines attached the images to what she considered motives and opportunities. I felt like I was on a television crime show.

"Pretty elaborate," I said. "But why is there a picture of the Wicked Witch on there?"

"That's Nicki."

Sure enough, even though she'd managed to procure actual photos of her other suspects, under Nicki's name hung the green-skinned, long-nosed witch from Oz.

"Jill!"

"I know. I know. I hung it before our talk at the hospital." She tore down the whole thing and flung the pieces on her bed. "I'll get better. I promise."

Just then, there was a knock at the door.

"Hurry! There's no time to explain." Jill pushed me toward the closet.

"Huh? What's this thing you have with hiding in closets?"

She opened the door. "We're not hiding. Just you."

There was another knock.

"Just a minute," Jill yelled as she shoved me in.

"What's going on?"

"Trust me." Her hand tightened around my forearm. "And when I need you, be there."

She tried to walk away, but I grabbed her wrist. "Jill?"

"I'll leave the door open a couple of inches."

"Why?"

She closed the door, almost all the way. "Just listen and be ready to act."

I backed into a pile of whatever she had piled on the floor and cringed. This was not like Emily's closet. Not neat and orderly. That was for sure.

Jill opened the door to the hallway.

Don stood there, a smile plastered on his face. "I was surprised to get your call."

I melted farther into the closet. Jill's clothes surrounded me. I could catch a slight scent of her perfume.

"Come in." Jill backed away from the door and let him enter. "We need to talk."

The desk chair scraped on the floor. "This doesn't have anything to do with the little episode earlier tonight outside the library?" Don said. "Because—"

Jill jumped in. "No, no."

"Nicki can be such a tease."

"This has to do with blackmail." There was a somber quietness in Jill's voice that said, *I figured it out.*

I held my breath.

"Look at this." She unfolded the list and handed it to him.

"I've seen it before." Barely glancing, he went to give it back, but she wouldn't take it.

"Yes, but now it makes sense."

Makes sense?

Don studied the list. After a moment, a shadow crossed his face. "Smart girl, aren't you? Maybe too smart for your own good. How long have you known?"

"Just figured it out. All this time I was looking at a list with my name blacked out."

"Name blacked out?"

She shook her head. "That's not important. It wasn't until I saw it in its entirety that I realized something."

"Really?" Don stood and began to slowly pace back and forth like a caged animal. "What was that?"

Jill snatched the list from his hand and pointed at the different lines. "The dollar amounts. Boomer—10, the President—50, Nicki—10 ... and now with me penciled in for 10. That just leaves you at 80. The amount after your name was higher than all the others. But it wasn't because she was getting more money from you. All the other amounts add up to 80. It's a sum. Emily wasn't blackmailing you. She was collecting for you."

He sneered. "Like I said, you're a smart girl."

Should I jump out now? What would Jill say?

If I made my move too soon, she'd never let me live it down.

"Emily was too nice to be a blackmailer," Jill said. "It's true. But, somehow, you forced her. She was doing your dirty work, wasn't she?"

Don stopped pacing and stood directly in front of Jill, towering over her. "It was a great arrangement too. Late last spring I found out about her pregnancy and put this knowledge to good use. She was so concerned for her reputation and for what it would do to Boomer, it was almost too easy."

Jill backed away a step.

"It was a perfect setup. Not only could I blackmail her, but I could also blackmail Boomer. But with him being my roommate, it might get sticky. Emily was the solution. At first, she wanted nothing to do with it. Then, when I explained that if she didn't help me, I'd not only ruin her life but his and his family's too, she saw the light."

"But why? Why blackmail? You weren't making millions off them?"

Don's eyes gleamed with smug delight. "Because I could. Because it was fun."

Suddenly the image of Mel Jenkins flashed in my brain. He was a sadistic kid who grew up in my neighborhood. His favorite hobbies were teasing dogs and pulling the wings off insects. I remember once when he locked his little brother in the shed for an hour, just to see how the poor kid would react. All this time, that's who Don reminded me of.

He shrugged. "Besides, I'm majoring in psych. Thought it would be a good study of human nature. How far could I push a supposedly good person."

"And Nicki and Dr. Spiner?"

Don chuckled. "I'm the one who got a copy of last semester's psych final for Nicki. I figured, 'Why not use this to my advantage?'"

Jill's brow furrowed. "Psych final?"

"As for the dopey president, I just happened to overhear a conversation between him and that secretary of his. It's amazing what you can learn when you keep your ears open." He gave Jill a look of admiration. "You caught me off guard the other day in the Tank. I thought you knew the truth, but instead, you assumed I was being blackmailed. Frankly, I ad-libbed a pretty good story, considering."

"So, it was a good setup."

"Yup."

"What went wrong?"

"Emily." He grunted. "That last night at the library, I went back. She was all tears. Said it was over. She couldn't handle it anymore. That was her problem. Too much of a conscience. Whenever she'd bring her collection, she'd have that fool list—Blood Money. I think she thought her cute title would guilt me into stopping the whole thing." He sneered at Jill. "Trouble is, I didn't care. When I went back that night, I caught her writing letters, confessing to everyone, implicating me! There was one to you, to Boomer, to Spiner, and to Nicki."

"Where are the letters now?"

"I took them. Told her there was no way I was getting in trouble for this. They're hidden in my room for safe keeping. Just a temporary thing. I planned to burn them in the woods. Didn't think it was safe to start a fire in my room, with smoke detectors and all. After the events of that night, I figured waiting a bit for things to cool off might be best."

"And Movie Night?"

"Movie Night?" Don asked.

"You broke into my room."

"No, I didn't."

"Really?"

Face it, Jill. You've got a messy room.

Don continued, his voice growing shriller, his words coming out faster and faster. "With Emily dead, I figured the whole thing was over. But no. You showed up. Couldn't leave well enough alone! Started showing that list around. I knew I had to get my hands on it."

This did not bode well for Jill. Don was starting to lose it. He rubbed his temple and took a deep breath. "I knew it was only a matter of time before you figured it out." In exasperation, he cried out, "And in the parking lot. Why couldn't you just let me run away once I had your bag? Why did you have to chase me into the woods? Why?"

She shrugged. "Instinct."

"When I stole it, I figured I was okay. With no list, there'd be no evidence."

"But it wasn't in my bag," Jill said in a matter-of-fact tone.

He threw his hands in the air and laughed bitterly. "Of course not."

Jill spoke calmly, sounding like her father. "You should give yourself up. Don't make things worse."

"Oh, sure. Confess to blackmail. Killing the president's dog." Don gritted his teeth. "You don't understand. I won't go to jail! I just won't!"

He's losing it.

He stepped toward her. "Give me that list."

"What good will that do? Jack has a copy."

"I don't care." His voice rose an octave. "I'll deal with him later." Don lunged at Jill, knocking her into the dresser.

I sprang from the closet.

Surprised by my sudden appearance, his mouth dropped open. He grabbed at Jill, probably to use her as a shield, but she kicked him in the shin.

My hand clamped on his shoulder and pulled him away from her. One quick shot to the mouth was all it took. He crumpled to the floor and lay there.

I shook my head. "I told you I didn't like him."

Chapter Thirty-Two

The police arrived within minutes of Jill's call. They carted Don away while Jill and I stood before her father, like criminals in front of a hanging judge. I let her do all the explaining.

Detective Thomas glared. "And you didn't think it prudent to tell me before this?"

Her head hung low. "I—I—I'm sorry. I just—"

He didn't wait for her to answer. "And you." He turned to me. "I expect this type of reckless behavior from my daughter, but from—"

"Sorry, sir. I made a promise. I was going to tell her tonight that we had to hand it over."

As the last officer walked out, Detective Thomas sighed. "I'm just relieved you're both all right."

"Don't you want to go with them?" Jill pointed to the door. I figured she was half hoping he'd leave, and the lecture would stop.

"No. Uncle Hank can take care of the preliminaries. We want to do this by the book. No way we're letting this one slip through our fingers. By the time Don is booked, calls and waits for a lawyer, a good couple of hours will have passed before any interrogation can begin." He pointed to Jill. "As for you, young lady, get home!"

She approached the overnight bag lying open on her dresser. "I was packing when I figured out the list. I'll finish up, and Matilda and I will be off."

He turned to me. "Hiding in the closet. Of all the—"

"It was her idea!"

"I wish you'd stayed in there longer," Jill said. "He never confessed to killing Emily. We never even talked about Caroline Webster."

"What do you mean?" I said. "Of course, he confessed."

Jill considered before answering. "No. I don't think so."

"But—"

Detective Thomas interrupted. "Never you mind that now. We'll get a confession out of him. Jill, should I have an officer escort you home?"

"Don't be silly. Don is in custody. Everything is fine now."

I raised my hand. "I'll make sure she gets safely to her car."

"No. You come with me," Detective Thomas said.

"What? Why? I've told you everything I know."

"This has nothing to do with the case." Detective Thomas and Jill shared a look. "I've got something else in mind."

Something else?

He placed a hand on her shoulder. "I know Don's in custody, but I'd feel safer leaving an officer here to make sure you get to your car."

Jill protested, "But—"

"No buts! You hid the list. Who knows what other secrets you're hiding—what trouble you'd get into if we left you alone?" He kissed the top of her head. "See you at home." He pointed in my direction. "Follow me." With that said, he walked out of the room.

I gave Jill a confused look. She shrugged, though the look on her face said she knew what her dad was up to.

"Are you coming, Mr. Hill?"

"O–Okay." I obeyed. As I left the room, I waved to Officer Grant, who had taken his station outside Jill's door

We entered the stairwell, and I asked, "Where are we going?"

"Thought you'd like to join me at the church."

"Church? Is something happening tonight?"

"The pastor and I meet once a week for prayer and Bible study. Been doing this for a few years now. He thought maybe you'd like to be a part of it."

The notion of prayer and Bible study with Jill's father kind of made my stomach ache. "Are—are you sure you don't want to get to the station?"

"With my job, our Friday study times are on-again, off-again. I don't want to miss this one. Besides, like I said, it'll be a couple of hours before we talk to Don." He looked at me and smiled. "Detective Phillips and I have decided to take a different approach on this one. We're going to let him sweat in the cell for a while."

"Kind of cruel."

"It is, isn't it." He chuckled. "What do you think? Bible study and prayer?"

I nodded. "I'm honored."

We made our way across the campus to his car. As we drove to the church, Don was the main topic of discussion. After a few minutes, I said, "I've been thinking about what Jill said. Did Don really confess to Emily's murder?"

"We'll discover the truth at the station."

We parked in the church lot and approached the building. A single light from the pastor's study window stretched across the yard.

Pastor Roberts met us at the door. "Welcome."

"Sorry, I'm late. We had a little excitement," Detective Thomas said.

We sat in the pews, me in the second one from the front with the pastor by my side. Detective Thomas sat in the first pew, his arm swung over its back as he turned sideways to face us and share the night's story.

"Well, that is good news," Pastor Roberts said once the detective finished. "I'm sure Emily's parents will be relieved to hear about it." He turned to me and gave a smile that stretched from ear to ear. "Well, Jack. It seems you and Jill had quite an adventure."

My face flushed. At first, I wasn't sure what to say. Then, in total frustration, I groused. "Detective Thomas, let me ask you a question. Does Jill drive you crazy, too, or is that privilege reserved just for me?"

After careful consideration, he replied, "I think she drives us crazy in different ways."

"Seriously! Let me tell you about her." I went on to describe Dumpster diving and clinging to the sides of buildings. Finally, I related the incident from earlier that evening, in front of the library. "You tell me. Why in the world was she so upset? She was the one who was late. By all rights, I should have been angry."

Pastor Roberts' eye twinkled just like Nicki's had done earlier. "You don't know, do you?"

"Know?"

The two men looked at each other. Then Pastor Roberts nodded. "Do you want to tell him?"

"The honor is yours."

"I think it's better coming from you." Pastor Roberts smirked. "Besides, I'd like to see how you handle this."

"Tell me what?" I asked.

Jill's dad gave a deep sigh. He crossed to the side of the sanctuary, where he retrieved a folding chair. Returning, he opened it in front of the first pew and sat facing us. "I have to say something, Jack, and I hope you don't take this the wrong way."

I leaned forward.

He looked straight into my eyes. "You are as dumb as a stump."

I blinked. "Pardon me?"

"I said you are as—"

"I heard what you said. I just don't know why you said it."

"The reasons for my daughter's actions are obvious."

"Maybe to you, but not to the average person." I rested my hand on the pastor's shoulder and smiled. "We're not all great detectives, you know."

"Er, actually Jack." Pastor Roberts grinned. "I think it's kind of obvious too."

I pulled my arm off his shoulder and slid a few inches down the pew. "Are you serious?"

"Let me give you some hints." Detective Thomas used his fingers to count his different points. "My daughter does not jog. The morning you found the body, she was there because she knew you jogged at that time of day." He moved on to the next finger. "You never told my daughter what room you were in. She discovered that on her own."

I straightened. "What? Is she stalking me?"

Pastor Roberts grunted.

Detective Thomas slapped himself in the head. "No, no."

"Are you sure?"

"Of course, I'm sure. She's my daughter, isn't she?" It looked, for an instant, like he was considering the stalking option, but then dismissed this notion. "Besides, she doesn't fit the profile of a stalker. A stalker would be obsessed with its victim ..." Detective Thomas winced. "Forget that one." He thought again. His face brightened. "A stalker learns his victim's schedule—"

Pastor Roberts cleared his throat.

The detective tried again. "Some stalkers will take every opportunity for chance encounters with their victim."

"Doug," Pastor Roberts interrupted. "Maybe you should quit while you're ahead." He leaned toward me and spoke slowly as if explaining something to a small child. "You see, my boy, sometimes young people may act like stalkers, but for a different reason."

Excitedly, Detective Thomas jumped on this explanation. "Yes! For a different reason. Here's another point for you to consider. My daughter does not like the idea of you finding Nicole Foster attractive."

I let this sink in, trying to put all the pieces together. Then the proverbial light bulb turned on. I asked in a dubious tone, "What are you saying? Does your daughter like me as more than just a friend?"

Detective Thomas threw his arms up like a Pentecostal preacher. "At last!"

"Jack, even I could see it," Pastor Roberts said. "I mean, besides the fact that she came up to me several weeks ago to ask who you were."

"She asked you who I was?" I said.

"Close your mouth, boy. You're going to catch flies. Yes. After church one Sunday."

"You think she likes me, too?" I said to the pastor.

With an exaggerated sigh, he turned to Detective Thomas. "Maybe he is as dumb as a stump."

"I am not!"

"She likes you." Douglas Thomas swallowed hard. "That was hard for me to say."

"Wow." I felt myself sinking farther into the pew, chewing over this new revelation. *She is kind of cute.*

Pastor Roberts nodded. "Mrs. Roberts was trying to tell you, she's a nice Christian girl."

I smiled as I reflected on some of our adventures over the past couple of weeks. My hand went to my right side, remembering her tender compassion as she touched my scars that night in my room. I awakened from my daydreaming to discover the two men staring at me. "But she drives me crazy," I announced.

"Well, many happy couples drive each other crazy," Pastor Roberts said.

"She asked you about me?"

"Yes," he answered. "Who you were. Where you came from." He smiled. "Why do you think Mrs. Roberts arranged for the two of you to drive to the funeral together?"

I shrugged. "I don't know."

"That woman's got a touch of a matchmaker in her." His voice was filled with admiration.

Detective Thomas added, "And you can thank my daughter that I never considered you as a serious suspect in Emily's murder."

"Why?"

"She saw your reaction when you found Emily. It was obvious to her that you were taken totally by surprise."

"And you believed her?"

"I trust my daughter. Besides, we received a glowing report from the marines. They say you're a hero."

"I'm not a hero!" The force of my voice took the two men by surprise. The pastor's mouth dropped. Detective Thomas's eyes widened.

My face warmed.

Chapter Thirty-Three

A couple minutes after Jack and her dad had left, Jill peeked out her door.

Officer Grant stood there, on guard. "Ready to go?"

"Not yet. Almost." She returned to her room, but after a second, stuck her head back out. "Jason, you know you don't have to hang around. I'll be all right. Honest."

"Sorry, Jill. If I left you, your dad would have me working third shift for the rest of my life as punishment."

"Fine."

Five minutes later, she was done packing. The two headed for the parking lot.

"Jack in trouble?" Officer Grant asked.

"Huh?"

"The way your father insisted he leave with him."

"Oh, that." Jill dismissed the officer's concern with a wave of her hand. "He'll be fine. My dad has something special planned for him. That's all."

"Seems like a good guy. You two make a nice couple."

"Thanks, but we're not a couple."

"Coulda fooled me."

They reached her car and Jill looked around. "Where's your cruiser?"

"It's in the other parking lot." Officer Grant opened the back door and tossed in Jill's bag.

She slid behind the wheel. "I'll let my dad know you did your job."

He smiled. "Thanks."

They paused.

Jill stared out the window at him. "See you later."

He stood still.

"What's the matter?"

He blushed. "I've got my orders to stay until you leave the parking lot."

Jill fumed. "My dad." She started the car and put it in gear. "Satisfied?"

"Almost." He pointed to the exit.

Even though she felt like she was being treated like a child, she understood her father's concern. "See you later."

As she pulled away, Jill spied Officer Grant through her rearview mirror, trotting toward the administration parking lot. "Well, that's that," she announced to herself.

She hadn't traveled more than a block from the school when a stray thought caused a sudden panic. She pulled Matilda to the side of the road. "Oh, no." She fumbled through her pocketbook. "Where is it?" Her phone was nowhere to be found. She had a funny feeling that it was back in her room, sitting on her desk. For a split second, she toyed with the notion of leaving it there, going the weekend without it. But that seemed like torture—so old fashioned.

Within a couple of minutes, Matilda returned to the school. Another three and Jill was in her room, grabbing her phone off the desk. As she went to leave, her stomach grumbled. An idea struck her. On a whim, she took out her cell phone and speed dialed Jack's number. It rang.

"Come on. Pick up."

He answered. "Hey. This is Jack."

"Hi, Jack. This is me. Listen—"

"I can't answer the phone right now, but if you leave a number, I'll get back to you."

Jill moaned. After the appropriate beep, she said, "This is Jill." She smirked. "Do you have your phone shut off again? You've got to work on that. I'm just leaving my room and was wondering if you wanted to go over to Ralphy's for a quick bite. I know what my dad had in mind, but figured you'd only be an hour, hour and a half. I could swing by the church and wait in the parking lot for you. Call. Let me know."

She sat on the edge of her bed, hoping he'd call right back. After fifteen minutes, she gave up.

Might as well go home.

Just as she was stepping through the door, her phone rang. She didn't even bother to look at the number, assuming Jack was returning her call. "Jack?"

But it wasn't him. Jill's face fell. She listened intently to the voice on the other end.

"I'll—I'll be right there!"

She dropped her bag and rushed out the door.

Chapter Thirty-Four

I looked away from a shocked pastor and said, quietly. "I'm not a hero."

"Jack," Detective Thomas said. "I have to confess, this is one of the reasons we wanted to talk to you tonight. Jill is concerned. She told me your story … about the explosion in the marines."

That explains the father/daughter look back in her room.

"I've been set up," I grumbled.

The detective's phone rang. He stepped away and answered. Listening for a few seconds, he said, "Okay. Thank you." Then he placed the phone in his pocket and rejoined us. "That was Officer Grant. He watched as Jill drove away from the campus."

I smirked. "Checking up on her?"

"She's a handful. I never know what she's going to do." He turned to me and smiled. "As a matter of fact, I'm not the only one checking up on people. Jill's so concerned about you, she pretended to be my secretary and returned a call to your hospital chaplain, Captain Evans, hoping to get more information about you."

"What?"

Detective Thomas chuckled. "Like I said, that girl is a handful."

I shifted in my seat. "What did she find out?"

"Nothing. Only information that was found in the official paperwork."

I hung my head. "Good."

"I think she was looking for more," the detective said.

"Jack, some good officers, including that chaplain, tell me you *are* a hero," Pastor Roberts said.

"But, I'm—"

He interrupted. "I've only known you for a short while. I've watched you grow in your faith. Still …" He hesitated. "I've also seen something dark, something hidden. You carry a burden, my boy. Since the incident with Emily, it's closer to the surface. I would never force you to talk about it, but maybe you need to."

I sat in silent agony, overwhelmed by memories. My past. My failure.

Detective Thomas prodded. "Something tells me Jill doesn't know everything about the explosion."

Pastor Roberts moved closer. "Maybe talking about it would help."

I closed my eyes and whispered, "I'm not a hero."

"Why don't you tell us what happened," Detective Thomas said.

I sighed, resigned to the fact that they weren't going to stop nagging me until I shared. But maybe they were right. Maybe Jill was right, and I needed to talk about it.

"Jack?" Pastor Roberts said, quietly.

I nodded. "Since finding Emily, the nightmares have returned. I know I'm not responsible for her death, but still—"

"Of course, you're not responsible." Pastor Robert's face turned grim. "I don't understand."

I swallowed hard. The words rasped from my throat. "That day … the explosion … it happened in a makeshift hospital. A building that had been converted from an old government office. When the bomb went off, my outfit was asked to help evacuate the patients. We carried, pushed, and dragged out about fifty people, mostly locals who'd been caught in some military skirmish. The bomb wasn't huge, but it was big enough to do some damage. The fire quickly spread. Once the patients had been evacuated, my lieutenant gave the call for us to pull back. Everyone was gathering across the street. I was on top of the stairs leading out of the hospital, about to walk away, when I heard a cry from inside. It was very faint. Hard to hear over the commotion. I couldn't understand the language, but the pleading voice made it clear. A child was calling for help."

Detective Thomas and the pastor moved closer to me.

"Lieutenant McDonald called from the bottom of the stairs, ordering me to join the others. But I couldn't … Not when a child was at risk. So, I ran through the front doors. The lieutenant screamed, but I didn't stop. The main hall was engulfed in flames. The fire … I can still feel it."

I choked on the imagined smoke.

Jill hobbled across the fog covered quad as fast as she could. Her ankle throbbed. Though mostly recovered from the twisting it took that night in the woods, it still hurt.

But she had to hurry!

She arrived at the building, the spot the caller had identified. There was no one in sight. It was dark. Closed.

"I'm coming, Jack." She climbed the front steps.

That voice on her phone sounded so urgent. Muffled, but urgent. She couldn't even tell if it was male or female. It hadn't identified itself, just said Jack was hurt. He'd fallen down a flight of stairs, and he was asking for her. Why hadn't he gone with her father? Jill imagined several scenarios. Maybe when her dad mentioned what he had in mind, Jack begged off. Maybe her dad got called in to talk to Don. Maybe … There were too many maybes.

She pushed open the door and was met with a wall of darkness. She tensed. They'd captured Emily's killer, right? At least that's what her dad thought. But was he right? She forced herself to be brave. There was nothing to be afraid of.

But it was so dark inside. Dark and empty.

Jill reached into her pocket and pulled out her phone. She proceeded to punch in some numbers.

What's Jack doing in the admin building, anyway?

"Are you all right?" It was Detective Thomas talking.

"I'm fine." I coughed, clearing my throat. "It's … I remember it like it just happened."

Pastor Roberts retrieved a bottled water from his study. I drank.

After a moment to regroup, I continued. "I calmed my breathing, trying to hear any sound that would lead me to the child. Then I hollered out. Again, I heard the cry, so faint, so small compared to the roar of the flames. I followed it to its source, one of the large wards. A small boy, maybe ten years old, was crouched in the corner. The flames were spreading across the wall behind him and creeping across the ceiling. It looked like the whole room was about to collapse.

"'Come with me.' I extended my hand, but he stayed frozen. I lunged forward through the smoke and picked him up. At first, he struggled. 'It's okay. I'll take you to safety.'

"He thrashed, his big brown eyes filled with terror. I'm not sure which frightened him more. The fire or me."

"It must have been terrifying for him," Pastor Roberts said.

I nodded. "I hugged him close. 'Trust me.'

"The flames and smoke were unbearable now. The exit was no more than fifty feet away. I smiled at the boy, trying to offer as much encouragement as I could. For a second, he smiled back. I think he was starting to trust me. We'd almost reached the exit. It was practically close enough to touch."

I froze. That terrible moment replayed in my brain like it had hundreds of times.

"That's when the second explosion hit." I ran my fingers through sweat-drenched hair. "They say the first explosion must have cracked a gas pipe. When the flames hit the leak, they ignited it. The impact slammed me into the wall. I blacked out. The next thing I knew, I woke up bandaged practically from head to foot. I spent five months in the hospital." I sucked in air through closed teeth. "Surprisingly, I'd received very few burns. The wall I smashed into collapsed around me, protecting me." I shook my head. "The doctors said that was the good news. The broken leg, a crushed hip, five broken ribs … and this,"—I lifted my shirt, revealing the scars on my side—"were the bad news."

Detective Thomas didn't react.

Pastor Roberts, however, looked like he was about to throw up. He quickly recovered. "I'm sorry, Jack. You—You took me by surprise."

The two men stared at my scar-covered side.

"A couple of pieces of metal and wood got lodged in me. The doctor says the pain will subside over time. Outside of the hospital, you two are the first people who've seen my scars … except for Jill, that is."

Detective Thomas gasped. "You showed those to Jill?"

"Quite by accident, sir."

The concerned father continued to give me a wary look.

"As I was saying, I spent five months in the hospital, recovering from the physical and emotional scars." I looked at Pastor Roberts. "That's where I met your friend, Captain Evans. His counsel was a tremendous help. He led me to the Lord. After my recovery time, I received a medical discharge, and as you know, came here to start college."

"So, you are a hero," the pastor said.

I stared at the floor and mumbled out the words, "Tell that to the boy. He didn't make it. I lived. He died."

"But what about the others?" Pastor Roberts consoled. "You saved the others."

"He did more than his share." Detective Thomas pulled out his notebook and removed a letter. "I thought this topic might come up tonight. Wanted to be prepared. According to his commanding officer, 'Corporal Jackson Hill showed courage and commitment far beyond the call of duty. After the explosion at the hospital, he singlehandedly pulled or carried fifteen civilians to safety. When the call to evacuate the area was given, Corporal Hill risked extreme personal danger to life and limb and rushed into the building to save more lives. It is my opinion that he exemplifies what it means to be a United States Marine."

My fists clenched. My mind raced to that boy. "I told him everything was going to be all right. It wasn't."

I winced when the pastor placed a hand on my shoulder. "You can't let this eat at you."

"I know, I know. And I was getting over this. I really was. But seeing Emily's body opened up all of those old memories." I looked at Detective Thomas. "I see that boy's eyes every day and say, 'What if I'd gone a little faster? Tried a little harder?' And then Jill was attacked in the parking lot. I failed her. I shouldn't have let it happen. You don't understand—"

Detective Thomas scoffed. "You're wrong. We all have 'what if' stories. What if we had done things differently? What if we had been somewhere else or tried harder or—" He shook his head. "There are dozens of them. As a police officer, I could tell you tales. Victims I couldn't save. Innocent children who, even after I'd tried to be a good influence in their lives, grew up to get hooked on drugs."

"Or as a pastor," Pastor Roberts joined in, his tone laced with quiet compassion. "There are lost people who I did my best to lead to Christ. Sometimes they listen. Sometimes they don't. In all of this, the key is to keep on trying. Don't give up."

I bowed my head. "I never want to lose another one."

"There's no guarantee." Pastor Roberts spoke with great remorse. "I wish there was. But there isn't. God gives us gifts and abilities. We do the best we can, but there will always be one who won't listen. One we cannot save. But that shouldn't stop us from trying. From serving our Lord in the best way we know how. Again, I stress, don't give up!"

Jill's shoes clicked on the tile floor. Using her cellphone's flashlight app, she made it about ten feet into the dark building before she stopped and listened.

A quiet ticking sounded from down the hallway, by a staircase whose metal steps wound to the lower level of the building. A faint glow rose from below. Then she heard a voice, a whisper, but couldn't quite make out what it was saying.

"Jack?" She stepped closer.

The voice stopped. The ticking grew louder.

"Hello? I received a call ..." She peered down the staircase.

That would be a stupid thing for me to do.

All at once, the ticking stopped. The silence deepened.

A really stupid thing to do.

Stupid or not, her foot reached down a step. Then another. Slowly she descended until she was at the base of the stairs. An open door led out of the stairwell and into the hallway. She whispered into the darkness. "Jack? Are you there?"

Just then, a light clicked on at the end of the corridor in the last room. "In here."

Relief washed over Jill at the sound of the familiar voice. She stepped through the door and down the hall.

Halfway to the room, the light shut off.

Jill froze.

That's when something hard and heavy knocked her to the floor.

Everything went dark.

The sanctuary felt warm and comforting, like the Lord himself was there. The two men sat—one to my left and the other to my right—with their hands on my shoulders, praying for me. What a blessing to know I wasn't alone. I was surrounded by others who knew what it was like to suffer loss and the grief that came with it. Maybe they were right. Maybe I was too hard on myself. But knowing that didn't make the pain go away.

They finished.

I wiped away a tear. "I thought I was dealing with this."

"Emily's death had a profound effect on you," the pastor said. "Your scar is so new it was ripped open. Give it time. Give it to the Lord and know we're here when you need us."

Detective Thomas's phone rang. He rose and walked a few steps away. "Yes ..." His back stiffened. "What? Are you sure?" He rubbed his forehead as he listened. "Keep me posted." He clicked off the call.

"What's wrong?" I asked.

He shook his head. "Why does my daughter always have to be right?"

"What do you mean?" Pastor Roberts asked.

"Don's already talking. He's emphatic that he had nothing to do with Emily's death."

"What?" I stood.

"He didn't even wait for a lawyer. Said we have him dead to rights on the blackmail, but that was it."

"He's lying," I said.

"I don't know. Detective Phillips is pretty good at reading people."

I snorted. "Sure. He thought I was the guilty one."

"He has a feeling Don's telling the truth."

I stared at the ceiling. "Jill's going to go nuts."

"I should probably tell her." The detective punched a number in his phone. He listened for a moment. "She's not answering."

"Could just be a bad signal," I said.

"Come on!" He raced for the door, his once emotionless face filled with fear.

Chapter Thirty-Five

I barely closed the passenger door before Jill's dad threw the car in gear and roared off. We left Pastor Roberts standing by the church in a cloud of dust. Detective Thomas almost pushed the gas pedal through the floor. With one hand, he white-knuckled the steering wheel, while frantically pressing the buttons on his cell phone with the other, redialing. "She's still not answering."

"She always answers," I said before realizing the implications of my statement or what effect they'd have on a worried father.

"I also tried the house phone. Nothing."

"You think she's still at the school?"

He nodded.

"But Officer Grant—"

"I don't care what Officer Grant said. She might have doubled back for some reason."

We swerved into the college's parking lot. There was Matilda. As Detective Thomas turned the car into the spot next to her, some papers fell from under the visor.

I scooped them up. Something caught my eye— something familiar. "What are these?"

A distracted Detective Thomas barely glanced my way as he opened his door. "Pictures from Caroline Webster's crime scene."

"Hold on." I grabbed his arm. Sure enough, there were images of the dead body—photos of blood on the rocks. But one picture stirred a memory—a pendant. Heart shaped, outlined in diamonds. "Was Caroline wearing this?"

"No, it was found under the body."

I felt a cold chill. "I think I know who Caroline's murderer is."

The first thing Jill became aware of was the pain at the base of her neck. Instinctively she tried to reach the spot but couldn't. Something held her hands firmly behind her back. The more she struggled, the more it cut into her wrists.

She tried to open her eyes, but the room was spinning. She squeezed them closed and tried again. Even then, it was a slow raising of her lids. The spinning had tapered off. She was in some kind of storage room. Its walls were lined with old tables covered with cardboard boxes filled with who knows what?

As her mind cleared, she became more aware of her surroundings. She was secured to a wooden chair, her hands tied together with something. It didn't feel like rope. Too stiff. An old lamp was lying on its side on the table to her left. Its cord was missing. *So that's what I'm tied with.*

"You couldn't have left well enough alone." Ms. Fielding stood under the only source of light in the room, a single bulb hanging from the ceiling. She clutched a knife in her hand. "Young Mr. Hill almost convinced me it was over. But I'm no fool." She leaned in. "No one hurts my brother."

"But—"

"No lies! You haven't given up your witch hunt."

Jill shook the pain away. There seemed to be some slack in her bonds. Slowly, she began twisting her wrists, working at it. "There's no witch hunt. I only wanted to know what happened to my friend."

"You mean Emily? You're no better than her. She was trying to ruin Roland, too. After all he's done for this school, his legacy will not be ruined."

Jill worked at the slack, pulling her hands apart to stretch and loosen it, but it didn't seem to be giving much. "And Emily was going to ruin it?"

"Yes! She'd found out about the dementia. Was blackmailing us. But I was too smart." She tapped a finger on her temple. "I watched for days, learned her habits. Then one night, I waited by the Dumpster for her to empty the trash. Stupid police. They'd jump at the obvious." She scoffed. "Dumpster Killer, indeed."

"You—You killed her?"

"Try to keep up, dear." Ms. Fielding's mouth pulled taut. "I had no choice. She wanted to hurt Roland."

"No! You've got that wrong. It wasn't her. It was—" She cut short. Even if she didn't think much of Don, there was no way she'd make him a target for a crazed murderer. The unbalanced look in Ms. Fielding's eyes only verified the fact that Jill might not make it through the next hour. If only she could work this cord loose. Her voice quivered. "You don't want to do this."

Ms. Fielding laughed. Not a maniacal, throw-your-head-back type of laugh, but one a woman of her position might do if told a humorous story at a school function. Quiet and dignified. It was unsettling. "But I do want to do this. I have no choice, don't you see. I must protect Roland. Emily got in the way. She had to go. Caroline—"

"You killed her, too?"

The woman nodded. "She wouldn't stop harassing my brother. It made his condition worse. Then when she showed him the letter from the lawyer, saying she had a chance to steal our property, I knew I had to do something." She lowered her voice to a whisper. "I called her that evening and said the president had a change of heart and wanted to meet her right away. She came to the office, but he never showed." She gave a quiet laugh. "Of course not. He never knew about the arrangements. When she left, I followed her into the woods. She didn't even see it coming. One swing with that rock and she was down. All neat and easy." She tipped her head and considered. "Made a kind of gurgling sound as she lay there." Again, she chuckled. "You almost caught me, by the way, traipsing through the woods the way you were. I'd barely escaped before you and that tin soldier raced in."

There was no remorse, no guilt showing on her face. Just a pleased smile.

Jill stared at the woman in disbelief. "Ms. Fielding. Please. You need help."

"I don't think so. I just need to tie up some loose ends."

Once I told Detective Thomas about Ms. Fielding's necklace, we split up. He drove to Dr. Spiner's home, hoping they'd be there. I went to check all Jill's usual haunts. Maybe she just had her phone shut off and that's why she hadn't answered. Wouldn't that be ironic? After all the ribbing I'd taken, I'd finally be able to give some back.

Oh Jill, how I hope I can rib you.

I checked her room, the Tank, and anywhere else I could think. All turned up empty.

No Jill.

Where could she be?

Standing in the center of the quad, I gazed at the sky. "Lord, please help me. Please!" Then I looked around. "Jill! Where are you?" My scream bounced from stone structure to stone structure. It ended in unanswered silence. My eyes darted about, looking for any sign of hope.

The darkened buildings mocked me as if knowing she lay helpless behind one of those windows but refusing to give a clue as to which one. My heart pounded in my ears. It reverberated off the sidewalk, beating the words, "Give up. Give up. Give up."

Off in the distance, I heard voices. Detective Thomas said he was going to get in touch with campus security and the police station. It was probably some of them joining the search. I don't think they were having any luck either. Maybe she wasn't even here. Maybe she went off with a friend for something to eat. I was about to retrace my steps, go back to our residence hall and do door by door search, when a slight beeping caught my attention. The quad was empty, desolate. Where was it coming from? It beeped again, and I traced it to its source. My cell phone. I checked it.

Two missed calls?

How could I have missed two calls? The stupid thing had been in my pocket all the time. It never rang.

Jill's name flashed up. My heart sank as I fumbled with the buttons then held the phone to my ear.

"You have two new messages," the computer voice said.

"Hurry up," I yelled.

"First message," the voice said.

"Jack. It's me."

Such a feeling of relief swept over me. Just to hear her voice. The rest of the message was something about going to Ralphy's. Is that where she was?

The message finished. The phone said in that emotionless computer voice, "Second message."

"Jack? I'm comi ... Hold on ... so dark in there." Her voice cut in and out like the wind was blowing against the receiver, interfering with the signal. She sounded frantic. Then a door squeaked open. "Why are ... admin build ... anyway?"

I looked toward the large stone structure.

Admin? I'm not in the admin—

My spine chilled, and I tore off toward it. Racing up the stairs, I crashed through the front door. My sneakers skidded on the tile floor. It was dark. Taking a lesson from Jill, I pulled out my cell phone to illumine the area.

In the dead quiet, I stopped, waited, and listened.

Jill, where are you?

As if in answer, a scream came from somewhere at the end of the hall.

The stairwell.

"Jill!"

It took three leaps to get down the flight. When I entered the storage room, my stomach soured. About fifteen feet in front of me, Jill sat in a chair. Ms. Fielding was behind her, a knife pressed against her neck.

"Jack," Jill said. "Don didn't kill anyone. It was all Ms. Fielding."

"One step closer, I'll slit her throat." The woman's eyes were wide and wild.

"You're going to anyway." Jill said.

Grabbing a handful of Jill's hair, Ms. Fielding yanked her head back. "Shut up."

Jill yelped. A tiny line of blood traced along where the knife touched her neck.

I winced. If Jill wasn't careful that knife would sink deeper. "Honestly, Jill." I hazarded a couple of steps toward them. "You should learn to keep quiet."

She glared at me through tearing eyes.

I focused on the crazy woman. "Ms. Fielding, please. Let her go."

She pulled harder on Jill's hair. "Stay back!"

I stopped. "The police are here. There's no way you'll get away with this."

She sneered. "I must protect my brother."

"Protect me?" Dr. Spiner stood behind me by the door, a confused expression on his face. His voice took all three of us by surprise.

"Roland? What are you doing here?" Ms. Fielding, with a look of uncertainty, took a step toward her brother. But then she seemed to have second thoughts about leaving Jill unguarded and returned to her post.

Dr. Spiner's finger stroked at his chin. "I—I went for a walk. That's all. Saw this fellow entering the building. Wanted to investigate. Am I in—"

"Roland!" Ms. Fielding screeched as she pointed at me. "Grab him. He wants to hurt me."

"What?" Dr. Spiner dazed eyes suddenly filled with anger. "Why would you want to do that." He marched forward and reached for my shoulders.

I backed up. "No, Dr. Spiner. I don't want to hurt anyone. Don't listen to her."

"But she's my sister. She always takes care of me."

"Sir. You don't understand."

He lunged forward and shoved me through some folding chairs which were stacked against a support column, scattering them across the floor. My hand shot up, seeking to balance myself. As it did, it slapped into the overhead light, sending it swinging back and forth like a pendulum. Parts of the room swung from dark to light. Dark to light.

Dr. Spiner continued his assault until I was pressed against the cold, hard wall. "Why do you want to hurt my sister?" His hands closed around my throat.

"I don't," I said, choking the words out.

"I won't let you."

"Stop him, Roland. Stop him!"

The man was muscular. Well built. It was obvious he'd kept himself in good shape. Even so, I brought my arms up inside his and broke his hold. Then spinning him around, I twisted his arm behind his back.

"No, don't hurt him!" Ms. Fielding wailed as she stormed toward me.

Quickly, I pushed Dr. Spiner at her. His foot caught on one of the fallen chairs, and he toppled to the ground.

Ms. Fielding, fierce and savage, stepped around him and came at me, knife raised to strike. "You hurt my brother!"

Before I had a chance to figure out how I was going to disarm her, something thudded against her head. She fell.

Every few seconds the light swung that way and revealed Jill standing over Ms. Fielding, a large lamp in her hands. "I got loose. This was sitting on the table."

I knelt by an unconscious Ms. Fielding and checked for a pulse.

Dr. Spiner, who seemed to have injured his leg in the fall, dragged himself over to us. "Please don't harm her. She's my sister you know."

"She's going to be all right," I said. "You stay right here with her. Okay?"

He nervously shifted his eyes from me to Ms. Fielding to Jill. Finally, he nodded and gave his full attention to his sister, stroking her hair and whispering to her that everything was going to be alright.

I stood and faced Jill. "Are you okay? That was quite a move you made, whacking her like that." I smiled, expecting her praise for my rescue.

But instead, she poked my shoulder. "I should learn to be quiet?"

"Ow, that hurt," I said, rubbing the spot. "I didn't mean it. Just trying to protect you."

"And where have you been?"

"What?"

"I left voice messages for you." She stood, hands on her hips, an accusing look on her face. "Did you have your cell phone turned off again?"

"It's not my fault," I whined. "I must have been in a spot where I didn't get good reception."

With a smirk, she raised an eyebrow. "Oh, really?"

"Hey!" I pointed to the brother and sister on the floor. "I rescued you. You should be thankful for that."

"Well," she nodded in the direction of Ms. Fielding. "I can take credit for that one."

"But if I hadn't gotten here when I did, she'd have—" I stopped, not wanting to put into words what might have happened.

Jill touched her neck, and her fingers came away red from the slight cut. She looked down at the knife on the floor. Suddenly, her chest began to heave. Quivering and sobbing, she rushed forward and threw herself into my arms.

I held her, caressing her hair. "It's okay. It's over," I whispered.

Then something unexpected happened. As I held her, I softly kissed the top of her head. She looked up, those big, beautiful, blue eyes staring into mine. She pulled me closer.

We kissed.

A few hours ago, I'd kissed someone else. There was no pleasure, no feeling of romance or love. This kiss was different. Holding Jill ... kissing her. It felt right. For a wonderful moment she nestled against me.

As I held her, I smirked. "So, you kind of like me, huh?"

She pulled away, looked up at me and smiled. "You figure that out all on your own?"

"Well … no, but … I mean—"

"Jack."

"What?"

"Shut up and kiss me again."

I did.

Fifteen minutes later, I sat on the front steps of the admin building. The police had responded swiftly to Detective Thomas's call. The entire quad flashed with the strobe-like effect of two cruisers. I watched as they escorted the brother and sister from the building.

So sad.

The relatively few students remaining on campus— maybe thirty or forty—had come outside, beckoned by the sirens and flashing lights. They gathered, watching. Each person was probably figuring another murder must have taken place.

I shivered. One almost did.

By the side of the building, Jill sat on the back of an ambulance, being checked over by an EMT.

"Are you okay?" Detective Thomas approached me.

"I'm fine."

Dr. Spiner and Ms. Fielding had reached the cruiser and were being loaded in. The president looked dumbfounded.

"Go easy on him," I said to Detective Thomas. "He really didn't do anything wrong."

An officer climbed behind the wheel and drove away.

Detective Thomas took a deep breath. "Jack, as we were telling you at the church, sometimes you lose one. Sometimes, you save one. Well, today you saved one."

I nodded and felt a distinct measure of satisfaction. "It was nothing." I stared down at the sidewalk.

"No, Jack." Something about his voice caught me off guard. It cracked with emotion. "It was something. The one you saved is very important to me. She's my girl. My baby.

Whether you want to admit it or not, you're a hero in my book. Thank you." He turned and went back to his duties.

Well, I'll be. The Old Man of the Mountain does have feelings.

Then I did something I'd already done several times in the last fifteen minutes. I said a quick prayer. "Thank you, Lord." When I looked up again, Jill had left the ambulance and was standing across the road, talking with Nicki.

Uh-oh.

Nicki looked mildly curious and confused. Eventually, she smiled. Jill extended her hand. Nicki looked at it for a moment. Then they shook and went separate ways. Nicki noticed me watching. She waved, then walked toward some of the onlookers as Jill crossed to see me.

"What was that all about?" I asked.

She feigned innocence. "What was what all about?"

"Don't give me that. I saw you and Nicki."

"So?"

"There were no fireworks. No yelling."

"If you must know," she huffed, "you were right. I haven't given her a fair shake. As a Christian, mine is not the job to condemn her, but to be a light to her."

I smirked. "What sage advice."

"Don't get a swelled head." Jill sat on the step next to me. "I apologized to her for my behavior and told her I hoped we could be friends."

"How did she take it?"

She paused, then shrugged. "Pretty well."

Various officers came in and out of the building, approaching and speaking to Detective Thomas or Phillips. The students were scattering, losing interest. Now that the guilty people had been taken away, there wasn't much to see.

Jill reached over and rested her hand on top of mine. At first, it took me by surprise. Her bashful eyes looked at me, hesitant as if asking if this move on her part was all right? Was our kiss a fluke? A result of the stress and emotion of the moment?

In response, I wrapped my arm around her and gently pulled her closer. She nestled against me. The kiss was not a fluke.

"You know what?" She said. "One thing doesn't make sense to me?"

"What?"

"Abbott and Costello night. Who broke into my room?"

I laughed. "Jill, I will admit you were correct about the list being important—"

"Of course."

"I will even admit you were correct when you said Don didn't confess to being the murderer."

"And?"

I faced her. "Jill Thomas. No one broke into your room. You are simply messy. Your room always looks like that."

"Well ..." Jill sat up, about to protest. She paused and blushed. "Maybe you're right."

We went to cuddle closer when she pulled away and removed a letter from her pocket. "Wait! Look what my dad gave me. It's from Emily. They found it in Don's room. It turns out, Emily wrote one to each person on the list."

"She *was* coming clean, then?"

Jill nodded. "With all that had happened to her over the last few months, she was going to take a break from school. Before she did, she wanted everyone to know the truth. What we found in the Dumpster must have been rough drafts. I haven't read mine yet." She stared at the envelope for a few seconds before opening it. She turned to me. "Listen to this—

> Dear Jill, I want to thank you for the friendship that ..."

She paused. "I can skip this part. It's kind of personal." Scanning further down the page, she pointed to a spot and began reading again.

"I have a confession to make. Don Henderson has been blackmailing people and using me as his go-between. The reason I'm telling you is that somehow he found out about your previous problem after the car accident. He knows your dad is a detective and that this would cause embarrassment for him. So, he came up with the notion of adding you to the list at ten dollars a week pay off. This was the straw that broke my back. I couldn't bring myself to take money from you. I've already been hurting enough people. Instead, I've been paying the ten dollars myself. I felt, this way there was no harm done. But I was wrong. I can't help but feel he must have discovered your secret through a conversation I'd had with Boomer. I'm writing to tell you how sorry I am that I hurt your Christian witness in Don's sight."

"Excuse me, Jill." Detective Phillips approached. "Could I see you for a minute? I have a few questions."

She got up, and the two stepped away.

"Jack!" Boomer rushed along the sidewalk. "Are you okay? I just heard."

"I'm fine."

"I can't believe it. Ms. Fielding!"

I nodded. "All to protect her brother. I think she's a bit unhinged if you know what I mean."

"And Don was the real blackmailer." He shook his head.

"I should have known." I cringed. "Something about him—"

"*You* should have known?" Boomer sat beside me. "What about *me*? I was his roommate."

"He was very good at what he did."

"Man! I never would have guessed Ms. Fielding." His eyes brimmed with tears. "She … killed …" He clutched an envelope in his hand.

"Is that from Emily?"

He nodded. "I haven't read it yet." He looked down at his shaking hands. "I guess there's no time like the present."

"If you'd rather wait until you're alone."

"No. I may need the moral support." He tore the envelope open and unfolded the letter. As he read silently, his lips formed into a smile and he wiped his eyes.

"You okay?" I asked.

He nodded, then read to me.

"Dear Boomer, I want to apologize for the way I've been treating you. I'm not talking about the blackmail, though that was a terrible thing."

He skimmed the page. "She goes on for a few lines and explains about Don." His finger ran down a couple paragraphs. "Here!

I'm talking about the way I've treated you since I lost the baby. At first, I blamed you, but I was wrong. We had an argument. It was a heat of the moment thing. Who can blame us, though? We were filled with fear about our lives being turned upside down. I've asked God to forgive me for what we did, and I'm sure that he has. The fall down the stairs was not your fault. I want you to know how much I love you. I'm going away for a short time."

Boomer choked up. When he spoke again, the words
came out slowly and with difficulty.

"I need to get away from the school and all the bad memories. But I promise I'll see you again. Remember that! I'll see you again. Please forgive me and hold tight to this truth—I love you. Emily."

He stared at the letter for a moment. Then, with great care, he folded it and put it in his shirt pocket over his heart. "I love you, too," he whispered. He bowed his head and closed his eyes. "I love you, too."

"Are you okay?"

Boomer sniffed back a tear. "No. There's a lot to work through. I'd like to ask one favor of you, though. You said I needed to tell my parents about this. I'd like to. Would you go with me, for moral support? I don't expect you to talk or anything. Just drive with me and be there."

"Sure." I wrapped my arm around his big shoulders. "I'd be glad to."

Jill had finished with Detective Phillips and stood across the way with a couple of friends. They were involved in an animated conversation. I could only imagine the questions she was answering about her harrowing experience.

"You've had quite an adventure, haven't you?" Boomer said to me.

"I guess I have."

He looked over at the group of girls. "So, tell me ... You and Jill?"

I smiled.

"She's pretty," he said.

"Yes, she is."

He scratched his head and chuckled. "If the two of you get together, it won't be easy."

"Why not?"

"You and her?" He sang in a nursery rhyme type of way. "Jack and Jill went up the hill ... Are you ready for that?"

Jill looked across the road and caught me staring at her. She grinned and waved.

Suddenly, life seemed pretty good. "You know what? I think I am."

THANK YOU

Thank you for taking the time to read my book, *The List*. If you enjoyed it, there's a few things you can do for me.

—**Recommend it** to a friend.

—**Review it** on Amazon. It's my goal to get one hundred reviews!

—**Keep an eye out** for the next in the series of Jack and Jill Mysteries.

—**Let me know** what you thought of the book by contacting me through my website-jeremiahpeters.com.

—**Check out my first novel,** *A Message to Deliver.*

Again, thank you!

Acknowledgements

So many people had a hand in the writing of this book, both through encouragement and sharing of their expertise. I'd like to mention a few.

Thanks to my editor, Judy Hagey, for ferreting out my many mistakes in spelling, punctuation, and basic use of grammar. Her hard work was truly appreciated.

To Connor Aversa who showed me the right buttons to push (literally) to get that magic box we call a computer to work properly.

To my friends who critiqued this book—Christa Handley, Jodie Peters, Clarice James, Ralph David James, Cricket Lomicka, and Michael Anderson. They offered advice and many kind words.

To Jennifer Peters for her willing assistance in properly preparing this book for publication.

Especially to my wife, Jodie, for her patience and support through the writing process. She puts up with my different (odd) personality and pushes me on ... in a loving way.

www.ingramcontent.com/pod-product-compliance
Lightning Source LLC
Chambersburg PA
CBHW071532110726
47908CB00007B/1848